STARDROPPED

Golden Sun

For my loving husband

Edited by Madison Stoltzfus

IBSN: 9798574105283

CONTENTS

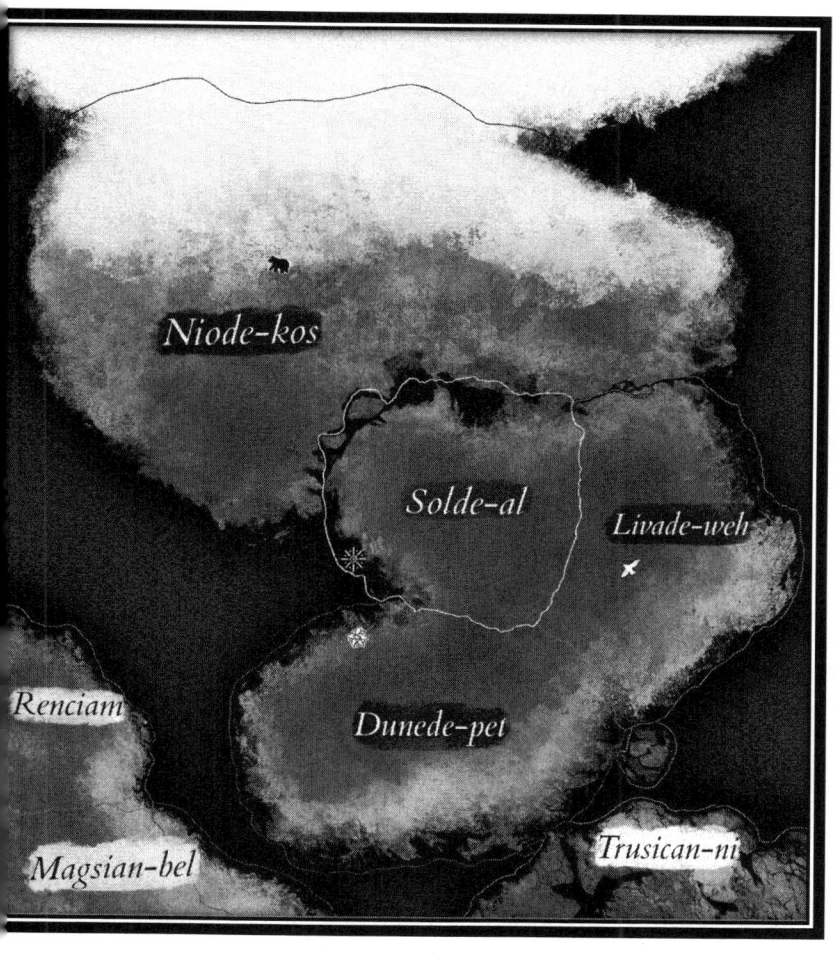

Sol-DEE all   Liva-DEE weh

NEE-o-DEE Kos   Dune-DEE Pet

CHAPTER 1

The Towers were the only home I'd ever known. Not that I had ever been allowed to leave and find another one. That was a distant wish.

The Towers stood alone with their backs to the foothills of mountains where wine grapes grew, and their front facing the glittering ocean. To either side were fruitful farmlands and small towns. The main road started and ended at the Towers' walls. On a clear day, the tall walls of the distant capital city could be seen, but most days they were a promised mystery. The location of the Towers was, if I was being honest, pretty idyllic. That was when I managed to look past the reason we were kept there and the chains around my wrists.

We were the mages of the Towers. It was where we had been raised, dropped off by our parents the moment we had shown unusual capabilities. We were our own family while the rest of the world viewed us as liabilities.

We waited. Studying and training in life skills as we waited one day for someone to come take us back to society to be wives, mothers, or professionals if we were lucky. The idea was to keep us under someone at all times, someone responsible. Or at least, that's how I viewed it. Many of my fellow mages viewed meeting someone to take them away as their chance to find love and purpose. After all, the individual has to choose them from all the other mages of age. A romantic notion of love at first sight. If a mage was not picked before her twenty-fifth year, she stayed behind to take care of the next generation of baby mages so that one day they could leave. It was all a big cycle, the only way out to be chosen.

My gift was not considered desirable. I was classified as a destruction mage, though they had never given me a name for my powers. I had a large array of abilities whereas others had only one or two, but none of them made me anything except a hazard.

As far as we could tell, I was indestructible. I'd experienced some pain, but it had never caused me harm. I was much stronger than my frame would suggest to the point it would have been comical if I didn't also have a way of making those around me feel waves of fear. When I felt a powerful emotion of any kind, every part of me glowed with a white-hot light from within, starting with my hands. I had been told it was difficult to look at me when it happened; like looking at the sun. I was known to defy gravity, leaving the ground behind, even when I didn't burn. My crowning power was catastrophic. I could use an explosive, radiating fire so hot it could melt metal in seconds. So forceful were the waves of it that it leveled anything near me. I had spent my life trying to control that power and had failed so many times the Mother Mage had kept me separate from the other girls. I had never wanted to hurt anyone, so I shunned emotions like they instructed. Through years of practice, I had learned to detach myself from my feelings by reading while the others my age practiced their powers.

Nonetheless, I was at the age where I was included in the lineup each time a man came to take one of us away. I was always passed over with displeased looks. The next time I would stand in line would be a special occasion, but I expected no difference.

The announcement had been made three days ago. The king of our home country Solde-al was coming to the Towers. The only things I knew about him had been what I'd heard from the other mages who had been allowed more freedom than I ever had. He was looking for a queen. King Zandorian Al had had a wife before, but she had died years ago. The people had been waiting for him to choose another. No one had expected him to want to choose a mage.

Zandorian Al was a mage himself, which was incredibly rare for a man. It was well known powers were carried by females primarily. Only a few men had ever been able to do anything beyond a simple sleight-of-hand trick. Of course, whatever his power was, it had worked out well for him. He was a living marvel that had won battles far beyond the capabilities of his father or his father before him. He had kept the country safe, and we had prospered for it. To me that was honorable but not a reason to look forward to his visit.

It made my head hurt how the mages of my age had gone into an excited flutter at the news and had only become more excitable as the visit came closer. I had shrunk myself against the walls and hidden in stairwells with books about history to avoid the parades of bright robes and eccentric hairstyles. This was a feat as I was a head taller than all of them, and that head was bald and glowed with my own dim radiance.

My sister mage Aurelia had been the only one who could get me to put the books down long enough to get dressed the fateful morning of the visit. I was grateful, of course. The robe of dusty blue was beautiful but not on me. It made my yellow-white eyes look sickly. That was probably for the best.

Aurelia had the most subtle but useful gift of us all. She manipulated emotions. I had also seen quite enough evidence to suggest that she could read minds, but she waved those accusations away with a giggle every time they came up. She swore up and down that she had never used either power on me, but I knew there had been times during a temper tantrum where I had become inexplicably calm. I didn't mind that she had done it on those occasions. It was better for everyone if I did not envelop the surrounding area in energy hotter than fire.

She stood in front of the mirror in her room, twisting and twirling to fix every angle. Her ruffly soft pink robe was a perfect choice.

"Do I look alright?"

"Yes." I reached out to straighten her necklace, centering it between her collarbones, careful not to touch her skin with my fingers. "Perfect."

"You think I have a chance?" She sighed, looking in the mirror. "Oh, it's no use, look at me. I'll mess it up somehow, I know it." She held her face in her hands.

"You'll be wonderful, I know that. If any of us have a chance, it's you."

She studied my face and knew what I was alluding to.

"No, you know I won't use it for that." She sounded sure of herself, but I saw her resolve melting as she fixed her soft brown hair to hide her pointed ears, a fruitless task as all mages had them but only a few could hide them. Aurelia was not one of them and neither was I. "But if I don't? What if it all goes horribly and I'm left an old woman with no one who loves me?"

"That is impossible because I love you. Since we were kids, you know that. No matter what, I promise."

Aurelia nodded and smiled weakly, smoothing out the front of her robes.

"Alright, I love you too." Then a crease of concern formed between her eyebrows. "Don't think that means you get to be a single old woman, either."

I rolled my eyes, "Auri, no one can even touch me, how-"

"Don't start, Skye. Sure, you're not the most traditional and your powers are intimidating," she skipped the words terrifying and disastrous, the usual set that accompanied talk about my abilities, "but that doesn't give you an excuse to not at least try for the future you want!"

"I can't have that future. And what if I want to be a love-less old woman? It's realistic."

6

"Then that's your decision, but I'll know you're lying to yourself. I know all your secrets, remember?"

It was true. I had told her everything, always. I had resigned myself to the near fact that I would likely be taking care of young mages for the rest of my life. I'd always known that I really did want a romantic adventure, a family, and just a little bit of power for my own. Even if that power was just within my own home, I wasn't unreasonable. But that had simultaneously felt like a hope and a wish that I knew would never come true. My skin was so hot it burned, and it got hotter based on my emotions. No one could touch me.

I ran my hand across my smooth bald scalp as I thought. I had never had hair a day in my life, but it always bothered others much more than it bothered me. My hand was warmer than it should have been. I tried to breathe deeply, slowly. I had no reason to be nervous today.

The morning was bright and warm as we passed through the arching open air halls. The tower gardens were beautiful, and the mage that helped them stay that way, Ferona, soon joined us. She wore pale leaf green, of course. Nerial was at her side as usual, her light purple hair curled and piled high. They talked with Aurelia in excited chatter. They paid me no mind, and I was alright with that.

7

At the end of the hall, the greeting room doors were thrown wide open. My sister mages were a whirling mass of color as we gathered. There were six of us, a few less than the larger classes of the younger mages. I preferred it that way; less people to want nothing to do with me.

When I stepped through the threshold, I was approached by our youngest Mother Mage.

"Wrists," she demanded. I held out my hands, showing her the thick iron bracelets. The heavy chain connecting them pulled at my back. I had grown so used to them I often forgot they were there at all.

She struggled with the locks.

"I can do it," I suggested. She shook her head. After two more attempts she stepped back, giving me a single nod. I heated my hands to white hot, pulling the bracelets off with my fingers as if they were made of wet clay. The chain fell with a heavy sound on the stone floor. Several people looked my way, startled. I picked up the chain and handed it to her.

She took them gingerly. Another Mother Mage took the key from her and undid similar ones on my sister Cerprilis who was more a feral beast than a mage. We were the only two destruction mages in our age.

Aurelia was busy talking to the others. I rubbed at my wrists, not wanting to bother them.

8

"He is ready, you know what to do," barked one of the Mother Mages. She was Mother Nai, the oldest and most demanding. I'd gotten a specific warning from her three days ago that I was supposed to be on my best behavior for this visit. It didn't surprise me at all that she would be involved today to see that it all went perfectly.

We all lined up. I ended up between Aurelia and Zifira, second to last. Aurelia was pretty in her blushing, soft way, but Zifira was devastatingly beautiful. She had long dark waving hair and eyes the color of dusk skies set deeply above her sharp cheekbones and jawline. She wore a silky dark gray robe. I knew from experience Zifira was the way her summoned storms from the ocean were: dark, cold, and unkind if you weren't careful. But if she liked you, she was the most loyal friend a person could have. A fantastic gift giver too, according to Aurelia.

The wide doors to outside opened and a small entourage of well-dressed men entered. I picked them out to be a general, two record keepers, a man who looked like his job was to be muscular, and an old man with a very deep frown and deeper brown skin. A figure taller than all of them by two heads stood in the middle as they moved inside. He wore a long deep green robe with golden stitching, a dozen gold chain necklaces around his neck that gleamed in the sunlight from the windows so he appeared to glow. The king of Solde-al. Zandorian Al.

My sisters took in a hushed collective breath. I could feel their thinly veiled excitement in the air. I was sure Aurelia could feel it tenfold.

He talked to our most senior Mother Mages first. His voice carried across the room. The sound of his voice was like dark velvet with a hint of an accent I couldn't place. It curled around his words with grace and depth.

Then he turned to us. His eyes were yellow. Darker than mine but only by a shade or two, making them more gold than yellow. That took me by surprise only as long as it took for the rest of his good looks to sink in. He had the darkest, thickest brown-black hair tied in a knot to show his pointed ears and a short, well-kept beard. His skin was warm and deeply tanned. A concerned heavy brow was softened by a kind upturn to his lips. He did not appear as old as I had expected, only a year or two older than us though we all knew he was closer to seven years older. My mind grappled with the math to figure out how that was possible. My fingers and cheeks were getting too hot. I had to calm down.

He started at the end, as was usual when we were visited. He asked Ferona her name before nodding and moving on politely. With Nerial, he asked a second question. "What is your power, Nerial?" Of course, I had no doubt he already knew. No man came here blind. He had been given all the information he would ever care to know about us in a stack of papers to be studied before he arrived.

Still, Nerial and King Zandorian were both infallibly polite, undiscouraged by the redundancy. I could hear the excitement in her voice as she described how she could move objects with her mind; the same tone it took on when she got to help cook a meal instead of study. Then he moved on to Cerprillis. I broke formation to look down the line at Nerial's face. She was doing a terrible job hiding the disappointment on her beautiful features. I snorted in anger at the arrogant king, earning me an elbow to the hip from Aurelia. He knew who he wanted, he needed to stop playing with the emotions of everyone else. He stopped again at Zifira, asking her name.

"Yes, the ocean storm." He nodded to her politely, wearing a knowing smile. I hated it. I moved my eyes to look straight forward.

Then he stood in front of me. I hated to admit to myself that he was even more attractive this close. I could see the twist of red line tattoos along the sides of his neck like vines and the shallow healed scars. The gold of his chain necklaces brought out the swirling glitter in his golden eyes.

"What is your name?" He sounded smug, his smile a little bigger than it had been before.

"Skye," I said without formality. I hope he heard my projected indifference and not my heart pounding.

"Of course. I am sure you know you are incredibly unique?"

I let my eyes narrow. "I'm aware."

"Amazing. Tell me, Skye, how would you use your power as queen?"

"No."

"No?" He raised his eyebrows, taking a step back. There were low whispers all around us.

"I won't indulge you. We both know you should be asking any of these other women. Please stop wasting our time." My hands burned. I fought for control.

"Why should I not ask you?" he asked calmly.

I took a deep breath, "I'm not a good choice for queen. I have a temper with no tolerance. I have a power that's wildly destructive, even when I can control it. I am quick to abandon all diplomacy in favor of speaking my mind. I would defend and conquer with strategy and duty, but I am merely a strategist at best or an uncontrollable weapon at worst." I paused, stilling my hands, "I would not make

12

a good queen, no matter how much of a living legend my king is."

Zandorian listened a moment longer then laughed. "I am no such thing. The only thing I have accomplished is victory in a few scrapes and luck enough to inherit my mother's power." He shook his head. "As for your star-fire and opinions, I see no problem with that. I am a king that says his mind, I do not see why a queen should not do the same."

"What did you call it?" I asked under my breath. I was stuck on one word.

"Star-fire, your power. We will have plenty of time to discuss it. Mother Mages, please gather Skye's possessions, we will both be leaving shortly."

I was stunned into silence. Had he just said those words? My name? My thoughts were flooded with denial, confusion, anger, excitement. A spreading numbness dulled my emotions before they ripped through me and my surroundings.

Then Aurelia was there, hesitantly wrapping her arms around me, still leaving a small bit of empty distance in most places. I couldn't hurt her, I remembered through the haze. I had to keep myself in check.

"Oh Skye, this is amazing! He chose you! You're the queen!"

Some part of my mind made my head nod and my lips smile to mirror her face full of joy.

"But Aurelia... you..." the words died on their way out.

"There's another man here today, he's a general or something. I still have a chance of not being a lonely old woman, so don't worry about me! Go on, I'll see you soon enough, I promise!" She practically shoved me towards the doors leading outside with her aggressive waving. I walked without feeling the ground.

I was outside the Towers for the first time in my life as I took my final step off the stone stairs. Everything felt like a dream. It didn't feel like I had thought it would every time I'd dreamed of leaving. It was heavy and empty, like everything else.

I moved not two more steps and I was swarmed by people. Two seemed to be there for the purpose of writing down every detail. The others were carrying robes, trying to hold them up and out to me.

My aura of fear grew. They went quiet. I walked to the nearest carriage, the nicest and largest one. I grabbed the door handle. I left my hand on it longer than I should have, letting it heat to glowing.

"Leave me alone," I snapped in a low voice to all of them. I pulled the carriage door closed behind me

14

with a slam before anyone could follow me in. For their sakes, I hoped they wouldn't try the handle.

The floor of my life and my plans had been pulled out from under me. All because this king had said the words. Who had given him the right to ruin everything? The answer was that the Towers, my Mother Mages, and the entirety of Solde had given it to him.

I sat for a minute, head in my hands. I heard panicked voices outside, then the smooth gold tone of Zandorian's voice, "I will speak with her, do not worry."

The door opened, to my surprise. He wasn't fazed by having his hand on what I knew was still a red-hot door handle. He sat across from me.

"I should clarify some points of our arrangement before you reduce my convoy to ash." His eyes moved from my glowing hands to burning eyes. He looked in my eyes without fear, which on its own was unusual for anyone. He spoke calmly with a reverent tone to his voice, "I do not expect you to love me. I have full intentions of letting you be whoever you want to be to myself and the people of Solde. A general, a conqueror, a scholar. Anything, Skye. I could not stand to let the most powerful and talented Stardropped rot in that place of subservience. You were who I came here for today. Please disregard my distracting theatrics. You know it was the only way I could get you out and give you the power I know you deserve."

"So, I am not your queen?"

"Yes, you are. You will rule as my equal in every way I can provide if that is what you want. But I do not decide the status of the other facets of our relationship, that is your choice."

I sat back in my seat, feeling the heat ebb from my hands. I was suddenly much more alright with the situation. I could be a queen without the drawbacks. Or at least, that was what I was hearing, words too good to be true. He sounded truthful, but I was suspicious. This was unheard of. Mages didn't get to negotiate the terms of their captivity.

"Why are you giving me a choice?" I asked.

"Well," he smiled, "we both know if I denied it to you, you could level this country as revenge. But beyond that..." he looked down, taking a deep breath. His voice was lower when he spoke, more ragged, "It was a choice my mother never had. It killed her. I swore I would extend all the choices I could to the next Stardropped."

"Is that what I am?"

"Yes, undoubtedly. Although, I will admit I am surprised I ever got to meet you. There is only one Stardropped at a time, like the other mages, and since

I can use star-fire I feared you would not appear until I was long dead."

"So that's what you can do." That explained the door handle. The gold eyes. Why he wasn't afraid. What caught me was that he had inherited it. Mage powers weren't inherited, they appeared from nowhere when their user was a baby. That made him doubly unusual.

"Yes. Only a fraction as powerful as my mother or yourself but useful nonetheless. But we have so much time to discuss all of that. Let's focus on our next task of the day- your announcement."

"Oh." I looked down at my wrists, rubbing at the ghost of my bracelets. Even in my initial shock I had not remembered that particular bit of pageantry.

I had heard of it being done. A passing moment of exposure so the people could see who would give birth to the next king or queen. That's all most queens did, in this country and others. I was determined that if this was my fate, I would not exist to do that.

He was far from revolting in looks, but I knew nothing of who he was. Surely there was something horrible about him that would give the newly named star-fire in my chest a reason to destroy him and his life, not add to it.

"We will get through it as quickly as possible."

17

I thought of all the people I had just alienated outside. The words felt silly in my mouth and my voice sounded small, "Do you think they'll like me?"

"Of course, you are the Stardropped."

"You keep saying that as if it's an answer. I don't know what that means!" My hands were hot again. He said we had time, but I couldn't stand to not know. I'd spent twenty years not knowing. Twenty years of suffering for it, convinced something was horribly wrong with me. If he knew what I was, a mage with her own name like a title, I needed all the answers he had.

"I knew you would have been sheltered in the Towers but..." he trailed off. "The Stardropped is an outstandingly powerful mage. Your power has shaped history. Presently, from the point of view of the people, the last time there was a Stardropped as queen, they got me as the next king. And I am sure, per our earlier conversation, you know exactly how they view me. A living legend, as you put it. So to see you by my side- I can not think of anything that they would be more accepting of."

This was not how my life was supposed to be. I wasn't supposed to be by anyone's side. I was supposed to be a Mother Mage, jaded by my job just like the rest of them. But suddenly I was wanted and I couldn't reconcile with how impossible that was. This wasn't real.

"I don't have to do any speaking, do I?" I asked.

"No, no. Unless you would like to?"

"The only thing I want more than to not speak is to not be here."

"I understand, but surely you understand why I am doing this. You could not stay in the Towers forever."

"I think in time I might be grateful, but not yet."

This man had a motive hidden behind his golden exterior. The men that took mages from the Towers had vile plans for them, a truth my sisters chose to ignore but I didn't. He was too good to be genuine. No one wanted nothing in return, especially not kings.

CHAPTER 2

"There is the palace." He nodded to the view out his window a few hours later. I carefully leaned over to look past him.

It was a hundred times larger than the Towers. The warm stone structure was set on the edge of a cliff face, threatening to disappear into the ocean at any moment. Every arched window reflected the sunlight and every open air walkway swirled with billowing curtains. I counted at least eight towers. It was beautiful, but my mind wondered which tower I'd be trapped in now. None of them, I reminded myself. I would sooner destroy every tower in the world than go back to one.

The carriage rolled to a stop. Zandorian opened the door and stepped out. He offered a hand to help me down. I made a point of floating down on my own, my feet not touching the ground at all.

He broke the long silence as a woman I had seen outside the Towers before approached us. She had been one of the people I had snapped at.

There were streaks of gray in her hair and slight lines under her eyes that deepened with her smile.

"This is your maid, Eda."

"Wonderful to meet you, my queen."

"Eda, I'm sorry I was rude."

"No apology needed, my queen." Those words sounded so strange to my ears. She said it like a name.

I followed them both inside the overwhelmingly large front doors as the rest of the people dispersed.

"Go get dressed, I will meet you there when it is time." He disappeared down one of the halls behind a patterned curtain.

I didn't know where "there" was but I didn't want to meet him anywhere. Maybe I could lock myself behind one of these doors and never leave.

"My queen, this way," Eda said. I followed her. She didn't deserve to deal with me doing that. What if they blamed her? I had no way of knowing what her punishment might be.

I didn't pay attention to where we went too closely. I was too caught on the colors. For every bit of plain the palace was on the outside, it was twice as colorful inside. Every room and hallway was a new set of patterns and color pallets. I chose to look mostly at the floor instead. I didn't want to be deceived into liking it here just because it was bright. Beautiful places held wrong doings just as well as plain ones.

I focused on Eda instead. We stopped outside doors made of red glass and metal.

"I am very sorry I was rude. I was upset," I apologized.

"Of course, no apology needed." She opened the doors and held them open for me to enter. "Pick a new robe, my queen."

I was dazed by the colors and patterns of the garments before me. The glitter of the jewelry that was just as colorful. My eyes hung over the shoes with their extensive beading and creative styles. I'd never have the heart to wear all these beautiful things only to destroy them by accident.

I settled on a black robe with a taller, upright collar. As I pulled it down I saw it had a gold chain belt around the middle but chose to ignore it. I didn't want to think about what it meant if I put myself back in chains immediately after leaving the others behind. Otherwise, it suited my mood perfectly. Something dramatic but simple. Eda helped me take off the blue robe and pull on the new one. She didn't flinch when she accidentally touched my skin, and for that I was grateful and impressed.

"Are you a mage?"

"Fire mage, my queen." Of course, that made sense. I wondered how much heat she could withstand. I wish I knew, I didn't want to get too comfortable and hurt her by accident.

"And you work as a maid?"

"I used to be a weaponsmith with my husband, but I had to give up the business when he died and my sons wanted to sell it. The king offered me this job because I was uniquely suited, as he put it."

"Do you want to make weapons? I can dress myself." As I said it, she put a heavy necklace around my neck.

She smiled. "Part of our arrangement is access to all of the kingdom's forges and any materials I could want. Better than I've ever had before." Her eyes were excited. "I'm happy with my situation. Your king is incredibly considerate and compassionate. My husband was not. You're very lucky."

That made an unfortunate amount of sense. Years ago, I had been told by Mother Nai that most of the men mages left with were not good people. They were wildly successful businessmen, diplomats, generals, and apparently kings. Those titles did not lend themselves to selfless men that didn't have a wild hunger for power. I wasn't sure I was one of the lucky ones.

She moved away. I looked at the necklace for the first time. It was not one chain, but several smaller gold chains twisted together. At the end was the star of the Al family, the most powerful symbol in Solde-al. It all felt much more real in that moment.

"There, all done. Let's get you in place. Follow me, my queen." I did, messing with my necklace and the lengths of fabric trailing behind me off my new outfit onto the stone and tile floors. When I looked up again, we'd stopped.

"Wait here, my queen. The king will join you soon."

She shut me in a room with several doors. I had no idea where I was other than that I'd counted three flights of stairs. The walls were decorated with paintings of past kings and queens of Solde-al. They all wore serious expressions. Two caught my attention for the simple fact that they included three and four people instead of two. The one with four would have been Zandorian's grandparents and two other spouses, I'd read their names before. His grandfather had been responsible for several famous battles. Famous because of how unfair they had been in Solde-al's favor, only to be lost. His grandmother was a mage, but I couldn't remember what power had been hers. I wondered which ones were Zandorian's parents, but I couldn't see yellow eyes in any of the faces.

The large doors opened again. Zandorian came in wearing a deep red robe, gold thread embellishing every flowing edge with stars. He had pulled his hair down. It surprised me how long it was, soft waves falling to his mid back. He wore a necklace like mine, except that his was larger and included the stars of the six regions as smaller pendants down either side of the chain. I recognized the same necklace on several of the men in paintings behind him. It all looked incredibly official and intimidating.

"Wonderful choices." He smiled. "Let's get this over with," his voice had an edge of distaste. He must not like this much either.

Two men opened the doors, revealing a beautiful balcony. I was detached from it all again. The only thing I felt was Zandorian's hand lightly around mine.

"Forgive me, we will need to keep up appearances no matter what you choose. Otherwise, some might question your title," he said in a low voice only I could hear. I was stuck on the fact that he could hold my hand. He didn't shy away or recoil from the heat. I looked down at our clasped hands, amazed. I let myself warm to a more comfortable temperature. When he didn't react to that, I let my hand reach glowing hot for just a moment. Still, he was unbothered. He looked over at me briefly, trying to read my face.

He led us out onto the balcony. The size of the crowd beyond surprised me. It was easily more people than I had ever met, although that wasn't saying much. They looked up at us with eager faces, hands braced to applause. I only distantly felt their eyes on me. My mind wasn't experiencing any of it. I was staring at the middle range where I could only see the flower arrangements that topped the balcony rail, the rooftops of the city, and the distant blue sky. I felt myself being pulled back inside.

He dropped my hand as soon as we were out of sight of the crowd. My only anchor, gone. I was floating freely away from myself now. I was both grateful he had dropped my hand and wished he would take it back.

I watched him look down at his hand. Had I hurt him after all? Looking closer he was adjusting his rings, nothing more.

"Back down stairs, then. I will give you a tour." I followed in silence, again trying and failing to figure out where we were in the building from what I had seen outside. I was almost at a breaking point from following and moving through this day. All I'd done was follow and sit and follow.

"Skye!" And then I was faced with a small and incredibly familiar friend.

"Aurelia, what are you doing?" I stepped away to keep her at an arm's length.

"Oh Skye, it's wonderful! Vitsef loved me, we knew in an instant it was meant to be, soon as he looked in my eyes." She didn't stop smiling, but I swore I saw the smallest, quickest wink. "It was so beautiful. He's Solde's highest general, he serves directly under the king, that's why they came together. We get to see each other all the time!" I realized exactly what she had done. Had she done it for me?

"That's wonderful," I hesitated on the word wonderful, but she didn't seem to care.

"You look amazing. I wish you'd let me dress you in stuff like that."

"The Towers never had anything like this."

"Well yeah, but it would have been fun to think about!"

She looked past me and I followed her gaze. Zandorian was walking away from the man that was now Aurelia's husband. I remembered briefly glancing over him at the Towers. He was of average build and slightly over average age; his face had a few lines and his blond beard and short hair had hints of white. She could have ended up with someone physically worse, but I had nothing but a bad feeling about the rest of the situation.

"Oh, the king is coming back. I'll let you go, but I wanted to tell you!"

"Bye, Auri," I said weakly. I didn't want her to go. Zandorian had kept his distance, letting us talk. I appreciated that. But now he was back in front of me,

27

offering his hand again like he'd done for the carriage. I didn't take it this time either.

"Most important destinations first, I think," he said with another smile, putting his hand down and leading the way.

I saw several halls and rooms through a haze. I knew all were aesthetically beautiful, but my mind couldn't fully process them. I was thinking too many other thoughts. Most of them involved fire.

Everyone I had thought was there to protect the king gradually disappeared. Not a single stationed guard, no one following ten paces behind us. Some very important men visited the Towers, and never had they been without personal bodyguards.

"You don't have guards?"

"No, no. It would be more a danger to them than helpful to me." He laughed, "You will not have any either, unless you want them," he offered, more serious.

"I don't." I liked my chances of being able to handle anything that came up when it came to my personal safety. What I could do was nothing a guard wouldn't get in the way of. I also knew I did not like the idea of being followed around, my every movement watched. The first part of my life had been like that. I didn't want it to continue.

We walked past the doors that went to my closet, farther down a hallway that gradually changed from red to gold and pearly white tiles covering the walls and ceiling. I noticed the way their designs swirled and reflected light from the openair arches, the gentle movement of the white curtains in the ocean breeze throwing shadows so they seemed to move. They looked like star-fire.

Zandorian opened a large, heavy metal door into a plain and narrow hallway. Then another door, opening on another identical hallway. I was getting nervous. Behind the third door was a large, comfortable bedroom like any other, but windowless.

"Here is your room. It is built to withstand your firestorms, hence the doors. They only lock from the inside, do not worry." His words were so soft, back in that reverent tone. "Through that door," he pointed to another heavy metal door across the room, "are stairs that lead further underground to another room that was constructed for emergencies, whether that be a particularly powerful firestorm or a hiding place. I will never bother you here unless you ask." I looked around. It was all much nicer than anything I had ever seen before, but in a subtle way. When I looked back at him, he was watching me closely. For less than a second, his eyes darted to the bed. Every one of my thoughts became exactly how this fireproof room would come down in rubble if he tried to touch me. But then he was walking out the door.

"Anyway, I thought you would like to rest before seeing the gardens or my study or the library. I will leave you."

"There's a library?" I was excited by the idea of more books to keep my mind occupied, but I also wanted out of that room.

"Of course, I could not live without it."

"I want to see it."

"Are you sure? It has been quite a day"

"I thought I was allowed to pursue whatever I want. I want to see it."

"Alright, that is fair." His words were passive, but there was excitement behind them.

We walked through an incredibly large and well-manicured courtyard garden. Fountains and lanterns decorated the stone walkways that weaved their way between the hedges. On the other side of the walkway that cut it in half, I saw the racks of weapons and some practice targets in a grassy open space. I wondered how often that was used, or was it for show?

We stopped at two large wooden doors intricately carved with geometric patterns and large polished brass handles.

"Here is my own pride of the palace, as requested."
He opened the doors to an enormous library. The air
left my lungs in a sigh.

Three levels tall with a wall of windows. The view
of the glittering sea was similar to the one from the
Towers. I ran my eyes over the shelves of books and
up to the ornate balconies above. Several doors lead
off into reading rooms, each one with its own obvious
theme: plants, art, the sea, and so many others. It was
all exquisite in every way. It had more books than the
Towers by far, each one a work of art. I walked
between the tables and plush chairs arranged in cozy
gatherings to look out the windows. Sheer cliff was
on the other side. Turning around I got to see it all
again, even more magnificent now that I could see
the curving staircases and the extent of the ornate
labels on the glass doors that protected the books from
the world.

Zandorian watched me with interest for a moment
before he walked to an open door,

"Here is a room I think you will enjoy. Historical
battle maps, military histories, some antique
weaponry. Admittedly, the weapons were the only
thing I found interesting here as a child, but I have
come to appreciate the rest."

He was right. He had just listed some of my
favorite subjects. The cases and racks of beautiful

weapons were impressive. The books and scrolls were marked with small gold plaques above their shelves, the dates and names in the most intricate lettering. I looked up at the enormous map that covered the far wall. It was the kingdom of Solde-al drawn in extensive detail in blood red ink. My kingdom, I realized.

I sat with that thought for a moment before it curled into anxiety about how little I actually knew about it. I rattled my brain for trivia.

Historically, I knew Solde's economy was largely dependent on wine, agriculture, gold, jewelry, and textiles. Whether Zandorian had made any changes, I wasn't sure. I'd have to find out. Guessing from the contents of my closet, it hadn't.

A map of the De continent and beyond was spread out on the square center table. I looked it over. It was pathetic how much I actually knew about the current situation between all of the countries. The Towers got information several years too late unless it was about a marriage, and even then I was only handed books that were at least thirty years old. I ran my finger lightly along the borderlines. They had moved since the most recent book I'd gotten my hands on had been written. Of course.

Something about the broken islands in the bottom corner bothered me. The Trusican-ni Empire. It looked like a landmass that had crumbled like bread. I was thankful it wasn't a part of our continent. I'd likely never have to think about it too seriously unless something was incredibly wrong.

"What are you thinking about?" Zandorian asked, moving to the side of the table across from me.

"If I'm going to do this, I need to know what's going on."

"Fair. Know that every time I leave, it is to go handle whatever our usual forces can not. Usually somewhere in here." He ran a finger across our northern and western border. I wondered what exactly he meant by "handle," but he continued before I could ask. "Truthfully, we are always fighting someone, and for the past decade it has been Niode-kos.

"Our neighbors to the north, Niode-kos, have far fewer resources. Our neighbors to the East, Livade-weh, have more but no substantial military force, so Niode takes from them. Our southern neighbors, Dunede-pet, have an interest in keeping them up here, so they help us. I try to maintain our borders and help out Livade. Our current largest fear is that Niode will turn its sights to us only, bringing the fighting here. We can handle them, but I do not look forward to it. Especially if you decide to become involved."

"They can't hurt me."

"I am not worried about them hurting you." The way he said it, I was sure he was aware of the imbalance of power I would have over an army. He probably knew better than I did. "Today that is all you need to know. We can get into more fine details in a couple days in time for your first council meeting. The rest is much more boring. Finances and whatnot. I would not blame you if you do not want to go at all."

I doubted that it was boring, but he seemed decided. I wanted to get my hands on everything I could. If I was to be his equal, I had catching up to do.

"I'm going."

"Alright, I will make plans for it then." I didn't know what plans he would need to make if it was a standard meeting, but I heard footsteps behind us.

I turned around to see the dark-skinned frowning man I'd seen at the Towers. He had his gray hair cut close to his scalp and wore a deep blue robe with pressed pleating and clean lines that mirrored the slight ones around his eyes and forehead. His ears had a mild point to their top that was common in mages and their children. Now that he was closer I saw he was on eye level with me, making him slightly taller than average. He kept his hands folded behind his back as he spoke.

"Zan, I suspected it was you. No one else leaves the door open." He had the same accent as Zandorian, though slightly thicker. I also noticed he'd called Zandorian by a nickname. What kind of relationship did they have? Surely more familiar than a king has with his servant.

Zandorian smiled warmly to greet him, an expression he did not return.

"Kaniel, this is Skye."

"Skye the Stardropped. I am very happy I could meet you and be one of the few who have the privilege to know two and a half Stardropped in their lifetime." He looked at me appraisingly without one hint of happiness. It wasn't offensive, but it was awkward.

"Skye, Kaniel raised me and taught me my entire education for subjects that were not combat. He will be more than happy to help you with whatever you want to learn."

"A devoted learner, hm?" Kaniel asked.

"Yes," I answered.

"Everything that Zan said is true with one stipulation; if you burn even one cover page, you will not be allowed back in this room," he sounded quite matter of fact about it. What kind of librarian could keep a queen out of her own library?

"Kaniel, really," Zandorian quietly reproved.

"No, Zan, you know my rules. After your mother lost me that entire shelf I have to set precautions, remember." Kaniel looked directly at me. Somewhere, as if from a dream, I remembered that was a joke, a flash of a smile crossing my face before I could stop it. Kaniel's face fell into an even deeper frown. What was that?

"Alright, I think she understands," Zandorian said. Kaniel nodded and walked away. I was not certain about that man. Something was off about him under his put together appearance.

"Skye, are you hungry? Kaniel says my mother did not need to eat, but I do not want to assume." He was right. The Mother Mages had tested it. I once went eight months with no food or water and no issues. I still enjoyed eating it anyway.

"I like food."

"We have excellent cooks. I usually let them use their best judgment, but if there is something you hate or prefer, please let me know." He started to walk out of the library. I followed.

"Seems wasteful to have them make one specific thing for just me."

"I promise they will not mind. It would be probably a nice change from the handful of enormous single dishes they usually make for everyone on staff. I have not asked them to make anything special in a very long time."

I didn't know where we were going. Occasionally he looked back to make sure I was still following. We went down more long hallways with their colorful swirling curtains and spiraling staircases hidden behind unassuming doors. Again we stopped, this time at an iron door.

"Here is where I eat my meals and spend most of my time."

The room was actually much smaller than I had expected, looking more like a sitting room than a dining room, even with the table with six high back chairs on one side. Bookshelves lined the far walls and cushioned armchairs sat before an ornate fireplace. The walls that didn't have bookshelves had paintings of landscapes and the night sky. The windows were tall and narrow facing the ocean. Each windowsill had a plant or three in ornate containers, including the one with a large desk in front of it. The desk was littered with papers and colorful inks. I looked up. The ceiling was tiled with sparkling golden stars.

"It's cozy. I was expecting to eat in a hall," I tried to not sound like I was demanding it. I'd spent enough of my life sitting in a dining hall with other mages. The small space was a welcome change, even if unfamiliar.

"Oh, we only use the halls for events. You are welcome if that is what you would like. I much prefer it in here. The view is better and I do not feel so lonely." He seemed to realize what he'd said and studied the hem of his sleeve. For a moment I was empathetic. I knew what lonely felt like.

There was a knock at the door.

"Ah, perfect timing." Zandorian pulled the door open and moved to stand against the wall. I did the same, putting an armchair between myself and anyone's way.

Several large dishes of food were brought in and the table set by a handful of people dressed plainly in yellow and red. I received several curious but slightly fearful glances. One young woman in particular jumped when she saw me. I hoped that reaction wasn't going to be a constant.

Once they'd left Zandorian closed the door and sat at the table in the chair at the end facing the door. I followed suit but sat at the farthest chair on the opposite side. I didn't want to sit any closer to him than I had to and give him the wrong idea about where I stood.

"I hope you like it." He gave me a small smile and turned his focus to the food.

Everything was spiced and colorful, even the white fish and vegetable soup. The Towers had never had food that looked so wonderful.

At the Towers, the four oldest years of mages rotated who helped the Mother Mages make food for the younger years. That usually meant we got simple recipes and little else. I was never allowed to help, even when it was my year's turn. I read the instructions to them sometimes, usually to Nerial who hated reading. Nerial had been the best cook, but that was attributed to the fact that she could have the pots and pans move on their own using her power to control objects with her thoughts. She had been a one woman kitchen team. I missed her. I missed all of them.

I'd all but forgotten about my own situation when Zandorian started talking.

"Skye, what is your favorite color?" he asked.

I thought, stirring my soup with a spoon. I looked up into his eyes and decided on a truthful answer.

"Gold. And black."

"I also favor gold. Red and green are close seconds."

He hadn't connected that I'd said gold because it was the color of his eyes. Good.

***

Later, I laid in my bed and thought of all the ways this could go. I was still convinced he wanted me so he could control me. It was the only way this made sense in the mind of an ambitious king. He could own the world with me on his side, but I wouldn't go along with that. The fire in my chest wanted that, but my mind did not. It said if he tried to control me, I could level everything, kill everyone he ever loved, just as he'd said. Or I could play a slower game. I could start making changes behind his back and closed doors… slowly destroying his kingdom. That thought made me cringe but the anger in my bones ached. It wanted that. I didn't.

There was a part of me that was removed from the fire entirely. That part was dazzled and dizzy by the sound of his voice and those eyes. The way he told me the answers to everything I asked. He promised he wanted nothing in return, not even love. I wanted to believe him. Deep down I wanted a romantic adventure, a family, and just a little bit of power. But that life wasn't for me, it never had been. I was meant to burn and destroy. I was the Stardropped Queen of Solde-al.

CHAPTER 3

I didn't sleep well. My room was too quiet. I missed the constant sound of waves and ocean winds. I even missed the distant sounds of my sisters stirring in their sleep. They had annoyed me for years, but now I was too alone.

After several hours of sleeping on and off I gave up on being comfortable. On my floor, a small box with the brand of the Towers caught my attention. That must be what the Mother Mages had given them when Zandorian had asked for my possessions.

I opened the box and started rummaging through my things. I'd never had much, and most of it had been burned to ash at some point. Two notebooks had survived, but only because the mages had confiscated them. I supposed they realized it was time to give them back. I wasn't incredibly angry that they'd kept them. I'd never had a place to keep them where they wouldn't have been burned with the others.

Should I keep them in here? Or hide them in the library? I could hide them on the shelves in Zandorian's room, but the idea of him reading what I'd written inside as a young teenager made me shudder. I decided on the library. There had to be a place to slip them in with the other books.

I found three robes: gray, light gray, and black. They were plain and worn. I doubted I'd ever need those again and laid them aside for when I needed something I wouldn't feel bad about burning.

There was a single silver ring on the bottom. I had had it for as long as I could remember, but I had no idea where it had come from. The Mother Mages had held onto it since I was fourteen. I had been sure they'd taken it to sell. I was glad to see it, again finding myself thinking of where I could hide it to keep out of harm's way.

I pulled out my eye makeup and went to the mirror. I licked the tip of the brush before dipping it in the black. I drew the brush across the top of my eye lid and out with a flick. I'd worn my makeup this way for years. I found I unsettled people a little less when I wore it.

My doors opened one by one. I spun, my free hand burning.

"Good morning, my queen," said a warm, deep female voice I recognized from yesterday.

"Hello Eda."

She came into my room and shut the door behind her. I calmed myself. She was allowed to be here. She was here to help.

"Ready to get dressed?" she asked. I finished my makeup and followed her to the closet.

Looking around, I saw significantly more black clothes than I had thought there had been before. Had I not seen them, or had they been added? Then I saw the jewelry. More of it was gold, I was certain of that. I would have to keep an eye out for changes tomorrow. I put my silver ring in among the others. It looked plain and out of place.

I picked out a black robe with sheer black sleeves that stopped at my mid arm and spilled onto the floor to join with the lengths of fabric flowing off the back. It wasn't as regal as the one from yesterday, but it was beautiful.

"Eda, do you know the palace well?" I asked as she helped me navigate the garment.

"Well enough, my queen."

"Would you mind walking around with me? I didn't get a complete tour yesterday, and I don't want to get lost." That wasn't entirely true. I was sure Zandorian had done his best at getting me oriented, I simply hadn't taken any of it in.

"Of course."

I felt less bad about asking Eda to accompany me as I realized just how labyrinthine the layout was. It was deceptively simple on the first floor, but I found it impossible to remember which door concealed a stairway to go up. When Eda showed me one, she said it only led to half the second floor. What kind of paranoid ancestors did Zandorian have?

When I thought about it more, it made sense. The countries of the De continent had been pushing and pulling at each other for a thousand years. The last two hundred had been the worst. I knew the Al family had been in power for about six generations. They had united the six smaller countries that were now our regions into what was now Solde, but it had not been a bloodless endeavor. In war it was important to make your leaders hard to find and harder to kill.

I walked us down past where the gardens ended, towards where we'd arrived yesterday. On one side of the entrance, two enormous doors were open to the largest room I had ever seen. They had not been open yesterday, I would have remembered this sight. The ceiling of the room was covered in iridescent tiles of a thousand warm colors arranged in mind-twisting flower and star patterns. I had to see it all.

"Can I go in there?" I asked.

Eda furrowed her brow, "My queen, did you just ask my permission?" Asking what I could and couldn't do was a habit that would be hard to kill. The Mother Mages had always kept me on such a tight chain I'd had to ask their permission for everything.

"Right, I'm going in there." I tried to say it with authority. I still felt ridiculous, but I figured I had time to practice.

The arched windows had the Al star set into the top in red and gold glass, throwing the colors onto the floor so the design covered every inch of it. The floor was made of squares of polished stone with veins of crackling black and red in its warm gray surface. Between the squares was gold to fill the gaps and smooth the surface. It was so beautiful I was nearly moved to tears, my hand on the side of my face in awe.

"Eda, how are you?" I heard the one sound that could have distracted me. That smooth gold voice.

He wore a deep red robe and his hair was braided today. The shade of red made it look as if his tattoos were a part of the garment. He wore three gold chains around his neck, each one dotted with ruby pendants. I also noted at least six rings. Did he always dress this way?

He smiled, "I see you found the grand hall." His voice bounced off the walls.

"It's beautiful," I whispered.

"It is now."

"Has it not always been?" I asked, looking out at the ocean through the clear sections of the windows.

"Not until very recently," he said. I nodded. I wondered how much of this was his work or if he'd not had any involvement at all.

"What's it used for?"

"Only the most important parties. Of course, you could use it for whatever you want," he offered.

I couldn't think of anything that could do this room justice. I chose to leave it instead. Zandorian followed.

I hadn't properly taken in the enormity of the domed entryway yesterday, either. It had to be the collective height of all the floors the palace had, if not more by a floor or two. The windows that circled the top let the sunlight into the dome. I swore it moved, or maybe it was the angle of my neck to look up at it making me dizzy. I hadn't noticed I had left the ground till I looked down again, falling the small distance to put my feet back on the stone floor.

I looked out the open front doors, down to the large homes, tall gates, and the city beyond them and then to hills and open blue sky beyond that. The world was bigger than it ever had been before.

"What's stopping me from walking out these doors and never coming back?" I asked Zandorian.

"Nothing," he shrugged, pushing the door open wider. "I couldn't stop you if I wanted to." He walked around me and back into the entryway, throwing out his hands. "I wanted to give you your title and any material thing you could ever want for. What you do is up to you. But, I do hope you will be up to the task of helping me make Solde-al better."

"And ending a war."

"Yes, that too."

I took ten steps out. I felt the sunlight and the breeze. I heard birds and people going about their day. As I went to step down the first stair, I realized I didn't want to leave, not really. Here I was a queen, and out there I was a nothing but a force of devastation. I couldn't make anyone's life better if I left, not even my own. The star-fire agreed as it flared at the thought of staying. Here I could end and start wars, collect titles, and burn without repercussions.

When I turned back I remembered another benefit of staying. I wasn't excited by the idea of leaving everyone I knew behind. Especially the only person who could hold my hand.

Zandorian looked incredibly anxious, fidgeting with his rings. I saw a few small star-fire sparks fly as he did it. His expression changed to delight when I walked back to his side.

"Any dinner requests?" he asked.

"No."

I couldn't see Eda anywhere. I was confident I could find my way back to my room but I was sad she'd left.

"What is wrong?"

"I'd planned on walking around but my tour guide is gone."

"I think I might be able to help with that," he said. I nodded once and started off in a different direction.

I kept up my plan of wandering, this time with Zandorian following me instead of Eda. I felt some guilt asking him questions everytime he was starting to leave, but I didn't want to be alone. He didn't seem to mind much. He let me into rooms that were locked and told me about shortcuts I never would have thought to try.

The doors here didn't all depend on keys like they had at the Towers. I imagined it was because they were in a palace with access to the best locksmiths in the world, not to mention the Al's paranoid history. Some had dials, some had multiple knobs, and some had tricks hidden in the woodwork. One had a metal bird that required its wings to be held closed while pushing on the door to open it.

48

Zandorian explained each one of them while he did it. I wasn't sure I would ever remember how to open all of them. I was thankful when he said some of the more important ones did in fact have keys that I could get my own set of.

I tried another door that was unlocked, and the room beyond made me pause more than any other since the grand hall. It was larger than I had expected when I'd opened the door, a small hall between unused bedrooms. It was open and light and one side was entirely doors that lead out onto a sunny veranda. What caught my eye was the ceiling. It was stars in a blue night sky. They were exaggerated like they would be in a children's book and slightly dusty, but I loved them.

"This is nice."

"It is," he said. The other rooms he had elaborated on, but in this one he stayed quiet. I lingered as long as I could before he got restless again. I would remember this one.

***

"Why is giving me a choice so important to you?" I asked at the end of our second dinner together. I wanted to question Zandorian every time I could. If his answers changed, it would be easier to spot lies, pull out his motivations.

"I firmly believe everyone needs them. It is what makes us different from animals. They simply are what they are. We choose who we are. Well... not all of us. My mother did not. I did not. My first wife Dezura did not have a choice at first, and when I gave her one she was in it to be queen. She never got that. Maybe Ashanm made her one in her next life. She was very religious."

"You're not?"

"No, I could never when I know so much about a different goddess. A very real one I see evidence for all the time in everything I do." He held a small collection of sparks in his glowing hand. "This is not something I should thank Ashanm for. It is something I should thank my mother for. What do you think?"

"I'm not religious. It never appealed to me." I gathered my thoughts, deciding to be honest. He'd been honest with me. "If there was something that controls my life, made me this way... it's not a force I want to worship." Somewhere deep down I knew there was one. It had been my mother too. A formless, faceless being of creation on the edge of an ancient memory. I knew nothing about her except that she was a cruel thing and the reason I was here. The memory faded quickly into nothing, leaving me anxious.

"Do you hate who you are?" he asked, very somber.

I thought of how the fire in my bones felt like I could have anything I wanted. How I knew in an inexplicable way that I was meant for things so much larger than this, the thirst for more power and change burning in my chest. But I also thought of how I ached. How my mind was exhausted from repressing my emotions. How it twisted itself into loops. I didn't have an answer for him, instead staring forward into the fire burning in the fireplace across the room. Maybe it felt like I did… we would both consume until there was nothing left if given the chance. I couldn't dwell on that any longer, and he was talking.

"I am simply trying to get to know you, forgive me."

I got up and left, heading for somewhere I'd find when I got there, probably my room. I still wasn't convinced he didn't have a motivation for all of this. When he said I could leave, it hadn't seemed like he had been lying, but I didn't know him well enough to be sure. I hoped he was genuine. This place was magic… I would hate to have to level it.

CHAPTER 4

I woke up to Eda opening my door the next morning. I must have made up for my lost sleep from yesterday. On the edge of remembering, I knew I'd been dreaming of wild-fire covered hills. I was glad I didn't remember it well as I looked at my singed pillows and blankets.

"Good morning, my queen. The king has requested your presence in the gardens as soon as you're ready." I didn't particularly want to know what he could possibly want. I knew those flowers were beautiful, but they'd look just as nice burned to nothing if he tried anything.

We walked to my closet. I led the way this time, opening the doors myself. The room had changed again. Even more black robes. I wondered if tomorrow they'd all be black. At this point I was worried it was wasteful. Where were the others going? Was that something a queen should worry about at all?

I had other things to worry about. I pulled one down without much consideration, putting it on. It was black and tight and flared out from somewhere around my knees.

I found Zandorian in the garden a few minutes later. He wore deep green, blending in with the foliage. The same large amount of gold jewelry with an additional earring today. That made me wonder about my jewelry too. Where did it go when it disappeared?

"Good morning, Skye."

"What are we doing?"

"With your first official meeting tomorrow, I thought you would like to research the current affairs."

"I would."

"Good, I will show you where it all happens." I followed him up a flight of stairs and to what I guessed was the northern side of the palace. The halls became progressively less decorated and the doors became more formidable.

"When the meetings are over and votes cast, the work moves to the office. Most things are accomplished during the days in between." He stopped at a metal door with a heavy lock and interesting details across its face. I could pick out the star symbols for each of our regions set into it in a map-like arrangement. "Everything you would ever want to know about how things are currently running can be found in here."

The room was small and lit with natural light through the barred windows. The space seemed nice, but I was overwhelmed. It was organized and messy all at once. There were very clear sections in the chaos; maps in one pile, lists in another, stacks of records in yet another. Most of the cluttered feeling came from the fact that every piece of paper was not stacked neatly or put away on the shelves, instead left to float around among the others. That would have to be fixed if I was to get anything done.

"I do all official business at that desk. Sometimes it bleeds into the study but I try to keep them separate. I will have to get better about it now that we share, hm?" I ignored him and shuffled papers, trying to figure out what each pile held. He continued,

"We will get you your own desk, but for now that table is yours." I followed his gesture to the one clear surface in the room. I was thankful for that. He settled into his own spot. I saw now how the piles radiated from his chair outwards. That made sense.

I kept up my searching. I wanted to know exactly where we stood in this war. Finally, I found what I wanted. A list of battles, their outcomes, and their commanders. I looked down the list, carrying it to my table and chair. Some battles had stars next to their name and location. Those drew my attention first. Some had only a handful of losses on our side and enormous losses on the other side. Eight of them, we had gained numbers. How was that possible?

"What do the stars mean?" I asked Zandorian. He put down his pen and came over to the table.

"Ah... I hate looking at it like that." He ran a finger down the list of losses on both sides, shaking his head. "Mmm, how do I say this in a humble way... the stars are where I was. I am not proud of what I did there."

"If this is the result why aren't you out there now?" I sounded angry. I wasn't, I was genuinely asking. He clenched his jaw and walked back to his desk.

"Forgive me for not wanting to slaughter entire towns worth of Niode soldiers everyday of my life," he growled. I'd made him mad. Fine, but I had more questions.

"You could end the war. At that point does it matter what you want if it saves lives?"

"There is a world of difference between having the ability to do something in theory and watching every one of them die when you do it," I heard a small snap. He kept his back to me. "I will never be that person again. If that is who you want me to be, I am sorry for the disappointment."

Again. So he had tried it my way. The fire itched to tell him I would do it and not think twice, but that was a lie. He was made of star-fire too. If he couldn't do it, he had a good reason. I couldn't do it either. I gave him time before asking the most pressing question on my mind as I looked at the list again.

"How are these numbers positive?"

It took him a moment to answer, finally turning around.

"I offer them a choice, when I can. They can come back to Solde with us. In Niode, being a soldier is one of the only occupations that pays a livable life. The way Kos handles his country it does not give them a choice, but Solde-al can."

His entire reputation made much more sense to me at that moment. A force of destruction, but a merciful one that offered forgiveness and new beginnings. The star-fire in my veins hated that he didn't destroy them all. But I loved that he didn't.

I focused on the list again, but I couldn't think about it properly. My eyes kept going to the stars. After a few failed tries I folded it up and put it away, going on the hunt for financials. That was an area I was much less versed in, but it was as important as any other, if not more. I'd have to learn quickly.

As I flipped through the thick stack of folders I'd found I could only get basics. Despite everything going on, we were still well into profits. That didn't feel correct.

"Can you help me with this?"

"What is it?"

"Finances."

"Ah... I will tell you now, I am horrible with money. Kaniel did his best but I never fully got the hang of it on the large scale." He smiled but I stayed stoic. That was a bit of luxury I'd never considered. I didn't pretend to be any better, I'd only lived in the Towers where everything was provided, but I would go as far out of my way as possible to make sure I could handle this.

"I could arrange a meeting with the treasurer for you? It would not be until after tomorrow's council."

"That would be good."

"Good. You will be better than I ever was. You are much smarter than me. I look forward to hearing your thoughts." I kept my face blank but that was one of the nicest things anyone had ever said to me.

I went back to the papers, turning my attention to trade. Dunede-pet was our largest trade partner by far, followed by Renciam. Renciam was a beautiful place of deserts and emerald rivers. Their purely democratic way of running the country had been in place for over three hundred years. I had enormous respect for them. I wished Solde-al was more like that.

Our elected officials were lifetime representatives, and the ones I'd read about had been from already powerful families. Even if everything was put to a vote, that didn't mean it represented the people well.

Close to an hour later I heard Zandorian get up from his desk behind me. I turned around to look at him.

"I have to leave. You are welcome to stay." He handed me a large metal key on a gold chain. "Lock the door when you are done. That is your key." I took it, holding it carefully. "Will I see you for dinner?"

"Not sure." I was, but I didn't want him to think I was too eager to see him. He nodded and left.

I immediately set about rearranging and organizing. Several hours later the sunset in the windows reminded me I'd said I wasn't sure about dinner. Putting down what I was going through, I admitted defeat for the day.

Sitting down at the farthest seat for dinner again, I pulled some of the dishes towards me. I ate in silence until I remembered what I'd meant to bring up.

"I noticed my robes are being replaced."

"Do you not like them?" He looked concerned.

"I love them, but it seems wasteful. Where do the old ones go?"

"They are altered and given away to people who need them. Sometimes sold." That made far more sense than I had thought it would.

"The jewelry?"

"Recycled, made into other pieces. Again, sometimes sold if the piece is particularly impressive. The jewelers both love and hate me. I let them keep enough materials that I would like to think it is more love."

"Do you tell them what to make?"

"The jewelers, usually not. The tailors, yes, nearly every garment. I have more opinions when it comes to designing clothes... one of my hobbies."

"So all of those robes, you designed?"

"Most of them."

"Wow." That was genuinely impressive.

"I keep the designs in the tall files on that shelf, if you want to go through them." He pointed to one of his larger bookshelves. "Keep in mind I have had years with nothing else to do. And exactly no queens to burn through them," he laughed.

I laughed too. It was a strange feeling. I hadn't had a reason to laugh in a very long time. The way he looked at me, I realized it was the first time he'd ever seen me fully smile. I hid it quickly, but he stayed dazed. I could dazzle him too.

"But honestly, do you like them? The dresses?"

"I do."

"Too much black?" he asked with a raised eyebrow.

"Not enough," I answered. That made him smile.

"I would not have thought the queen of a country known for colorful fabrics would have such an aversion."

"It's less about my aversion and more that I know black is easier to make. I feel less bad burning it than a beautiful pattern."

"Skye… you do not have to worry about that. But if it makes you feel better, that is how it will be."

I stared out the window for a long time, sinking a little more comfortably into my chair. My thoughts of burning the palace to the ground had substantially ebbed today. I found myself rubbing my wrists again, a little surprised not to find chains. It gave me a thought,

"You should tell them to stop making bracelets. I don't wear bracelets."

"Never?" he asked.

"Never again."

CHAPTER 5

I fully expected the whole of my closet to be black robes after the conversation last night. I was right. This morning, all but a handful of red robes with gold accents had been replaced with black. The red would likely stay permanently as it was the national color of Solde-al.

My jewelry was entirely gold now. If it was set with stones, they were blood red or sparkling clear. There wasn't a single bracelet in the whole assortment.

I got dressed quickly, picking out a deceptively simple piece that grew when I pulled it on. What I had thought was safe with a single fabric unfolded into flowing sleeves and cascading layers.

I went to the place where I'd been told the meeting room was, just across from the gardens on the second floor. I was glad to see others waiting there as well. Aurelia was waiting with her husband. He had both arms around her. My stomach lurched as I remembered their dynamic. I shoved it out of my mind. It wasn't my business. If she was happy, I was happy for her.

I was suddenly aware of how grand my clothes were compared to hers as I felt them billowing around me and dragging the ground in lengths as I walked. No one else was dressed like this, not even Zandorian. I didn't hate the feeling, exactly. It was nice to have something quality of my own. But I did hate the attention I was sure it was drawing. It wasn't positive attention. Not that I ever drew much of that anyway.

Walking in from the main hallway was a familiar face I would have never expected to see. I almost ran to her. Aurelia peeled herself away to meet me there.

"Zifira!" Aurelia called out.

"What are you doing here?" I asked when I reached her, my voice accidentally cold.

"I'm Navy Commander Rolten's wife now. I left a day after you and Aurelia." She did not look happy, but I had never known her to be one for smiles. She pulled at the collar of the tight blue and red dress she was wearing.

"Seems the king has started a trend among his council…" Aurelia said.

"So it seems," Zifira said.

Having a mage had always been a status symbol for these men. It didn't impress me. Mages were expensive because the Mother Mages had decided they wanted paid for their efforts and then some. If a man could afford a mage, it meant they were not only disgusting but also flaunting their wealth. With maybe one exception. I caught sight of Zandorian outside the doors, talking with two people. I counted six gold chains around his neck and nine rings on his hands. No exceptions.

Zifira walked closer to me, only a few inches away, speaking barely above a whisper, "I am thankful for my situation, but I swear I will sink his ship if this man crosses me again. Can I count on you to help me should I have to?" I saw in her eyes how serious she was.

"What would you like me to do?"

"You are queen, protect me. Know I will not unless it is to protect myself."

"You have my promise, Zifira." We exchanged nods and she backed away. Aurelia took the opportunity to strike up the conversation I knew she was itching for.

"Hey, Skye, why didn't you go to your party? Vitsef said Zandorian was making excuses why you didn't want to go and I know you're not the most social but–"

"I'm sorry, what party?" I asked, cutting her off. My mind was reeling. I had no idea what she was talking about.

"Oh Ashanm, he didn't even ask you?" She put her hands on the sides of her face, then quickly dropped them, "Well it doesn't matter now I guess. Do you want to show us around while the boys talk?"

"Maybe another day. I'm actually going to talk with them."

"Really? Wow," she drew out the word with an impressed tone. "I guess Zifira and I are on our own. We'll find something to do." She weaved her arm through Zifira's so they were linked at the elbow. It didn't look like an action Zifira appreciated much.

"The library is beautiful," I suggested, pointing the direction they'd need to follow to find it.

"You and your books!" Aurelia called back as they started their walk away. In a selfish way I hoped they were impressed by my new home. I knew I was.

I turned back to the space and found it empty of everyone but Zandorian waiting beside the closed door. Was I late?

"Ready?" He smiled and pushed the door open.

"No," I said, walking into the room.

It was windowless and lit with bright lamps hanging from the ceiling. The only furniture was a single long table with twelve seats. Most of them had been filled in by the men who'd been outside, now free of their attendants. Every one of them went silent. I looked to Zandorian as I made for my seat at the table. The higher back and its position directly to his right made it obvious.

The last of the ones standing sat in what I imagined were their usual places. I heard the mumbled whispers. I could only make out a few.

"He brought the mage…"

"She's like him but worse."

"My newest wife says she could make the city into rubble with a blink. Don't look her in the eyes." That had to be Zifira's husband. I couldn't see who had said it. He wasn't wrong, but it had nothing to do with eye contact.

Zandorian leaned forward to talk to just me.

"This is our usual group." He made a vague gesture to them as he started to introduce them, "Our Navy Commander Rolten, High General Vitsef, International Trade Officer Daner, our Treasurer Nelser Hu, the six representatives of each of our regions. You can see what star they wear. They will not all be here every time, but they are required to vote on national matters. I asked them all to come just in case."

"In case of what?"

He stood up, ignoring my question. Then he was talking and I didn't care.

"Welcome back everyone. Today is-"

"My king, why is she here?" Interrupted one of the old men. I matched the voice to the whisper about not looking in my eyes. Poor Zifira. Rolten barely fit in his robe. He had a dried drip of wine on his chin and I was sure it would not be alone before the night was out.

"She is queen, and she has a vested interest in the wellbeing of the nation."

"You never let Dezura come to our meetings."

"Dezura, although lovely in many ways, did not spend nearly two decades studying history and stratagem as Skye has." He looked at me with kind eyes and a proud smirk. "She was also never queen, as you remember."

"A mage studying something that's not child rearing? I don't believe it," Rolten chortled, looking down the table to the others. He got a few small smiles in return and my eyes ignited.

"I have the power to destroy armies, I wanted to know how to do it in the most effective way possible. If you are uncomfortable with me having that knowledge I suggest you take a look at your own hobbies, not criticize mine."

My gaze didn't go to the faces around me for their reactions, just to the end of the table. Zandorian sat back in his seat, grinning as if I had proved his point.

"Since it is her first meeting, I would like to know if there are any changes Skye has in mind." He looked at me expectantly. They all did, but in much more bitter ways. I took in a breath.

"I would like to give all mages of age the freedom to leave the Towers without the stipulation that they leave with a husband or job. They should be free to leave on their own terms as individuals."

It was a snap decision to bring it up at that moment, but the idea was well thought out. I'd been thinking about it for years. What I wouldn't have given to have been allowed to walk out and never come back... but now that I had left and had the power, I owed it to every mage who would think the same as I had.

There was a pause of silence, then the whispers.

"Think of the damage mages cause, my queen."

"I have never avoided causing damage because I was under the jurisdiction of my mothers or the king. I have restrained myself with my own self control. All other mages can do the same by the time they're twenty if they are taught how to do so."

"My king? Surely you don't agree. It is the way mages are handled and it has been working quite well.

The last thing we need is mages without ties causing chaos," Rolten argued.

"I know a mage that can cause chaos, you should try to handle her," I mumbled under my breath. Zandorian put his hand on the table in front of me, a subtle reminder that it was best if I kept my composure. He stood up from his seat.

"I do. I completely agree with Skye. Free mages could help the country. If Skye thinks this is the best solution, I trust and support her. You all should do the same. Any questions?" There were low mumbles but no questions. "Ready to vote, then?" He looked at each of them in turn. Aurelia's new husband looked like he was thinking hard, his hands clasped on the table in front of him.

"Vitsef?"

"Yes."

"Rolten?"

"No. The last thing we need are mages ruining everything," Rolten said. I'd remember that.

"Nelser?"

"Yes." Nelser the treasurer looked nervous, his eyes darting around the room.

"Daner?

"Yes, I suppose." The trade officer looked bored.

"Haullen?"

"I vote yes." I picked him out as the representative from the Northeast. He had dark hair under a low purple hat. He was younger than many of the others.

Two more yes voted from the West and Southeast, but they were caught up in their own whispered conversation. A no from the Northwest, and I saw Haullen sit up to throw a nasty look at him. Now that I looked at them closely, I saw a resemblance, even if the age difference was large. They had to be father and son. The Southwest representative looked around the table and said no, but I watched him watch the others for their reactions. I guessed he was either a people pleaser or unpopular with the rest of them. The Central representative followed suit and voted no, not looking up from something he was writing feverishly. That put it back around to Zandorian. I held my breath even if I knew what it would be.

"And I vote yes, of course." That was enough by one. It would pass. The table looked up from whatever they were doing. I heard the whispers start again, the most notable a harsh scoff from Rolten. Then Zandorian was standing again and they fell silent.

"I will notify the Towers of the change of policy. I will expect signatures from everyone who voted yes before you depart. That will be all for today, thank you."

They rose from their seats and started to file out. I stayed in my seat, head in my hands. It had worked? My sisters were going to be free? It hadn't sunk in.

There was a shift beside me, and I realized Zandorian hadn't left. He was still in his seat, watching me with a proud smirk.

"That went surprisingly well, good job."

Surprising? I wanted to say something in return, but nothing felt right. How could I say thank you and fuck you in the same breath? I found myself smiling nervously back instead.

***

At dinner reality had set in enough that I was able to think again. I remembered what Aurelia had said earlier.

"Aurelia asked me why I didn't go to a party. What is she talking about?"

"Ah…that, regrettably, was our wedding. I did not go either, obviously." It took me a moment to make sense of that sentence. We hadn't gone to our own wedding? I wasn't upset but I was confused,

"Why did it happen if neither of us were there?"

"Those parties are never about the couple. They are about gossip and free drinks. I did not tell you because I knew you already had too much to think about. The last thing you needed was to hear all of the comments they would have made, especially from people you already had to meet at a later time."

"What comments?" I asked. His eyes glowed and his hands went into fists.

"Much like the ones they were spewing at the meeting today. I would imagine worse because they would not have gone ten minutes without someone comparing you to Dezura or my mother or any other woman. I did not want to listen to them either, so I spared us the torment."

He was right. I probably would have ended this entire thing then and there if I hadn't had time to adapt a bit before facing their judgements. Even today's meeting had been a trial at points.

"I will always ask from now on, I promise," he said sincerely. I was quiet. I had never thought I would have a wedding at all, so losing this one wasn't truly a loss. Judging from how he spoke, it wasn't a loss for him either.

"Are you upset?" he asked.

"No. Thank you for not asking me to go."

"You are welcome. Did your sister at least have a good time?"

"I didn't ask."

CHAPTER 6

I didn't need Eda's help today, but it was nice to see her. I found myself looking forward to seeing her more and more. She told me about a letter she'd gotten from her oldest son and all about her other two, though she said she hadn't heard from them in a long while. It made me sad for her, but she seemed to be shrugging it off the best she could.

I'd gone with a flowy black dress that swished and swirled around my feet and a gold chain necklace today. I was warming up to the more simple jewelry pieces. If I melted them, I knew it could be replaced without too much trouble on the part of the jewelers. It still felt strange to be wearing something expensive at all after years of little more than rags, but I liked it.

I had my mind set on the office today, bringing my key with me from the place it hung in the hallway behind my first bedroom door. Keeping it in my room was a wonderful way to melt it into a useless lump by accident. I hoped Zandorian wouldn't need to spend too much time in the office. When I saw him in the hall in full armor, I doubted it. The sight did make me stop in my tracks, however.

The large round chest plate was emblazoned with the Al star in extreme detail. He had three layers of plates from the tops of his shoulders to his neck, a red cape cascading down his back. He had two more plates on his forearms and another set that mirrored them on his shins. The pieces were all held in place by smooth steel sheets of chain that took the place of leather straps. Otherwise, he didn't wear anything between the metal and the skin of his chest and arms, making it very clear that the lines of his tattoos covered his entire body. The helmet under his arm was a shape I'd never seen, many sloping points making the top into a three-dimensional version of the Al star design. As he got closer I realized his pants were made of entirely small and tight chainmail and held up with the same kind of chain belt. It was all a smart solution for being able to use star-fire without burning clothes. The craftsmanship of the whole ensemble was outstanding, even if it did show some light wear.

"Good morning, Skye."

"What's going on?"

"I am leaving for a couple days to go visit Wertrick Pet in Dunede. You are welcome to come with me if you wish."

"I'll stay here," I said. He nodded, looking slightly disappointed. "Why are you going? I thought when you left it was to go to the front. Unless that's what this is about." I pointed to the armor.

"It usually is. I will be completely honest, I am not entirely sure why he has invited me. I suppose I will find out." He shrugged. "The armor is much more conducive to flying there instead of wasting everyone else's time with travel." He could fly like I could then. I'd only done it a handful of times over the open ocean so the Mother Mages could document what I could do. I imagined he was much more practiced.

"And if it's a trap?" I asked.

"I am not worried about that. I do not trust Wer much, and he is not the brightest, but he would never dare," he said with a smirk. I remembered the lists of Niode losses and I didn't doubt him. "If you are staying I will set up a meeting with Nelser for you later today. He will be here for the meeting tomorrow as well if you would prefer then?"

"No, today is good."

"Good, I will let him know." He didn't move, fidgeting with the rings on his right hand, "I will be back in a couple days…"

"Alright." I crossed my arms. If this was his way of guilting me into going, it wouldn't work. After a beat he turned and walked away. It wasn't till he was long gone when I realized I probably could have been nicer and at least said goodbye.

I continued on my way to the office. Halfway there I heard a distant bang. It sounded exactly like a small star-fire explosion. I looked out the nearest window but saw nothing. If Zandorian had done anything disastrous I imagined I would hear about it soon enough. An hour passed and I heard nothing. I did receive a note from him telling me when and where Nelser would meet me. It was dropped off by a nervous looking young man dressed in a red uniform that had nearly run away as soon as the note was in my hands. Judging by the lack of pleasantries surrounding the enclosed message, I extrapolated that Zandorian had thought I could have been nicer with my goodbye as well.

I met Nelser in the entryway of the front doors a few hours later. He was a small man that looked even smaller as he walked between the enormous doors. His orange robe did not match the purple-pink of his sash. He had folders tucked under his careful arm and a small pen case in his other hand.

He gave me a polite half bend when he saw me.

"Nelser Hu, my queen. We haven't formally met."

"Thank you for meeting me."

"Of course, my queen. I was surprised to get the request. I was expecting Zandorian to be with you, however." His eyes looked at the space behind me with hope.

"He's currently traveling to Dunede. I'm the one that requires the assistance, his presence is unnecessary." I moved so he would look at me. "Would you prefer the meeting room or the office?"

"The meeting room if that is agreeable, my queen."

I nodded and headed in that direction. He had already said one thing I had questions about.

"The Hu family? You once held the Central region, yes?"

"Yes, a very long time ago. There is only myself and my sister now."

"That seems to be the unfortunate way of things with the old families, from what I've read."

"Yes, but we are still standing, unlike the Xi and Ve families." He sounded proud. He should, he had a family he could trace back to royalty. I found myself unusually jealous of that before remembering exactly what I was doing and who I was.

I sat down at the end of the long table. I had no idea if I was allowed to be in Zandorian's chair, but I didn't think anyone would dare tell me I wasn't. Nelser sat down two seats away and began to pull papers out of the folders he had brought with him.

"What exactly were your questions, my queen?"

"More than anything I'd like an overview. I've never been formally educated in money management outside of a household budget and even that was sparse. You can imagine the Towers never imagined I would need to know more than that."

"They didn't?" he asked quietly, pausing.

"No." Why was that unusual? Maybe he wasn't well versed in how the Towers worked. I would respect him more if he wasn't.

We poured over the different trade agreements and what percentages they were to the income of the nation. The main exports had stayed much the same, as I had guessed my first day. I noticed Nelser had nervous hands, curling and uncurling them as he spoke.

Then we moved on to different sets of taxes. I was surprised to see the system I'd last read about had changed drastically to a system I had never seen. Only businesses and their interactions were taxed, not individuals. Judging by the rest of the numbers, it was working very well.

By the time we got around to the palace's own microcosm, Nelser had started to stumble with his words. I took my eyes off the accounts to look at him for the first time in a long while. He was visibly sweaty. I knew my body heat could be overwhelming in a small space, but this room was huge and I was calm.

"My apologies, my queen." He gathered his papers with shaky hands and left the room. I watched the doors shut after him. What had I done wrong?

I shrugged off the interaction and tried to move onto something nicer. I wandered to the library. I drifted to the different floors, looking into the reading rooms. It was all just as impressive as it had been my first day. One alcove had a feature that made me stop. My favorite board game. Tiny columns painted four colors, two colors on either end that fit into the crisscrossing diagonal rows on the board. It was a strategic game. The goal was to end up getting all of one colored column across the board and into a corner without getting in the way of your opponent's movements, lest your piece be flipped over and become theirs. This set was much nicer than the one the Towers had, the pieces made of four different colors of stone instead of wood. I moved a few around until the stairs creaked behind me. I turned around to see Kaniel, a game piece still in my hand.

"Good afternoon, Skye."

"Hello, Kaniel."

"Do you know how to play?" he asked, walking a couple steps closer.

"Yes."

"Are you good?"

"I'd like to think so." I had played with Aurelia and lost less than half the time, but she did cheat and anticipate my moves based on my moods. Or so she said. It was one of the things that made me near certain she could read minds. I held the tiny column tighter and tried not to think about her abilities.

"I am quite good at it myself. I was given an award for it in my academy days." He didn't say it as a boast, he said it like a neutral fact. Everything he said was neutral. "I remember Zan's mother never liked it. She did not have the patience."

Frustration flashed through me. I wanted to throw the little piece in my hand as hard as I could. But the feeling faded away into nothing a moment later, and I couldn't find a reason for it. I set the piece down carefully.

"It's a good thing I'm not her, then," I said.

"Yes, it is. You are very different." He picked up the pieces I'd moved and put them back in their resting places methodically. He studied my face for a moment before walking away to the other side of the floor. "I am sorry if you are compared to Serana too often. She was beloved, and although you are distinctly individuals, it is hard for those of us who knew her to fully separate the titles of queen and Stardropped from her memory. Especially myself."

"And Zandorian," I said. Kaniel shook his head.

"No, he has it right. He only knew her until he was barely six. Zan only knows what I tell him, and he is using that information to make your life the best he can." He walked around the top of the stairs, farther away. "To him, you are a real person he likes immensely, and she is nothing but a faded memory I have idealized. Very different."

"Why are you saying this?"

"Because it is the truth. And you are angry in my library. I would rather it stay standing."

Before I could respond he disappeared into one of the reading rooms, shutting the doors behind him. I did believe him that Zandorian did think of me much differently. I also believed that Kaniel did not and I would have to deal with his strange attitude towards me forever.

I found it comforting to know Zandorian's mother's name had been Serana. No one had told me her name, and her portrait was nowhere I had seen. I realized I had been starting to feel the seeds of worry my first day. The worry that I would simply be a shadow of her, especially when I'd heard her brought up so often. Not that that was usually a problem Stardropped had; I didn't cast shadows, and I doubted she had either.

CHAPTER 7

I knew there was a meeting today and I was determined to be there, whether they had come to terms with my presence or not. There were two regional representatives along with Nelser, Vitsef and Rolten. Their conversations died as I walked through the doors. I sat down in my chair. They looked at me in suspicious silence. Rolten was the first to speak,

"My queen?"

"Yes?"

"Why are you here?"

"I thought Zandorian explained it well. Do you need a reminder?"

"I think this is a bit beyond your expertise." My aura of fear kicked in. Nelser Hu started sweating again. That answered yesterday's question; he hadn't been hot or sick, he was afraid of me.

"I'd like to decide if it is for myself, thank you." I pulled it back. I needed them to tolerate me, not be so terrified nothing got done.

They talked through which towns needed the most fortification, how many Livade communities were getting support and how much. It was the simplest meeting I could imagine. Then the conversation changed to one small island community.

"There's nothing we can do for them," Rolten scoffed.

"Why not?" I asked.

"They're practically on the Niode border. They've been trapped for nearly two years. We can't keep hold of the land, my queen," Vitsef answered.

"Then to take them back would be a good thing," I said.

"My queen, we don't have the manpower. Especially not for a position where more Niode forces could arrive at any time. We clear them out, more come take their place," Vitsef explained.

"It's a wonderful thing we only need to evacuate them instead of continually fighting Niode off the land then, isn't it?"

"My queen?" Vitsef sounded unsure.

"In two years no one has thought that we should remove them from their situation? No one once thought that when we run transports only miles from them once every month?"

"Why are we responsible for staging a rescue?" Rolten asked.

"If you question that then why are we fighting this war at all? If we stop going out of our way why not pull back from the whole thing, let everyone fend for themselves? You two would enjoy the time off, I think. Spend more time with my sisters?" I snapped, looking at Rolten and Vitsef. They were quiet. "Good, we'll evacuate them."

"And where will they go?" After a long pause Vitsef realized his mistake, "My queen."

"I believe we just finished discussing some unused barracks, yes? Is that enough room? I heard a hundred beds."

"That is correct, my queen," answered one of the regional representatives, the one from the Southeast.

"How perfect."

I sat back. They could discuss the exact logistics without me. I made a note to check back on it before and after the transport of supplies was scheduled. If this didn't get done without a legitimate excuse I'd know they were refusing to listen to me.

When the meeting ended, I was faced with absolutely nothing to do for the rest of the day. It would have grated on me if I wasn't so used to entertaining myself while my sisters had lived their lives.

I made a mental map and remembered an entire wing of the palace I had never been to. Or rather I had been my first day, but my mind had been miles away. I wandered in its direction, and when I looked up I found myself in another room of paintings. This one had the curtains halfway closed. It looked like it included more casual portraits than the ones I had seen the day I had arrived. The subjects wore colors other than red, and the poses were widely varied. Some of the faces I recognized from before, particularly Zandorian's grandparents.

Their portrait was the largest. Meriah and Zian Al in the middle, their other wife and husband beside them, and their pack of children around them.

There was an obvious oldest son in the middle, probably early teens. Zian had his hand on his shoulder. He looked strong and angry, arms crossed and swords on his hips. He had dark brown hair the same color as Zandorian's, but his was cut close to his scalp. His ears were pointed like a mage's, which was common in children of mages, although they were usually less pronounced. On his chest gleamed a silver version of the Al medallion.

I checked the small label for names and dates. Sure enough, the middle boy was Zindraun Al, Zandorian's father. I guessed that was the only likeness of Zindraun I would ever see as I walked past a very large open place on the wall.

The next portrait was more interesting to me anyway. It featured a young Zandorian, no older than a late teen judging by the date on the label. He had no tattoos, no piercings and significantly less scars. The scar from under his right eye across the side of his nose looked new at that time, though. He wore a plain deep green robe and a smaller star medallion in silver exactly like the one Zindraun wore in the other picture. That must be what Al princes wore.

Standing behind his chair was the most beautiful normal woman I had ever seen. She could even surpass most mages, a significant accomplishment. Pale blonde hair, pale white complexion and pouty pink lips. She looked short with a perfect hourglass figure that was draped in a lush green dress. Dezura.

She was the opposite of me in every way. I was all tall, harsh angles and lightly tanned skin. I hoped more than anything that she wasn't a reflection of who he found attractive. If she was, I didn't have a chance. But I wasn't sure I wanted to have a chance.

Despite what I'm sure were the artist's best efforts, they both looked unhappy. Zandorian's eyes were dim. A flat, dark yellow without their swirling glitter or glow. I didn't want to look at it anymore. As I moved I saw my light shift on its surface. There was a subtle repair to the center of the canvas, a long raised line as if it had been ripped and sewn together. As I studied it closer I saw the edge of the frame hid the edges of burns. Had someone tried to destroy it? Judging by the burns, I could guess who.

I made it around the room, back to the first king and queen of Solde-al. It was much like the others, although the style was older and the canvas faded. Aphier and Zenos Al with their daughter Zaphier Al. I liked this one, largely because both women had been famously tenacious. Between the two generations, they'd united well over half of what was now Solde-al. Zaphier was the only female Al to have ruled Solde to this day.

Aphier's depiction made me pause. She was a mage, I could tell by her beauty. It was clear between her bright blue-white eyes and silver hair that didn't fully hide her pointed ears, but that wasn't what made me stop. She wore a different iteration of the Al star. Hers was inscribed with the delicate word "Mother" around the center circle. I wasn't sure what that meant, but I would remember to ask someone about it.

CHAPTER 8

The next morning I went to Zandorian's study to eat breakfast. As strange as it felt to be there without him, I couldn't bring myself to ask anyone to bring it somewhere else.

My spoon was halfway to my mouth when there was a heavy knock at the door. I put down my bite and opened the door. There was a young man with the standard armor of the gate guards. I had never seen them in the palace before. How had he found me?

"There is a mage at the front gate asking to see you, my queen."

"What's her name?"

"Cerprillis, I believe, my queen."

My brain recoiled at the name. Cerprillis was one of the nastier mages the Towers had ever raised, even if she was my sister. She was a feral mess men had a hard time looking away from. Her teeth were longer and sharper than they should have been, and she moved too quickly. I had expected Cerprillis to be one of the first to go of all our sisters. She was like me, a weapon. As volatile as I was, Cerp was fueled entirely by her hunger, and whoever offered her food held the key to her loyalty. The problem was that her favorite food was human blood.

As I reached the front doors, I saw her. I wasn't concerned with my safety, but I was worried about my guards on either side of the gate.

"Skye." Her red eyes flashed. She wore fur-lined robes as she always had. She said she liked the smell. No one else could smell what she meant.

"Cerp," I said flatly.

"Thank you for freeing me," her giggling words made me hesitate in that decision for the first time. I looked down at her hands around the bars of the gate and saw the dark red-brown of old blood underneath her nails. I couldn't let her leave in good conscience.

"Cerp, do you want to come in?"

"I would love to."

Instead of waiting for the gates to open, she climbed over them with bone chilling speed, landing at my side in a crouched stance.

"It's nice here. Big, but closed in," she said, straightening up.

"Let's go inside."

"Bye boys!" she chirped at the gate guards. I moved to put myself between her and them. She walked so quickly I found my feet hovering forward with each step I took just to keep up.

Once inside, I saw her stop and stare up at the entryway ceiling. She straightened her back and folded her hands politely.

"I enjoy the tile work, I've never seen anything like it." Her voice was clear and calm. I was able to stand by her side and watch as she looked like any other mage.

"It is beautiful, isn't it?" I said. She smiled a small smile that slowly cracked into a wild snarling one. There was the beast again.

She was back to erratic, walking in a serpentine pattern from column to column, running her hands down the tiles. At least if this kept her interest I knew she wasn't hungry. We'd called this manic state "fed" Cerp. She wasn't as likely to take a snap at anyone. That didn't mean much, though.

I watched as she stretched all the way up to grasp at the top of a set of blood red curtains, pulling them down and wrapping it around herself, pushing her hands through the fabric to wear it like a coat. I let her do it. If that was the worst thing she did with her freedom today, that was wonderful.

I'd never seen her without chains. They would have prevented her from doing something like that before. Unlike mine, Cerp's hadn't been for show. On more than one occasion they'd been the only thing between her and the person she was going to tear apart. Both of us had worn them for everyone else's comfort.

What was I going to do with her? I couldn't let her go back out there and hunt indiscriminately. My mind raced for a solution, then I settled on an incredibly obvious one. One that had worked all the years in the Towers.

"Let me go get Aurelia, I'm sure she would love to see you."

"Oh, Auri. She makes me feel fuzzy."

"Yes, she does." I saw a door that I knew went to a small guest sitting room and rushed to open it for her, "Wait in here, I'll be right back."

She looked me in the eyes in another moment of shocking clarity. "You know, you shouldn't trust Aurelia," she whispered.

"What?"

"You should trust Aurelia." The crazy was back in her face.

"That is not what you said."

"Sure it is, Skye," she giggled.

From anyone else that would have been cause for alarm, but I was never completely convinced Cerpillis knew what she was saying. I shut the door and ran to find Auri.

I found her outside the meeting room, just as I'd guessed I would. I lamented that I was absolutely going to miss this meeting entirely, but I had to take care of my sister. Aurelia looked excited to see me, but her face changed quickly.

"What's wrong?"

"Cerp is here, I need you." She nodded and followed me back to where I'd left her.

"What should we do?"

"Do you think she could live with you? You're the only one that can control her."

"Yes I think so... we have some spare bedrooms."

We found her sitting on the floor, ripping up her stolen curtains into very clean strips with her nails. She turned around when we returned, her unnaturally wide smile back in place. I hated that I could count all of her sharp teeth.

I leaned to Aurelia's side, whispering, "She said I shouldn't trust you, so she might be on to what you do to her. Be careful."

"I will, don't worry!"

Aurelia put on her dazzling smile,

"Cerp! How are you, love?"

"Hungry," Cerp hissed through a smile.

"Mmmhm, I bet it's a little better now, huh?" Aurelia asked. I shut the door, thankful that was over for now.

CHAPTER 9

I was in the library that evening. Instead of a text-heavy book I'd chosen one full of star charts. I could feel them as if they were real. The visual of them swirling and glittering was so vivid it comforted me. I could lose myself in it.

Kaniel has finally stopped his lurking and I was able to curl farther into the comfortable armchair in front of the table I'd laid my book out on. Then the doors opened and I was a long way from comfortable. Zandorian entered, looking around a moment before he saw me glaring from my seat.

"Ah, Skye, I did not see you. I will come back."

"No, it's alright." I straightened up in my chair, trying to clear away my scowl. This was the first time I'd seen him since he'd returned from Dunede. Considering how I'd treated him when he left, I wanted to be nicer. "What are you here for?"

"You are not going to believe me, but I was actually grabbing a book of flowers."

"I believe you, but it isn't what I expected."

"I have a soft spot for unusual flowers."

"The gardens make more sense, then."

"Yes… that was the first thing I had changed about the place when my father died. He had had the whole courtyard set up as an arena."

"What was the arena for?" I asked. Zandorian shook his head and made a disgusted face. I didn't push the subject. There was a story there, but it was not a pleasant one.

He disappeared for a moment and came back with a large book. He laid it on the table. Inside were wonderful colored illustrations of plants I'd never seen. Ferona would have loved it.

"I am thinking about trading for more of these. The red and yellow is too fitting." He pushed it across the table, turning it so I could see.

"They're nice. Why do they need to be traded for?"

"There are only two counties that have them, Renciam and Magsian. They are rare even in their native environments." I remembered Magsian as the country below Renciam, one that was largely desert and had a significant alliance with Dunede. But the fact that our highest concern was flowers made me think of something I'd meant to bring up when he returned,

"I'm not dissuading you from what you want, but what if we took more of the trade towards helping mages establish a life outside of the Towers? Instead of keeping it within the palace walls. I met a mage that was… not handling her freedom well while you were gone." I left out that there was a near impossibility of Cerp being a model citizen no matter how much help she was given.

"That is a very good idea. What do you suggest?"

"Well… maybe a committee to help them find ways to use their talents in a way that helps everyone? Every one of my sisters had something to offer the community. Ferona especially could help the farmers immensely if she was told who needed her help."

"We can make that happen, but the council will need to vote on it as it would be a national undertaking. People still fear mages and the damage they can cause when they are not controlled. It would be nice if they could show their value. Not that they should have to, of course."

He was right. We shouldn't, but that was the world we lived in. I wasn't even sure I wouldn't have to, but as we sat in our comfortable silence I doubted it for the first time.

He sat with his back to the window. As time passed the light faded and I found myself watching the sky instead. The sunset was turning the clouds a pale purple with bright pink streaks.

"The view is nicer toward the window," I said, breaking our long silence.

"I do not need the view. Unless that is your way of asking me to leave?"

"No, I was genuinely recommending it."

"A good recommendation, to be sure. It is beautiful."

He missed the sunset as it disappeared under the ocean horizon, fading down to a deep starry purple. I wished we could dim the light of the library so I could see out better. I would rather see the real stars than the ones in my book. I settled for them instead as the windows became mirrors in the night. Then I was distracted by sparks across the table.

When Zandorian was concentrating, he rubbed his first finger and thumb together. On occasion it made the smallest snapping spark.

"You better stop that before Kaniel sees you"

"Stop what?"

"That thing you do. If I dared even think about star-fire here he'd run me out."

"Oh, yes. Bad habit of mine." He took his hands off the table. I looked back down.

His leg touched mine under the table. I refused to move, and apparently so did he. It didn't bother me. It was nice. I had never had this happen with another person that didn't immediately jump away. Then he moved, and it was gone. I tried to catch a glimpse of his face, but he was already looking at me. I made a point of looking down at my book and moving so my legs were under me instead of the table. We sat quietly like that for a long time until I heard his book close.

"I know you read, but do you ever write?" he asked.

"When I was younger I did."

It was true. I'd written sticky, unrealistic romance with exhausted plots. That was back when I had accepted the lie that being a mage was a romantic situation and a kind man would come take us away to a life of flowers and honey and silk. I'd lost hope of that being my reality as I'd gotten older and the extent of my abilities had set in. At sixteen, I was told the truth by a disenchanted Mother Nai. She had told me the lives my sisters would leave to live would not be nice ones. The men who came to the Towers were kings and generals and diplomats, sure, but those jobs did not lend themselves to kind men. Consequently, I lost all urge to write my tales.

"Why did you stop?" asked my own silk-dressed king with a voice like honey, folding his hands over his book of flowers. I hesitated to give my answer.

"I lost interest. I'm not sure what I would write about now."

"Anything you want. I personally keep a journal and write about my own everyday life. It is not the most riveting, sure, but it keeps the mind busy. Not bad penmanship practice, either." He grinned. I'd seen his notes. As messy as the royal office was, his writing was beautiful. I'd attributed it to his artistic skill.

"Are you suggesting mine is bad?"

"No, no, but I personally am of the resolve that every line I make should be pleasing to the eye. Kaniel was a large influence in that."

"Kaniel seems to be an influence in everything you do."

"Yes, many things, to be sure."

I leaned across the table. "Are you just saying that because he can hear you?"

"I do not think he can, but I would say it either way." He leaned forward too, and I was suddenly very aware how close we were.

"I think he can. He's always watching." I leaned back but added a bit of humor to my voice. He smiled and leaned back as well.

At that moment, I realized I had missed him when he was gone. As much as I didn't want to believe he had the best intentions, I started to think that was true. If he didn't, he was doing a great job at pretending.

CHAPTER 10

I spent the whole day in the royal office. I had gotten a fair bit of organizing done. Thankfully, my real desk had arrived. It was a heavy thing made of black stone and curving shapes. It had a stand that could hold multiple books and a drawer for anything I wanted to keep close. I adored it.

When I sat down at the table for dinner I felt I had actually accomplished something. I was looking forward to the next day I could do something even bigger.

"How was your day?" Zandorian asked. I looked fully at him for the first time. His robe was dark gray with red flower patterns today. He had his hair in one braid over his shoulder with small gold flowers beaded in. Any other man would have looked feminine but he made it look like something Ashanm would wear; the god of creation was allowed to wear flowers.

"Fine."

"Do you want to talk about your plans for the committees? I would be curious to hear."

I'd been going over exactly what I would propose to them in my head, but I felt unprepared. I hadn't been over possible places of operation, which businesses and individuals should be able to communicate with the committee to request a mage's assistance, and I especially had not begun to consider how the mage abilities might play a part in the latter.

"I haven't figured out many of the details."

"That is alright, we can work on that. I give them half way done plans all the time." He grinned. I wasn't sure that was encouraging. I had seen the improvement in Solde-al during his time as king, however. Maybe there was something to that approach. "What do you have so far?" he asked.

"Well, I know we should try to establish committees in major cities and communities so wherever they choose to live the service would be available. That spreads the availability for assistance outside a specific region. That will also give all of the representatives incentive to go along with it."

"And what of our officers? If it is mainland Solde only they will not see the use. It is brilliant so far. I am simply warning you, Vitsef and Rolten are doubly as self-serving as the rest. And Daner is a utilitarian."

"I'm not worried about Rolten. He would vote against me if it was his own execution and I wanted to let him live."

"You are not wrong about that. There is also our dear Nelser Hu to consider. Have you thought about how it will all be paid for?"

"I'm still thinking that through, and I'll have to work with him after the vote, probably. Though I'm not sure he can handle going through another page with me after last time."

"Poor man." He laughed.

"I think the hardest part of the whole plan will be finding men who can work with the mages without drooling. They're all so beautiful it's distracting for normal people."

"Maybe." He didn't look like he agreed with me.

"All of my sisters are more attractive than I am. Even Cerp." He shook his head and thought hard for a moment.

"Forgive me for asking, but do you romantically prefer mages? Or other women?"

"No, romantically I don't discriminate between genders. It's the personalities that come with them that I don't like."

"Hmm, I think I understand."

"It's also not as if I have many choices if I'm not after conversation, so I try not to think about it."

"No, no, you do not. A stupid question."

"No, it was actually nice that you could forget that for a moment. Everyone else treats me like a sexless monster."

"You are far from being a monster."

"Tell that to the rest of the world," I scoffed.

"I do," he said sincerely.

The spoon in my hand glowed hot, bending as if it were a wilting flower stem. I didn't want to put it down and cause more damage, so I focused all my thoughts on cooling my hand so it would be a reasonable temperature again. It started to melt more. I folded it and crushed it in my fist, determined to keep it there until it was a safe temperature to put it down.

I looked up and he was watching me. We made eye contact. He raised his eyebrows and looked very pointedly back at his food. I was glad he didn't ask questions.

After dinner, instead of leaving I sat in one of the armchairs by the fireplace. I sat there a long while before he grabbed some papers and inks and sat in the other chair.

I looked at the fire while I listened to the scratch of his pen, then the soft sweep of paints. I knew I was useless for anything artistic, but I'd always admired those who could. Ferona had been the best artist among my sisters. Nerial gave it a fair shot, but she had always preferred to color in what Fer gave her.

I wondered how they were. Where they were. I imagined if they had left the Towers they would have left together, as they had always been inseparable. I hoped they were better off than Cerprillis, but that wasn't hard to accomplish. Aurelia might know where they were. Maybe they had written to her. It hurt a little to not know where my sisters were any more. My whole life I'd kept my distance from them, but now that we were apart I missed them.

"Do you like this?" He held up the drawing he'd been working on. It was a sweeping and delicate dress, the fabric intended to fade from black to red.

"Yes, but a lower neckline."

He made a face and fixed it to where I pointed. I couldn't tell if the face was good or bad. I remembered I couldn't care too much which it was, even if I had warmed up to him. I'd started to come around to the idea that maybe this was actually my life and he was real. The nice kind of real I could sit in silence with by the fire and feel something akin to peace.

CHAPTER 11

The next day I abandoned my morning work in the office and headed for the library instead. To my dismay, Kaniel was rearranging a shelf near my favorite table. I chose to ignore him as I sat down with a book about navigating by stars, but it was difficult because of how closely he was watching me. I'd turn a page and hear an exasperated sigh, and he had since moved to stand far too close, feigning the arrangement of another shelf.

"Kaniel, leave me alone."

"You look very frustrated with that book, Skye. I am watching for its own good."

"I wasn't frustrated until you started watching." I snapped the book closed. "I have never burned a book before in my life." He took the book from my hands, setting it on the table.

"And I will not allow there to be a first time. Calm yourself. I will leave this here for when you have calmed down."

"Calm myself? Does that seem like a wise thing to say to me?"

"No, but I know you will control yourself to make a point. I have read your file, I know you have anger problems until you have to prove something. While I reside over the books, I can say what I like to the Temper Tantrum Queen," he said it all in such a levelheaded way it made me want to scream.

I scoffed instead. He had read my file so he thought he knew me. No doubt it had an account of every fight I'd ever gotten into with a Mother Mage-every behavioral issue they deemed a problem. It made me wonder how large my file actually was. Likely the size of a large novel if it included the minor verbal altercations I had gotten into almost daily as a teen.

"Fine, say what you like, but Zandorian will as well and I'm not sure you'll enjoy what he has to say."

"Ah, yes. Go fetch the king I raised," he called after me as I left.

Kaniel was a rude man. I had little patience for rude men. Maybe he had known me in my last life but that gave him no right to treat me like a child. I was a queen, and I was not under his influence like Zandorian was. It was beyond me why he would keep a man like Kaniel around willingly, no matter what kind of relationship they had. Then again, maybe it was telling about who Zandorian was as a person as well. Even if I had warmed up to him, I still needed to be objective, and Kaniel was not a point in his favor no matter how I thought about it.

I found Zandorian in the courtyard practicing his swordsmanship with a young soldier I had seen around a few times. He'd been with him the day he visited the Towers, the one who had been almost too muscular. Up close, I realized they had some similarities. The same nose and jawline most notably. Zandorian was still far taller, while the other man had a stocky build.

They stopped as I approached, my robes swirling around me in the breeze no doubt making me look like a dark cloud intruding on their sunny day. I noticed Zandorian was only wearing pants, a stark contrast from the long sleeved robes he usually wore. I swore I wouldn't let that distract from my annoyance.

"Sorry to bother you,"

"You could never, Skye. What do you need?"

"Can you call off your librarian? He's about on my last nerve. I've been reading books my entire life and never once damaged one."

I saw how his eyes lingered, even as he made an effort to pull them away. I was suddenly quite aware of my exposed midriff, pulling my robes closed.

"Of course, I will speak with him."

"Alright, thank you." My eyes caught on the deep red tattoos across his arms, chest, and back. A handful of large pink scars were hidden among them. It did not help that the shadows of his muscles were just as eye catching. I was the one with lingering eyes this time.

"Do you need anything else?"

"No, that's all." A blushing heat rose in my cheeks.

"Good." He looked over to the man then back to me. "You have not met my brother Eran, have you?"

"I didn't know you had a brother." Why had he never brought up that he had a brother?

"Half brother," Eran corrected. "I didn't know either until about four years ago. My mother told me Zindraun was my father on her deathbed." His eyes were brown, so I had guessed they did not share a mother.

"And then you came here on a warpath."

"I did. Sorry about that." Eran looked apologetic between goofy smiles. That raised many more questions that I knew I wouldn't get answers for right now.

"It is alright, you pay for it now." Zandorian laughed and took a lazy swing. Eran dodged and swung back. Zandorian blocked his blade and shoved it away.

"Do you have other siblings?" I asked.

"Most definitely, but no others have come forward." He shrugged. Eran took another swing, this one harder. Zandorian caught Eran's blade in his hand. I knew their swords were likely dull, but it took me aback. Could I do that too?

"I will talk to Kaniel."

I nodded and walked away.

***

On my way to our usual dinner spot that evening I saw him on the practice field again, thankfully fully clothed this time. Before I could think much else about the situation he jogged to my side. Had he been waiting for me?

"I saw you were interested earlier today."

"Excuse me?" I asked, flustered. That made him smile.

"Swordsmanship practice. Have you ever trained with swords, Skye?" I realized with relief he was referring to the sparring I'd interrupted earlier.

"No, they were considered too masculine and bulky for mages. I trained in archery and using my power." I should be more honest, he would expect too much. "Well, the smallest fractions of it I could control and incredibly bad archery." That made him laugh.

"Using your power is likely enough for you, but I find swords entertaining. Want to try?"

"Against you? I don't think I will."

"You know you are indestructible and I could not hurt you. If anything I should be scared of you. If you land a hit it would be much worse than anything I could do." I hadn't thought about it like that. "But, lets focus on defeating him." He slapped a hand on one of the swinging wooden men on a stand. I fought a smile as I walked to the racks of weapons.

I ran my hand across the large, shining, pure metal sword on the top rack. All Solde blades were gently curved with decorative etching on their handles. This one was exquisite.

"Ah, that one is mine." He picked it up and gave it a twirl. He reached down and pulled one off a few rows down. "Here, this one will be more your size." It was about two thirds the size of his. "It is less about weight for you and more about distance. Let's start small till you get the hang of it. Anything much larger would be a problem, more wild swings. Hands here and here." He showed me on his own handle. I put them there. The leather wrapped on the handle started to smoke. "Ignore that, it is metal underneath," he laughed at my light panic. He put down his sword and led me to the nearest target, a wooden thing that looked vaguely like a man hanging from a chain from the top of its head.

"Take a swing." I swung and hit the dummy. It must've been a wild swing because his eyes were wide.

"That's one approach."

"Well tell me how to fix it!"

"Less back swing," he said. I tried again. It glanced off the wood with hardly a dent.

"More follow through, Skye. If you stop yourself you are wasting your energy and making your hits less impactful. You can hit harder than I can if you let yourself."

My next swing was harder but incredibly far off target, hitting the dummy in what would have been its hip, taking out a large chunk of wood.

"Maybe this is not your thing," Zandorian said, shaking his head.

I rolled my eyes, annoyed now. Of course I wasn't any good, this was my first try! Just wait till I had some more practice. I'd show him it was "my thing" because I wanted it to be. My hands were warm. I took one more swing down.

Without meaning to, I'd heated my blade to a near glowing point. It smoked where it cut the target nearly in half, leaving behind a few small sputtering fires. I dropped the sword. It bent as it fell to the ground, burning up the grass around it. More things I'd ruined.

"That was not bad. We can work on it."

I wanted to work on it not just because I liked it, but because we were doing it together without maids or brothers or librarians. It was probably just as well I had a way to defend myself that wasn't star-fire. Even if it turned out to be a hobby.

He shuffled his feet and walked back to the rack to grab his own sword, giving it a few lazy twirls.

"Can we try something? I am curious."

"What do you want to try?"

"Block this." He took a sudden swing at my head. I caught the blade in my hand. He leaned into it. I had to strain to hold it in place, but it didn't get any closer. The smallest star-fire blast rip through the air, but he was unbothered.

I grabbed the blade with both of my hands and pulled. He kept hold of it, his shoes dragging through the dirt as I pulled him closer. The metal started to give way under my fingers, and I let go. I didn't want to ruin this sword too, it was too beautiful.

"That is more what I was expecting. Small star-fire is usually my move. Took me years to figure out properly." I didn't find that to be something to be proud of. I hadn't meant to do it. It was lazy on my part, nothing but a slip up.

He hadn't backed away. I saw the burns the fire had left on his robe, still smoking in places. "I think I will have to talk to Eda about this, though." I looked back at his sword now as he led it up. What I thought would be small indents were large impressions of my hands. It had been bent back into a severe curve from him pushing down and me pushing up. It was a misshaped mess. I felt horrible.

"I'm sorry."

"Do not be. I wanted to try it and you reacted. My fault." He walked away to put it back on the rack. It didn't stay, hardly a sword at all. He laughed again.

He was so kind. It dawned on me that I hadn't been blamed for burning anything since I had arrived here. In the Towers chiding was all I'd ever heard. Everything I had ruined, he'd seen as inconsequential, even laughing at its demise.

I didn't fully trust him, but I was getting there. I was comfortable calling him a friend. A good one.

CHAPTER 12

The next morning had me far more nervous than I had been for the other meetings. Today, I would explain my plan and the council would vote on it. I hardly noticed as I went through my routine, though I was briefly distracted long enough to notice a nightmare I didn't remember had burned my pillows.

Zandorian asked me questions about my plan over breakfast and I answered them without thinking. I had to stay focused and his presence wasn't helping. Too much was weighing on this for me to dwell on how he'd braided his hair down the sides against his temples today or how he smelled like smoke and flowers...

The palace was shining and alive on yet another beautiful day, but it was lost on me. I only started to notice it fully as I stood anxiously waiting for Zandorian to open the meeting room doors and let us in. When he finally did, I went to my seat but didn't sit. I'd have the first words at the meeting today, as he had promised at breakfast. Once everyone else had taken their places and I had drawn their silent attention, I spoke:

"I'm proposing we establish committees in major communities across the nation to help free mages find where they can use their gifts to the best advantage of the community. These would be organized by the kingdom and their members paid as such. I'd work with Nelser to make sure that can happen with minimal impact to our current budget plan."

"Absolutely not. We let you give them freedom, now the kingdom is supposed to take responsibility for all of them? I can't support that reckless request," Rolten said.

"We can't treat mages better than the rest of our citizens. No," the Central representative said.

Why was this out of reach for the rest of the people? I clenched my jaw. I'd fight with them about that later.

"No. The mages choose to leave the Towers. They are responsible for their own adjustment to society," Vitsef said. As if the Towers gave us the skills to do that. I had made a mistake sending Cerp to live with Vitsef and Auri, I was sure that was why he was voting no.

Two more no's, each without an explanation. That was worse. I couldn't address their reasons.

Again the Northeast regional representative, Haullen, voted yes. I liked him. To my surprise, Nelser didn't let me down either. Zandorian voted exactly as he had said he would with a yes, but it was too late. There were too many no's. It wouldn't pass.

"Thank you for your votes," Zandorian said. I had to leave. The star-fire begged me to show them what would happen when they moved against me. I couldn't do that. I pushed it down, trying to separate myself from it as I left. It didn't work. My feet left the ground and the entirety of my arms burned. I looked at the gardens, begging myself to calm down. It was one no. I could withstand a no. But could my sisters and every mage who came after them? There was too much at stake for them for me to feel complacent in this.

I heard the doors open again but I couldn't move. If I moved I would snap.

"Skye, are you alright?" Zandorian asked softly from somewhere behind me.

"No."

"They are talking…"

"Let them. I couldn't care less what they think about anything, especially what they think of me."

"You do not mean that."

"Yes, I do. I don't respect their opinions." I felt the fire win as I turned around to face him. "They don't

115

fight for or live among the people! They sit in that room and think that alone is enough! They think I am a feral monster incapable of handling this title! Every time I go into that room I-"

He waited for me to finish my sentence but I couldn't. I meant my words but I didn't mean to fill them with venom. It was pure fire. I had to calm down.

"Skye, they are scared. Especially for their reputations internationally."

"I can handle being told no, I am not perfect. But to say no out of fear for their reputation? I can't respect that," I snapped. Zandorian took on the tone of a mediator.

"Let them sit with the idea for a while. And, maybe better, bring it up to their wives. I would love to see how their votes change in the days after the mage wives hear your plan."

"They sit comfortably with the idea while my sisters are left directionless."

He put his hand over his face in frustration. "Maybe we should not have freed them without thinking this through."

"You think their freedom could wait?! They should have waited in the Towers so more of them could end up like..." I thought of what Zifira had said to me. I couldn't imagine what she was subjected to. I shook my head. "Right now I'm not sure you're better than them." It was the harshest thing I'd ever said to him. I regretted it immediately. He was the reason I was there at all. He fought for his country harder than any other king. He cared about everyone. He wasn't like them.

"You are right." His voice was quiet.

I wasn't but I couldn't get the apology out. He turned around and went back into the meeting room, slamming the doors closed. My feet touched the ground again. I waited, breathing as quietly as I could, hoping to hear anything on the other side.

"The vote stands," said Zandorian, his voice muffled. That was all I could stand to hear. I knew that our laws said that there was little Zandorian or I could do once the vote was cast, but the fact that he apparently didn't even want to try hurt.

I didn't leave my room for the rest of the day. I expected to become a flaming figure of fury at any moment, but the fire never came. It burned high and hot but still contained itself to my body. I was thankful for that as the long hours passed and I found morning had arrived before my eyes had shut.

***

We ate breakfast in silence. I thought hard about skipping breakfast, but I found myself wanting it after forgoing last night's dinner. The food here was good enough I craved it even if I didn't need it. That, and it was something to do. After withstanding my heavy silence for close to an hour, Zandorian broke it.

"There will be a large gathering in the palace in three days. The Conference of Kings. I hold it annually so we can meet and discuss in person in a temporary neutral space instead of through couriers. It is a three day event. I would love it if you were at my side. I know this is not your type of event, but it is important. You will have the opportunity to meet many of the most prominent people abroad."

"I'll be there. I can't promise I'll be the most gracious host," I muttered to my plate.

"Be whatever kind of host you wish, Skye."

I finished my meal and left with my glass of fruit juice still in hand. I wandered the halls with nervous energy until it was time for the meeting of the day. I didn't want to go, but I knew they would take it as yet another tantrum if I didn't make an appearance. I wasn't happy with the situation at all, but they had to know I wasn't so easily sent crying. Those men would never get the satisfaction of thinking they had scared me away.

The space was much fuller than usual and distinctly more female. I spotted mages and regular women of varying ages. They were all dressed in finery, which made me think they must have a purpose for being here.

"Hey!" Aurelia called to me. I walked to her side but my eyes still glanced at the new faces.

"Hey… why are they here?"

"Oh, they're some of the council member's wives. I hear there's quite a stir going on. Vits said Zandorian said-"

I looked past her to three wives I'd never seen, then to Zandorian beside them, politely nodding. I saw at least two of them looking at him too fondly for my taste. I tried to remind myself not to care.

"I'm sorry, Auri, I need to go talk to them." I walked swiftly to join their circle.

"You are welcome to join us, although I will say today's topics are particularly dry. I would love to hear your views, all the same," Zandorian offered. I faltered for less than a second. I bumped lightly into his arm as I joined their formation. He turned to look at me. I offered a small smile as an apology. He returned it.

"Who are you all?" I asked, trying to be warm and friendly. I'd imagine the tone fell closer to neutral.

"Lira, a mage. I have command of all languages, sometimes even animal." She smiled and adjusted her pale orange hair. "Trade officer Daner's wife."

"Nice to meet you… unless we've met before and I don't recall?" She could have only been a decade older than me, maybe she had been at the Towers during a time when I hadn't been allowed near the older mages.

"No, my queen, I'm originally from Livade. The Citadel was my home, not the Towers." I nodded and looked at the next woman.

"Hani, wife of Haullen Cy. I'm not a mage but a mother of one. We had to send her to the Towers four years ago and it was the hardest thing I've ever had to do." I remembered her husband as my first supporter to free the mages. That made more sense to me now.

"What was her power?" I asked.

"She flies and floats. She always looked like she was underwater when it happened, but she is still my daughter," her voice broke at the end and I tried very hard to stamp down my own reaction. I had never fully considered that the parents of mages had not always wanted to give them up. I looked to the last woman, a normal woman as well judging by her rounded ears and plain appearance.

"Central Representative Raham's wife. I like the idea of everyone having equal opportunities and my husband seems to disagree." I liked her already.

"Glad to have you here. I need all the help I can get."

"Skye…" I looked back to Zandorian who was inclining his head to the now impatient looking council members, trapped outside by the closed door. I wanted to make them wait till I was well and ready to end my conversation, but Zandorian seemed to have a different opinion. Fine. I went and I sat in my seat.

"Welcome back my queen," Nelser said sincerely. He'd switched seats with Daner to sit beside me. That put me in a better mood.

"Thank you." I was extra careful to pull in my intimidation. Even as I did, I felt something like it coming from Zandorian at the end of the table. He was far more serious than he had been in the hall, the lights in his eyes swirling quickly. Something was wrong.

I looked to Haullen at the other end of the table. "I didn't know your daughter was a mage, Haullen." His eyes widened. "Your wife told me. They both seem lovely."

"She was," he said it like she was dead, fidgeting with his pen.

"I'm sure you're glad she gets to live in one of the only countries with free mages."

"I am," he said. I looked at Daner.

"I also did not know your wife was a mage. She has an incredibly useful power for your occupation."

"She does. She handles a large part of my correspondence."

"I'd love to see her around more. I'm glad she's here today. And yours, too," I looked at Raham. He met my eyes and nodded before looking past me to Zandorian. I followed his gaze and saw Zandorian giving him a glare I was glad I wasn't on the receiving end of.

The meeting went well, but Zandorian stayed stoic and menacing the entire time. The councilmen did a good job of working through the uncomfortable air, but I could see their nervousness in how they shifted and fidgeted when Zandorian spoke. By the end I couldn't focus on anything else. As the meeting concluded, I wanted answers.

I followed him out of the room, across the hall down the stairs, and to the first few feet of garden path. I nodded goodbyes to the women I had met before we disappeared between the tall shrubs.

"You weren't your usual self," I said. He seemed startled, a few sparks flying from his hands.

"It is nothing," he responded, slowing his breathing.

"Is it?" I asked. This was definitely not usual.

"I may or may not have threatened them yesterday." He tried to make it flippant, a throw away explanation. That certainly aligned with his actions.

"How so?"

"I told them I wanted them to go home and explain to their mage wives why they voted no to your committees."

"That's not much of a threat."

"It is. There is something far more motivating than threats of violence or the potential upheaval of their careers. I would imagine their wives will be utilizing that until they admit defeat and a change of heart. They have a power over the council I will never have." It took me a long second to figure out what he meant. Unhappy wives would be much harder to live with and even harder to get into bed. The genius wasn't obvious, but it made perfect sense. They'd change their minds within a few days. "If the vote has to stand for now, I want them to have to change their minds so when we ask again we get the right answer."

"I didn't think you would be so quick to manipulate your own council."

"It is worth it in this case. I do not make it a habit."

It made me slightly more apprehensive of my judgement that he was not, in fact, manipulating me. Making this happen would put him further in my good graces and he knew it. But, he was doing it in favor of the common good, and that was good enough for me.

I was in favor of the fact that the small braids were back for a second day, this time ending in gold beads on his shoulders. I let my hand brush his while we walked. When he looked down to check if it had been intentional, my heart started to beat harder and my fingers started to burn. I didn't know what it wanted. Did it want to burn our surroundings to nothing or to touch him again?

"Are you alright? You look…" he trailed off. He looked so tenderly concerned it nearly hurt. The heat spread up into my hands and the tips of my ears and the tops of my cheeks.

"I'm fine."

He watched me out of the corner of his eye for the rest of our walk; quick glances I noticed. I kept my hands firmly together in front of me. I knew I'd have to avoid being alone with him until I figured out exactly what that reaction was and how to keep it contained.

***

That evening I was taking off my makeup in front of my mirror. It was one of my least favorite tasks and I was glad to have Eda there to talk to. She was fussing with my bed sheets, yet another replacement set.

"What were you doing today, Eda?" I asked as casually as I could, like I would have if she had been one of my sisters. She paused, tilting her head in confusion but her expression happy to answer.

"I was making the king a new sword, my queen." I was thankful she said it with a grin.

"Sorry about that…I didn't mean to."

"It's quite alright. It's an opportunity to make improvements to my last design."

I remembered how much I'd liked the look of Zandorian's sword before I'd ruined it. I wished I could make something like that. Then I remembered that if Eda was one of the best sword makers in Solde, surely she could teach me.

"Eda, could I come with you to the forge someday? I'd like to learn."

"Of course, my queen. Whichever day you wish."

CHAPTER 13

The first day of the party arrived faster than it felt like it should have. I blamed it on the general whirlwind of activity the palace had entered. I wasn't directly involved, but I watched the changes happen.

Furniture was moved, curtains replaced, every inch cleaned. The workers moved about in teams, always careful to not disturb wherever I had chosen to settle. I had reverted to the strategy I'd used for years at the Towers, staying to the sides and less used halls and stairways.

Zandorian was as scarce as I was the entire three days. I saw him only twice after the meeting. After he hadn't shown up to breakfast or dinner the day before, I had asked for my meals in my wing on one of the tiny balcony alcoves for today. I didn't know if he was busy with preparations or if he still felt strange about my outbursts, but I would have done the same either way.

As the evening approached, I decided to find somewhere more secluded than somewhere a curious guest could wander into. It was the first time I had ever seen guards in the halls. I could hear guests arriving and getting settled in the suites on the floor above me.

I had no idea if Kaniel would allow guests into the library, but I doubted it. I slipped inside, closing the doors behind me. I nearly ran up to the second floor and into a reading room. It was the one that was textile themed. That I was thankful for. The theme included many plush pillows and a window seat reading nook with heavy curtains to pull closed.

I regretted not bringing in material of a different subject. I settled on a book about dyes and their ingredients. It was not riveting, and even if it had been, I doubted I could have paid it much attention. My mind was distracted. I caught myself looking out the window, watching the steady stream of carriages, guests, and luggage arriving. After a long while the traffic ebbed and the sun started its descent. Just as the lanterns were being lit, there was a knock on the door.

"Skye, Eda is here. She says it is time for you to get dressed." Kaniel. How had he known I was in here at all? Kaniel knew too much, it annoyed me. I

127

begrudgingly opened the door. Sure enough, there was Kaniel and an anxious Eda.

"Eda, do I have to?"

"I would never force you to do anything, my queen, but I do highly recommend it. We're going to need the extra time." I had no idea what she meant. Maybe I was so ugly she needed the time if I had a hope of looking decent. I agreed.

I nodded and let her lead me away.

"Have a good night," Kaniel said with a sarcastic tone as we left the library.

I was promptly put in a bath and instructed to scrub every inch. I had never been incredibly fond of baths. The water always evaporated too quickly for me to find them relaxing.

Before too long she ushered me out and back to my room. I was confused why we weren't headed to the closet. I was not going anywhere in the thin fabric I was wearing now, that was certain.

"The king already dropped off your outfit, my queen."

Sprawled across my bed was a mass of gold. I rushed to it and pulled the garment up to see. The dress was the longest and heaviest I had ever held. It had a chain-like pattern in the weaving, but flowed like the lightest fabric. Every thread was embroidered or beaded glittering gold. It reflected my light across the walls, giving my room a golden tint.

Eda helped me find my way into the lavish garment. Once all the folds were laid and my limbs through the right holes, I dared look in the mirror. The tall collar piece reflected my glow, the patterns in the fabric making a thousand iterations of the Al and regional stars, the long sleeves and cape made of a mesh of beads that looked sheer. I loved how I looked in it. I looked like a goddess. It was a distantly familiar feeling. I never wanted to take it off.

After comparing several potential colors, Eda put ashy black makeup on my eyes and a dark sweet berry color on my lips. She brushed fine gold dust on the tops of my cheeks and put my official queen's necklace around my neck. My feet were slipped into soft silk slippers with small raised heels while I held up the hem of my dress. Eda had said she couldn't move it all on her own. I didn't question her, it was a lot of fabric.

"There, all done, my queen." She had a huge smile. She must have liked it too. "You'll be meeting the king outside the grand hall."

"Will you be there?"

"Oh no, my queen. Tonight is an all-hands-help night for those of us who work here. We have our own party when all the guests are leaving happy."

"That sounds nice."

"Not as nice as the one you're going to. You best leave now to avoid being late."

"Can a queen be late?" I asked.

"I don't think she can. My apologies, my queen." She smiled wide and I tried to return it. As beautiful as I felt, anxiety bloomed in my stomach and the fire twisted around it. This was going to be difficult.

Moving through the halls, my dress made soft jingling and scraping noises as it dragged on the floor. It was at least three times as long as I was tall. I wondered how many times it would be stepped on before the night was out.

I met Zandorian in the main entryway outside the doors to the grand hall, just as Eda said. I was sure the huge open space would feel a lot smaller with so many people inside it tonight. I could hear their voices on the other side, a mix of yelling and laughter that made me nervous. I concentrated on Zandorian so I didn't have to think about it.

He wore a smaller amount of gold, his beaded over a base of deep red velvet in the same star patterns as mine. He'd tied his dark hair back away from his face but left the back free to fall down between his shoulders. I saw the Solde king's necklace back in place as it had been for my presentation. I was surprised how plain his outfit was in comparison, but this dress would have made anything look boring by contrast.

"Do you like your dress?"

"It is extravagant."

"Yes, true. It is an extravagant occasion. For what it is worth to you, I think you look beautiful. Like the sun," Zandorian whispered.

I believed him only because he didn't look at me as he said it. No one could look directly at the sun, no matter how beautiful they thought it was. Similarly, I couldn't stand to look in his direction for long, either.

"May I?" He reached his hand out for my own. I gave him mine, concentrating on keeping my composure. I didn't need the added problem of my new found reactions, whatever it was. He made it incredibly difficult as he ran this thumb absentmindedly over the back of my hand as he spoke, "Most of tonight is formality. The real transactions happen tomorrow behind closed doors and in deserted hallways. Tonight, we smile. Tomorrow, they make threats."

"Should we be worried?"

"Maybe. We will have to wait till tomorrow to know." His twitch of a smile did not reassure me, but the doors were opening and he was pulling us forward.

The colors of the hall were as impressive as they had been when it was empty, but the added stained glass lanterns and the hundred shades of fabric worn by our guests made it a jewelry box of colors.

We circled the crowd gathered in the center of the room. I tried not to meet any eyes. They were all also dressed lavishly, but none so much as me. I knew even without the glow of my skin that my dress was shining brighter in the lights and the colors reflecting off the tiles. We made two rounds before the music changed and Zandorian dropped my hand to begin greeting guests. I met so many people my head was clouded before long. The few I remembered were mages or men with mages.

I met an old mage that could heal the injuries of anyone she touched who was on the arm of the frail King of Livade, Dortes Weh. Another that flitted in and out of existence at different places with a Niode general. I met one named Clarina who could generate force fields. Her sky blue hair was not something I would forget quickly, and neither was her title as Queen of Niode. She was on the arm of a man that made my stomach lurch. He stunk of leather and had a set of thick silver chains draped from a nose ring to a set of earrings that covered most of his square, ruddy face. His smug way of looking up at Zandorian forced me to move all of my effort to controlling my temper.

"Quailen Kos, King of Niode-kos," Zandorian introduced him.

"Wonderful to meet you," Quailen's flat tone made it sound like it was not at all, and I had to agree. He held out his hands to take mine. I placed mine in his, overriding the reflex to deny him. The interaction lasted less than a blink. He pulled his hands back with a yelp and shook them before shoving them into his robes. His face was a thinly veiled expression of pain. I did not feel bad.

"Ah, sorry about that. Skye still struggles to regulate her temperature." Zandorian did not look sorry in the slightest. It was his turn to be smug.

"No real harm done," Quailen assured him with a bitter tone. I knew he was lying. The heat of my hands was enough to give most people a burn that lasted for days and I'd turned it up slightly for his enjoyment.

The interaction had drawn the attention of several people near us. They watched with cautious apprehension. One of them was Zifira who gave me a quick snort and the twitch of a smile. It reminded me of the two times I had scared away men at the Towers and she had been the only one to voice approval. She was used to this behavior from me, but the rest of them weren't. They were terrified of the new

Stardropped Queen of Solde who could burn with a touch. Good.

As we walked away from the Kos couple, Zandorian leaned down to whisper in my ear, "Our relationship with them is quickly dissolving. We will likely be at war with them on our own soil before the year ends."

"Oh… I'm sure I didn't help matters."

"It is far beyond a bad greeting, Skye, do not worry. What has me concerned is that they know about you and me, but they are still pushing at the borders as diligently as ever."

"I will handle it. You've spent months telling me I'm indestructible. They won't get far if they come here."

"You are amazing," he said it like a fact rather than a compliment. I floated on its sound until I was standing before another person I had to meet. This man was another I knew I couldn't stand the moment I saw him.

"This is Celevan Ni, Emperor of the Trusican Islands," Zandorian said, an undertone of a growl in his voice.

"Al…" was all Celevan said in greeting, with a slow, too perfect smile.

Celevan Ni was not much older than Zandorian, if he was at all. Short dark gray and black hair and a well-trimmed beard on a sharply angled face. He was a very good looking man with dark blue eyes that held no good intentions as they looked at me with deadly interest.

Then I saw his wife step out from behind him. She was a beautiful mage with dark skin and tightly coiled hair the color of garnet. Her dress was the same color, tightly clinging to her short and curvy frame. Her eyes were so kind I wondered what struggles had dug them so deep that they could hold that much good.

"What's your name?" I asked, my attention now completely on her.

"Hira," she did a polite half bend. "I think… you're the Stardropped. Can I try to shake your hand? My power is extreme cold." She held out her hands and I was happy to give her mine. She was able to hold onto my hands for several long seconds with complete comfort, much longer than anyone else that wasn't Zandorian. She giggled and I knew I was obsessed with her.

Zandorian pulled me away from her too soon, looking as if he was on a warpath. What had the Celevan said?

"Sorry. Let's talk to someone else," he scanned the room, finally pointing out a blonde woman dressed in silvery gray. "Wer brought his oldest daughter, you should meet her. She's one of my better friends."

As interesting as Wininer Pet was, I found my eyes drifting back to Hira. I wasn't going to forget about her that quickly. After a few moments Zandorian left to go do something else with Wininer, leaving me alone in the sea of people.

I saw Aurelia, draped in a deep rust gown that matched her eyes. She was talking to Kos and Clarina. It looked like the conversation had been going sour until their faces abruptly changed to calm and polite. I saw Aurelia smiling, her eyes a little brighter. She'd used her power on them. I wouldn't complain. Anything to stop even a fraction of the hostility. They quickly ended the conversation and walked away when they saw me approaching.

"Hey! Are you having a good time?" Aurelia asked, her smile wide and cheeks warm. She had always loved meeting new people.

"I'm having a time." I left it at that. Aurelia didn't need to know about the war's impending move closer to home or the war that was going on inside my mind as my eyes followed two figures in the crowd, one made of star-fire and gold and the other of cold and kindness.

"This is very fancy." She pointed her finger up and down at my outfit.

"It is, isn't it?"

"Did you pick it out?"

"No, Zandorian picks out my clothes. Has them made from his own designs. He's a very good designer, actually." She tilted her head to the side, pursing her lips.

"That makes sense. Vitsef said he's very particular about how things look. He is very artsy, isn't he?"

"When he has the time." I shrugged. If he was known for wanting things to look a way he found pleasing, that meant something about my clothes. Normally that would have made me upset, but as I looked back down at my dress, I knew it didn't bother me. Especially not tonight.

"I'm glad Vits doesn't pick out my clothes. I think I would be in men's armor or nothing. I don't know which he likes better," she joked. I smiled. "I'm going to get food. Do you want anything?" I followed her gaze to the small but high-piled tables of food. The arrangements looked more like art pieces than food in their fantastical shapes and colors. I didn't want to disturb them.

"I'm alright, thank you."

"Alright, I'll talk to you later then."

"Bye, Auri." And again I was left alone.

I watched the dancers with interest. I knew that despite all the differences between Solde, Livade, Niode, and Dunede we all danced the same. Like our shared language, I guessed it was a result of thousands of years of moving borders and switching allyship like most of these men switched wives. As much as I hated them for their complacency of how mages were treated in their countries, they moved gracefully, and that was something I could not do.

Zandorian wandered back to my side, looking in slightly better humor than he'd left in. He watched the dancers too for a while.

"I am surprised you are not drinking," he said in a joking way.

"I don't do that. Control loss," I answered, again sounding cold.

"I understand that completely." His demeanor changed as he shifted his feet and became much more interested in watching the party.

"Do you?"

"I do not drink either, for that reason."

"Really?" I was surprised.

"Yes, I made the mistake of being drunk once. Thankfully, Kaniel was there to… anyway." He looked darker for a moment, the light in his eyes slowing its swirls. His hands pulled at the fabric of his sleeves.

"I've never been allowed to even try it. Mother Mages told me I could never."

"You could try it, I would not stop you, but speaking from experience it is not worth it." He didn't look at me, watching the guests instead.

I wondered exactly what had happened and why he had done it in the first place. A firestorm or a fit of rage or maybe some other bad decisions? I didn't want to dwell on it. If he wanted to tell me the story, he would. My thoughts were interrupted by a man dressed in a red and yellow palace uniform.

"My King and Queen, the closing dance?" That sentence hit me hard. That was something I had to do?

"Yes, of course. Skye?"

"I was never taught to dance." My sisters had been. I hadn't been able to be close enough to anyone to practice, so I'd missed out on it like I had so many other skills.

"Fortunately and unfortunately, I was." He smiled. "You will learn. The good news is no one can see your feet, just walk quickly and follow." I heard them announce my name and his. I didn't have time to be nervous. He grabbed my hand and walked us to the middle of the rapidly clearing floor.

One hand on my shoulder, close to the base of my neck, and the other around my waist. I put one hand on the top of his shoulder and the other in the bend of his elbow. I didn't expect it to be as comfortable as it was. The music started again. We twisted and twirled like the patterns in the tiles far above us. He pulled me along like I was nothing.

Zandorian very much kept his hands off my skin, adjusting his fingers when they brushed. It would have been comforting except that he was thinking about it, and then I was thinking it would be alright if he didn't. He slid his arm so my hand was in his. I wasn't sure he couldn't read my thoughts. We made eye contact briefly, and my temperature rose, my hand heating until it was glowing in his. He leaned close to my ear, cheek nearly against mine.

"Are you alright?"

"Yes, why?"

"Not to alarm you, but the sleeve of your dress is melting."

I caught a quick glance down at my arm. Sure enough, around my wrists liquid gold was running like thick tears down my arms.

"Why is it not on fire?" I gasped.

"Gold does not burn, it melts." He laughed over my shoulder.

My mind struggled with the idea that I had been wearing pure gold all night. We did one more sweeping turn before we walked back outside into the entrance space. I took a quick glance back behind the closing doors. Dripps of gold glittered on the stone floor where we had danced.

"Skye, what is wrong?" He was too close. His hands were still in mine and his eyes looked like my robe; molten gold. I was breathing too fast.

"I… I have to go."

And despite every one of my intentions, I was nearly running away from him. I wound up in my closet. As carefully as I could with my shaking hands, I pulled off the spectacular gilded thing I was sure would haunt me for the rest of my life.

I ran to my bed and hid under my blankets, begging for sleep to end the night. After long hours of replaying exactly how the whole evening had gone, it was merciful.

That night I dreamed of him. I wore a dress made of a swirling nebula, young stars glittering against my skin. He took my hand and led me to the edge of a cliff where we looked out into an impossible expanse of galaxies and stars. I felt like I could reach out and touch them. They wouldn't burn me. He asked me which one I wanted. I couldn't pick one, I said. He told me that I could have them all.

CHAPTER 14

As soon as I opened my eyes in the morning, my feet hit the floor and took me to my closet. I wanted to see if it was real. The anxiety had twisted itself into wanting to see if such a dress was even possible.

The dress was gone, the only evidence of it ever existing were small glittering drips on the stone floor from where I had walked. I wondered if they'd clean them up or if they'd be there forever. I didn't know which I would have preferred. Eda opened the doors before I could decide.

"Good morning, my queen."

"Where's the dress?"

"I'm not sure, my queen. Although I think it's weight alone narrows down who could have taken it elsewhere without your knowledge." I nodded. She was right. We both knew Zandorian had taken it somewhere. Either that or an entire team of people had dared to move the incredibly hot, extremely heavy thing and successfully done it with impeccable stealth.

"Anything special I'm supposed to wear today?"

"Not that I was told, my queen."

"I think I'll go with red today, then." I pulled one dress down and held it out. She got it ready while I pulled off my sleeping robe. I put it on and looked in the mirror. I couldn't remember if I had worn a red like this before, but I did know I liked how it looked now.

"Is there a red lip color that would match?"

"Yes, let me find it, my queen." She opened a drawer of makeup I'd never noticed. She put the color on my lips as I put on my necklace.

"Do you know where I'm supposed to be today?" I asked, adjusting it so the Al pendant was centered.

"The king and his guests are eating in the grand hall this morning."

"Thank you, Eda."

I had never wanted less to be somewhere that my heart begged me to go. The idea of seeing a table full of monarchs, ambassadors, and entitled people made my stomach ache, but the idea of making him laugh again made it flip. I winched as both of the enormous doors were pushed open.

I was quite obviously late. Everyone was seated at the long table and over halfway through their food.

143

Zandorian was seated directly in the middle. He was talking to an older mage, the one that could heal with a touch. Our eyes caught.

"Skye." He stood up from his seat, and the rest of the table followed in a ripple. My cheeks went hot and not with star-fire.

He made a hand movement and an enormous chair that matched his was set at his side. It took too long for me to make it to my seat.

"How was your night?" he asked when I'd settled.

"Weren't you there, Zandorian?" chimed in an older and portly man dressed in the colors of our neighbors to the south, Dunede. This must be Wertrick Pet.

"No, Wer, unlike you I can afford to furnish more than one bedroom," Zandorian said with the same tone as a whip, holding out his goblet to indicate a joke.

My eyes had never been wider as I stared directly down at my plate, trying with all my strength to hide a laugh. Wer let out a room filling belly laugh, smashing his goblet against Zandorian's. What a strange relationship.

"You did not answer my question," he said quietly once Wertrick had moved on.

"It was fine." Was all I could answer. I knew it came out cold.

My eyes searched for more mages I recognized, especially Hira. I couldn't see her anywhere. Not even the emperor that she was with. Had they left?

I followed the flow of people out the doors as breakfast came to a close. I saw everyone breaking into smaller groups and drifting in different directions. I looked to Zandorian at my side, waiting for some kind of direction. I didn't have to wait long.

"Dortes Weh and I have some topics to discuss. You are welcome to join us." Only one other person? How easy it would be to end up alone. I had to avoid that.

"No, I have other things to do."

"Alright." He looked dejected but hid it quickly. He directed his attention to Dortes Weh and the mage he was with.

I wandered away from the larger crowd. I wanted to find out if Hira had left, or maybe find Aurelia or Zifira. I didn't make it too far before I found myself alone in a hallway, but when I turned back I found my way blocked.

"Skye of Solde-al... I have an offer for you."

Celevan Ni. Everything about him bothered me the same way his country did. Something from a hundred lives ago was unresolved, I could feel it.

He walked towards me, much closer than most people dared. I took two steps backwards until I felt a wall at my back. That didn't bother me. Walls weren't much of an obstacle.

"I want to offer you something better than your king could ever dream." I doubted it. "You could come back with us. I'd shower you in riches greater than that rag from last night. I'd make you my Empress instead of his queen."

None of that could be true. Trusican was large but not rich. A thousand islands with nothing but agriculture and fishing, its people torn by years of civil wars I had read about. Not that that would have swayed me. I'd rather let Zandorian use me for whatever he wanted than be near Celevan. I thought of the most scathing insult for an arrogant man.

"Who are you?" I looked past him and finally saw the elegant mage with the garnet hair and big brown eyes. "Hello, Hira." She smiled. I didn't know how to radiate fear but leave Hira out of it. I wanted her to like me.

"Celevan Ni, Emperor of Trusican." He had a crease of anger on his forehead. I stayed cool and calm.

"Ah, that makes sense. I'll make a note to take it when you fall."

"Excuse me?"

"It's inevitable with how incredibly stupid you are. Talk to me when you have something realistic to offer." I turned to doge past him.

"How dare you!" He grabbed my bare arm, trying to pull me back.

"If you want to keep your hand, take it off me." I let my skin slowly begin to heat to burning. Still he held on. I saw Hira's hand on his shoulder. I liked her a lot less until I saw how tears pooled in her eyes while doing it. This was her job, not what she wanted.

"Last chance," I snapped. He gripped harder, I saw the pain start to show in his face. And Hira's.

I hit his arm with the smallest burst of star-fire I could control. He wheeled back in pain, muffled howls. I ran away. Not for my sake, but his. If I stayed I would kill him. The star-fire ached to do it. It physically hurt to deny it. I needed to kill that man, but I couldn't. Not today.

When I looked up at the end of the hall, Eran was there with two women I didn't recognize.

"You saw what happened?" I asked. He nodded. "Good. Don't tell Zandorian." I didn't want to know what kind of delicate diplomacy I had just burned to ashes.

"I definitely will, that was badass, he'll be proud of you."

"I don't want to start anything."

"You didn't, he did. Don't worry about it." He smiled a large, goofy smile. "You should probably get out here, though."

I kept walking. I didn't know where I was going but I knew I didn't want to be alone and I wanted to be as far away from Celevan as possible. I was incredibly thankful to find Aurelia coming my direction not long later. I'd had a moment to calm down, but the star-fire's burn wasn't gone.

"Hey! How are you?" Aurelia met me halfway, closing the distance. "What's wrong?"

"I was grabbed by some arrogant emperor," I said. She didn't ask any further questions about it. "Let's keep walking."

"So, other than that, how are you?"

"Alright, you?"

"Great actually," she said.

It was the last thing I fully heard as she started diving into a story involving Vitsef and his first wife. Something about a summer house in Dunede and picking out new furniture. She was just getting into the very interesting realm of different types of wood flooring when I heard running footsteps behind us.

"Skye, please come quickly." Kaniel was at my side. I would have dismissed him but he looked like there was something seriously wrong.

"What's going on?"

"Zan has discovered a spy and is making a public example."

That was not the Zandorian I knew, that was fire. I gathered my skirt in my hands so I could run after Kaniel as he started back the way he came. I followed him through a route that twisted back towards the direction of the gardens.

Zandorian was yelling with the fury of thunder. "I welcome you here to speak as equals and you dare stoop to the level of bringing extra ears!"

I looked down from one of the open air halls overlooking the gardens. He was standing over a kneeling man, holding a sword. Sparks of star-fire were flickering from his hand at his side. His eyes were flaming, completely white with light. It genuinely scared me to see him like this, and it had nothing to do with Stardropped fear. Between the natural way he pressed the blade into the man's neck and the look on Zandorian's face, I was sure that this man would join a long list of men he'd killed for the same crime.

When I looked up, I'd lost Kaniel. I searched the doors, trying to remember the closest stairs down. I gave up and decided on the drastic option. I put one foot on the ledge of an archway and jumped. I landed down in the garden, only a few paces from him and the terrified creature kneeling in the gravel before him.

"Zandorian! Let's not do this," I called with as much authority as I could conjure. My voice had a volume and depth to it I didn't understand but I was glad to have. I moved to their sides without my feet touching the ground.

Zandorian had frozen, only his eyes looking at me. The star-fire flared in his fist. I grabbed his arm and pulled the sword away from the man.

"We'll give him a trial," I said, quieter now to reason with him. His eyes dimmed, returning to rapidly swirling gold glitter. The star-fire stopped.

"Do not think this is the end," he hissed as the posted Solde soldiers swooped in to drag him away. "That goes for whoever he is here for as well!" he called to the spectators. They started to disperse with the sound of muffled gossip following them. I realized I was still holding onto his arm and let go. He hadn't seemed to notice.

Zandorian threw his sword on the ground a dozen feet away. The grass burned away where it touched the handle.

"Years of killing spies and still they think they will hire the lucky one," he grumbled. He looked surprised to see me, his eyes going wide as they met mine.

"I'm sorry I took over," I said.

"No, thank you. I lost my temper. I have little tolerance for spies in honest places." His sad, quick smile made an appearance. "Skye, you can say no, but would you do me a favor and stay with me for the rest of the day?"

The exposure of us together would be good. We would look like we made our decisions together. The idea of being alone with him still bothered me. But apparently there were spies in the bushes. I'd remember that if I felt I was losing control. I nodded.

"Thank you." He looked from me to the palace behind me, "That was quite a jump."

"Was it?"

"Three floors up. I would say so. Enough to scare our guests, to be sure." I didn't have much to say about it. It wasn't impressive to me. He tried again, "Do you like that dress?"

"Yes." Suddenly I was rethinking my choice, "Why?"

"I am surprised. It is not black."

"I'm allowed to wear red."

"Yes, of course- I like it too, obviously." He held up his sleeve with a smile. And in that moment, as I looked from his robe to the skirt of my dress, I realized it was the same fabric. My heart skipped a beat, but I was angry I hadn't noticed at breakfast. I

151

wanted to change the subject before he read too much into it.

"Speaking of dresses, where did mine go?"

"I thought it best to move it back to the vault."

I was sad to know it was locked away, but thankful I wouldn't have to look at it. I didn't need a reminder of the night before. I didn't need a reminder of any of this. Especially Kos and Celevan and the way I'd nearly lost myself in the way Zandorian looked at me. I couldn't do this much longer, it was stressful.

All the same, I kept my promise and stayed with him. I stayed behind him at a distance like every other mage that followed around an important man. I had to admit to myself, I was tuning in and out of what was being said. After the end of the second short conversation with a queen named Kalara Bel, Zandorian turned his attention back to me.

"Skye, can you not do that?"

"Do what?"

"Stand behind me like the rest of them do. If anything I should be standing behind you."

"You're the one talking to them."

"You should be too. They have met me a hundred times, they want to talk to you."

"I don't want to." It was a lie but it was easier to explain than that I was fighting the star-fire down.

We had both lost control in the same day and even if no one had died, that made no guarantees that the next party or meeting or diplomatic visit wouldn't end worse. Maybe this one should and we could be done with it.

"Alright. Please at least walk next to me." I nodded once and stood closer to him.

I sat by him at dinner that evening and didn't talk to anyone. I did let him hold my hand to walk me to my seat, and it only added to my anxiety as the fire reacted to his touch again. After dinner ended, I left immediately without looking back.

***

The next morning I watched the guests depart much the same way they had arrived. I stood at the window of one of the reading rooms in the library. It wasn't in contempt or avoidance this time, instead in assurance that I had survived my first party and hadn't started any wars at all. As far as we knew, at least.

CHAPTER 15

The two weeks that followed were calm. Only one meeting. Zandorian and I had settled into a quiet routine. We didn't talk much, and when we did it was short. But I loved that we could be quiet together.

I had several more dreams about him. In some we danced to music that sounded like the winds of space. In some I nearly drowned in liquid gold while he laughed. In others I burned the palace to nothing while he stood behind me and held my hand. That one had burned my room's furniture to nothing and made my heart ache.

Our routine was interrupted not very long after it had started, however. The words that ended it came from a soldier that had intruded on our breakfast.

"My king, we need your immediate attention."

"Why?" he asked. I saw the angry Zandorian again as he handed him two letters. Zandorian's face darkened with each page. "Fuck- alright. Three days to get this figured out, I guess."

"What is it?" I asked.

He handed them all to me. A Livade town had been completely taken over by Niode. That wouldn't have been detrimental or urgent if we didn't also use that town as a pass through and supply hub for the entirety of the northeast front.

"I am the only one who can fix this in three days without losing too many more of our own."

"I could do it in a few minutes…"

"I know, but I do not think that this is the situation. I would like to leave the town standing. We need the supplies."

"Right…"

"I am sorry, Skye, I must go. I will write." I tried to hide my disappointment as he followed the soldier out of the room.

Why did he have to leave? I knew why. I knew I couldn't go, but it still made me uneasy. The palace without him wasn't much of a home for me, as wonderful as it was. There was no reason for me to be here.

There were no meetings. No news for me to catch up on except maybe what I would get from Zandorian about the situation he was handling. My next three days would be entirely clear.

I took the opportunity to let my curiosity get the better of me. I went to the shelves of designs, pulling some down to go through. He had said I could.

I hated the thought but I knew it was less about clothes and more to get to know him without being asked questions in return. After the gold dress, I doubted any of it would surprise me.

They were beautiful. The grander designs were my favorite. I recognized some from my closet. The ones that intrigued me were the ones for himself. Although largely plain, I did find some I could tell he had let himself have fun with. Of course, my eyes settled on a black one. It was supposed to be embroidered with thousands of swirling gold stars each one with a small diamond set in its middle. I wondered if he had had it made already. Why hadn't he worn it for the party?

One folder held outfits for me that wouldn't cover anything at all. I quickly shut that one and put it back. I didn't need to see those. But a part of me wanted to... I looked around even though I was sure I was alone, pulling it back out slowly.

Gold chains, sheer fabrics, deep necklines and skirts with slits much higher than they should have been. My favorite was one made of just a handful of small gold chains for its ambiguity as jewelry or... I shoved away the thought of its purpose.

There were some suggestive fabric patterns stuffed in the back that made me laugh. I could tell they were less serious because they were only halfway finished and sketchy at best, but they were fun. All in all, it was much tamer than I had been expecting.

I looked back at the everyday outfits for me. Maybe I could pull some out and leave them as hints. I flipped through, pulling out two.

One design caught my eye. The wrists were supposed to have bracelet-like cuffs that connected to the trail of the skirt, but they had been scrubbed out. I knew why, and the thoughtfulness struck me again. He listened to what I said. It showed in everything he did.

CHAPTER 16

Zandorian more than kept his word and figured out our three day problem in two. He arrived back home in the early morning, just in time to meet me for breakfast. I didn't say much more than good morning, but I was happy he was back. It was nice to be able to be quiet with him again.

I walked down with him to the day's meeting where he left me to talk to Haullen. Aurelia arrived with Vitsef later than usual, and she was ecstatic when she spotted me.

"Skye, come here!" She waved me towards herself. I did as she asked, trying to read her for an explanation.

"What's got you so happy today?" I asked. She clasped her hands in front of herself in excitement.

"I'm so excited Skye, I'm having a baby!"

"Oh, that's…" I found my eyes leaving Aurelia and meeting Zandorian's across the space. For a second my cheeks were warm for no reason I understood. He took it as an invitation to come over.

"Aurelia, wonderful to see you,"

"My king," she smiled. "I was just telling Skye General Vitsef and I are having a child."

"I am happy to hear it." His smile said he was happy, but his eyes were hard. Aurelia looked from him to me

"When are you going to have children, Skye?" I was too surprised to react. Did I tell her never and bring down our entire carefully crafted appearance and dash all possibilities in a single statement? Or lie for an even more unlikely timeline? Zandorian saved me, gently grabbing my hand to pull me towards the doors.

"Meeting is starting. Feel free to sit in the garden and enjoy the fresh air while you wait, Aurelia." I took a glance back to wave an apology to her. She waved back. I was glad she wasn't mad.

"Thank you," I whispered to Zandorian once we were far enough away.

"Of course," he whispered back. Then, quieter, "I have always thought that was a rude question to ask."

"She is my friend…"

"And that is information friends are not entitled to, even if they ask." He dropped my hand and adjusted his rings. "You do not have to answer anyone's questions."

He was right. I didn't owe her an answer right now, if ever. I'd have to think about it when my hands weren't white hot and shaking.

The meeting itself was markedly uneventful, though it was exceptionally long. I found myself tuning in and out. I was more imagining Aurelia and Vitsef's situation than listening, especially when Vitsef was talking. Did he have other children? What would Aurelia be like as a mother? I knew she had wanted a family and it showed in her current excitement. I tried to be happy for her.

***

By the time the meeting ended, the sun was low in the sky. I had done nothing but think myself into loops for hours. Their spinning was only stopped by a voice I'd made a point of ignoring during the meeting to prevent thinking too hard on my own situation.

"Are you joining me for dinner?" Zandorian asked as he walked out of the room. I'd nearly forgotten about dinner. I wasn't hungry, of course, but I did want to.

"Yes."

"Wonderful."

I made an impulsive choice as we arrived at the sitting room. I sat at the chair by his side instead of on the end.

"Change of scene?" he asked.

"Why do we have so many unused chairs, anyway? May as well get some use out of all of them." I didn't look at him as I took a sip of the fruity drink.

"Very true." I felt him watching me. "What did you think of Vitsef's new plan?"

"I wasn't listening to it carefully."

"Just as well, you will see it on your desk soon enough. It is not the worst one we have ever had, but I have concerns. I would be curious to know if you did as well."

"I'll let you know."

When our plates were cleared and our glasses empty, he moved to his desk by the window and picked up three letters with the official gold edging and red Al star seal. I watched him with curiosity.

"What are those for?" I asked.

"This one is to Vitsef about a group we have in Livade. This one is to a representative in our largest gold mine to tell them transport will be interrupted as we move soldiers closer to Niode. And this one is for turning down an invitation to a party Wer is throwing in Dunede. It is my favorite."

"Not into parties?"

"No, that is why I continue to throw ours. It is big enough I see everyone I need to, then I do not have to go to others for the rest of the year."

"I appreciate that. I don't think I could fake dance through another and talk to the same fifty people again."

"I could teach you to dance for real if that would help make the eventuality more bearable," he suggested. I thought of how close I'd come to burning even a gold dress to nothing.

"Not yet," I answered. He made a scrunched face. "What?"

"Nothing, you just said that like I do."

"Oh, sorry."

"No, it is just funny. You do not know Renci." Everything fell into place with that sentence. I had my answer. His mother was from Renciam, and Kaniel must have been as well. That explained the embassy Solde had there. But he was wrong, I had learned basic Renci for class when I was fifteen. At the time I'd thought of it as a useless thing to occupy some time. I'd forgotten most of it, but I remembered loving it.

"I do, actually. Only a handful of words, none of them useful."

"Oh? Show me?" He leaned towards me with interest. I saw the glitter back in his eyes, like sparks. I looked around and picked up an orange and green fruit from a bowl on the side table.

"*Merdan*"

"*Murdan*, but close." I said the rudest word I knew in response. He laughed. "That was perfect."

"*Ketani*," I said, pointing to the books.

"Good, but how about full sentences?" he asked. I answered clumsily. It was the closest I could get to saying *not very good* with the vocabulary I had. I knew I was wrong, but I didn't care, I'd made him laugh again.

"We can work on it if you like."

"I'd like that."

I fumbled my way through another set of random vocabulary words I hadn't thought about in years. It was a language I had only ever read and not heard and I was surprised by how beautiful it was when it was spoken correctly… or maybe it was his voice I liked. I couldn't separate the two now. He sounded so much more at ease when he spoke it, softer. It was like hearing his voice for the first time again and I was just as enamored now as I had been then.

When I looked up for what felt like the first time in hours I saw that the sun was long gone, the stars lighting the night instead.

"I should go to sleep." I got up from my chair.

"Of course." To my surprise he got up to open the door for me. He looked tired.

"Goodnight,"

"*Ar sem nedam*," he breathed quietly.

"What does that mean?" I asked, not having to try to match the breathless tone.

"Have a good night…" he murmured without looking me in the eyes.

I knew it meant I love you, but I'd never tell him I knew that. I took a breath then hurried away down the hall.

He'd gone so far as to use *nedam*, the word for romantic love. I would have much preferred *nudam* for love between friends, or even *nidam* for family. *Nedam* was a heavy word. It was the word only said to one or two people in a person's whole life.

My heart was racing and my eyes were burning. I shoved down everything those words made me feel. Maybe I had heard him wrong. Maybe I was wrong. After all, I'd learned it so long ago… but I had remembered them. At the time, they had resonated as words no one would ever say to me.

CHAPTER 17

I didn't get much sleep. I spent most of the night staring at the ceiling, watching my own light fade and brighten with my thoughts. When I did doze, I woke myself up in panic, feeling like I was falling.

I drifted to the library much earlier than I usually would have after pulling on yet another gauzy black robe. The sun was barely up to disperse the morning fog, putting the library in a dim blue light as I opened the doors. I searched for the language section, spotting the plaque on the second floor. The stairs took extra care in this gown.

I ran my fingers down the spines until I found what I wanted. I pulled out a language manual for Renci. It was old. I recognized the stiff grammar charts from what I had learned before. I didn't get much farther than that when Kaniel appeared from nowhere, as he always did.

"An interesting choice. Trying to relearn? I could help more than that book. Seri and I raised Zan so it was his first language. It would not be the first time I have taught it." I looked up at him. How close had he been to Zandorian's mother to call her by a nickname too? "But you've studied it before, I guarantee you remember more than you think." And for a moment I did. As I looked back down at the book I recognized the Renci words and the sounds they were supposed to make, but the words in my native language looked clunky and unintelligible. It faded quickly.

"I appreciate that but I'm looking for something more than trying to learn." I studied his face. As blank and annoyed as ever.

"Ah, I see." He watched me fumbling through the pages. "I still can not help at all?"

"No, Kaniel."

He left me alone and went down stairs. There was only a moment's pause before I heard the doors slam open and whispering voices in the language I was reading. I moved to the edge and peaked over the balcony. A ruffled Zandorian looked panicked, quickly talking to an amused Kaniel. His outfit was bedraggled, and it was the least put-together I'd ever seen him. Exactly no gold chains. His hair barely contained by a hastily tied ribbon, the waves turned to frizzy curls in places. I would have bet anything that he had thought he was getting here early enough to warn Kaniel in case I came looking for answers.

We made eye contact, and he took a step back. The panic quickly lessened, but I was sure it was an act on his part.

"She is upstairs," Kaniel said with more humor than I had thought he had, all pretense of whispering gone.

"Skye! You are up early." I hadn't slept at all because of him! I wanted to scream. I felt my hand glow for a second. I couldn't do that, not now. He ascended the stairs two at a time.

"You do not need that." He deftly pulled the book from my hands and put it back on a random shelf to our right. "So you figured it out, then? I do not take it back, but I do apologize for saying it and making you uncomfortable."

"Figured what out? Why would another language make me uncomfortable?" I feigned. If he could lie, so could I. I took the book back. He let me keep it, but I saw the smallest crease of concern between his eyebrows. Good. He'd kept me up all night with his slip, maybe I could return the favor.

"That my mother is from Renciam, so I am not full blood Solde." He wasn't lying, but he was quickly changing the direction of the conversation. It was a smooth transition, I had to admire that.

"Yes, I put it together last night. That doesn't bother me. Would have been nice if you'd told me

167

sooner, I've been trying to figure out your accent since we met." I held up the book. "I thought I would pick it up again. Kaniel offered to teach me, but I declined. I'd rather read more before subjecting myself to more *merdan– murdan* embarrassment." He smiled. He was buying it.

"Maybe you should reconsider Kaniel. He is better than an outdated book. These are not common phrases any more." He was so sure he'd gotten away with this. That was it.

"Common phrases like I love you?" I pushed past him and down the stairs. I regretted not staying one more second to see his expression.

He followed me down and skipped the last few steps with a jump. There were sparks in his hands. He slid in front of me to keep me from ignoring him,

"I am sorry."

"No, you're not!" I yelled with a force I didn't know I had. The fire flared in my chest. My toes left the ground in anticipation of burning. I had to calm down. Kaniel's eyes were digging into my back. I took deep breaths and held the book tighter. I could never burn a book.

The way Zandorian looked at me gave me pause. It wasn't terror or anger. It was awe. He didn't deserve my tantrum. He had lied, yes, and made my feelings about our relationship more complicated when I still wasn't sure I wouldn't bring the palace down because of one too strong emotion. But it had been for something that would have never been a problem if I could act normally. If I wasn't terrified of feeling it too.

"But it's alright. I'm just... I'm not there yet. Please don't start saying it." I could see him working through it.

"That is fine, I will not say it."

"Good." There was an awkward pause. I didn't want to leave. He didn't seem to want to either.

"Would you like to have dinner with me tonight in the garden instead of at our usual table?" He sounded anxious. I sighed,

"Only if you promise not to say it."

"I promise."

I nodded and left the library, letting the doors close behind me. I remembered the book in my hand. I didn't even want the book. I would rather the next thing he said be a complete mystery instead of that heavy phrase. But I had it, so I had to keep it out of principle if nothing else. After a long moment of deliberation, I decided I may as well use it. Renci had to be useful for reasons that weren't Zandorian.

***

I sat in the small reading nook off the main hall of my wing, a breezy, cozy place I'd never had reason to sit in before. Normally I'd go to the library, but right now I wanted to avoid every other part of the palace. I stayed there for a long time, watching the sun rise and fall with the glances I took up from my small stack of books and a notebook I'd started to fill in.

As much as I didn't want to think about him, Zandorian was right for saying writing about nothing was entertaining. I'd added a handful of terrible doodles as well, trying to draw maps of stars I'd never seen reflected in our sky. When I started to see the real ones in the Solde sky, I knew it was time for me to face whatever Zandorian had planned for our evening.

I debated whether I should put on something nicer or not. I settled on a dress with an outer layer covered in small stars. I loved how they caught the light in a realistic way. I decided I would look better with a dark smudge on my eyelids like Eda had done for the party. It wasn't as well done as what she had done, but I didn't hate my attempt.

As the gardens came into view I had to stop and take it in. It was incredibly beautiful. Every lamp was lit along the paths, their colored glass throwing a thousand colors across the walkways. I could hear the fountains and the whispering rustle of the leaves in the light breeze. There was a table set in the middle near one of the water features, the water decorated with flower petals, the smooth surface reflecting the night sky above and the flicker of the lantern light.

Zandorian had taken the time to put on a much nicer outfit than what he had thrown on earlier. I counted three plain gold chains and two matching bracelets. The robe under them was either incredibly dark blue or black. I couldn't be sure, but I could be sure that he made its simple design look wonderful. He had redone his hair into a half up bun, pulling it away from his face. I didn't like it. It made it easier to see him from every angle and still find no faults. The effect only worsened as I walked closer. I couldn't look him in the eyes.

"Skye, am I overstepping if I say you are beautiful?" I shook my head and hoped the low lighting hid my blush. "Then I will say it. You are beautiful." The way he spaced the words, they sounded like three others he had said. Or maybe I was reading too much into it. "Please, sit. I know we both missed breakfast." He gestured to my chair.

"That's your fault." I'd meant it as a joke but it only made him look down in shame.

"Yes, it is. I hope this makes up for it."

As usual, the food was delicious, but the presentation was unmatched tonight. It looked like the foods that had been at the party; more sculpture than a dish. I'd have to ask Eda who made this.

I finished my food a long time after him, but he didn't seem to mind. He kept his hands folded on the table and watched a place over my shoulder, not focusing fully. He seemed to return to the present when I set down my utensils. He took in my empty plate and nodded approval before speaking,

"Skye?"

"Hm?"

"I have more planned than dinner." My heart stuttered with what that could mean. From under the table he pulled out a long and thin red box.

"I had wanted to get you something, and could not quite decide. Jewelry and clothes would not do. You have every book in the library. Then I realized the answer." He opened the box. Inside was a smaller version of his own sword, just as intricate and well made. I took it out. It fit in my hand with grace and ease, catching the light on its mirror-shined blade. "Eda made it herself, the very best."

"I don't have words... thank you."

"You deserve it. Especially after the beating you gave our practice target," he laughed. "Even if you never use it, I like the idea that you have the option."

Thank you wasn't enough. My resolve to stay mad at him was melting like the gold of my dress. He watched me hold it a moment before putting the box down. He looked anxious again.

"We still have a second part of our evening. Walk with me?"

I put down my sword and followed him through the gardens, still in awe of all they had to offer in the night.

"I hear you like stars."

"What makes you think that?" I found myself doing a small spin so he would notice what I'd picked out for the evening. It made him laugh, and I found myself laughing too before a wave of embarrassment took over. I was acting like a child. I fell back into my usual indifference quickly.

"I asked them to set up something for stargazing. Let's see what they did, hm?"

We rounded a corner and were on the practice field, but it had been cleared of all targets and weapons. Instead it was just a grassy field where an enormous blanket and more pillows than I could count now rested. They'd done another wonderful job.

The pillows were piled so high I knew it would be easy to get lost in. I wanted to be lost in them. Bury my face instead of having to look at him. I laid down and stared up, completely ignoring that he laid next to me and that I felt our hands brush. I hoped he had the sense not to push this. I didn't know if I could handle it.

"Tell me what you know about them," he said. I had to look at him in disbelief for a moment. I was so glad he wanted to listen. No one had ever cared before.

I pointed to each one I knew anything about. Which ones were stars and which were galaxies. How each moved in the sky, how bright and what color it burned. I knew things I had never read, like that many of them burned hotter or cooler than myself. How some were close to death in a brilliant explosion and some were just starting out in life. I was sure I sounded insane. I couldn't explain how I knew what I knew, or even fully what I meant, but he had asked.

After a while he stopped asking questions or agreeing. I was boring him. When I looked over to make sure he was there at all, he was looking at me. He smiled and suddenly I was much more accepting of what he had said last night. I believed him. I didn't see what he would possibly have to gain from listening to my rambling if he didn't truly mean it.

My heart was beating fast. I found myself thinking maybe this conflict was all for nothing. All I had to do was kiss him. Maybe I would enjoy it and I could leave all my qualms about our relationship behind. I found myself leaning my head closer. He did too.

But I couldn't, I wasn't sure I wouldn't burn the entire palace to the ground if anything went wrong. I turned my head to look back up at the stars. He sighed beside me. Had I upset him? I reminded myself it was fine if I had. Then his smooth voice,

"Let's walk." It seemed like a spontaneous choice, but I didn't object. Maybe he had planned something else. I hoped not. I already had too many feelings to sort out tonight. I took his hand to help me up and followed him.

I had never been to this part of the building before. We took two grand stairways and one small tightly spiraling staircase hidden behind an unassuming door. When I stepped out, I was on the very top of the palace in the cool night air. We made our way to the very edge where a low balcony rail separated us from the sky. I wasn't completely sure what we were supposed to be doing, but I was happy.

Looking at Zandorian, he was too. For the first time I saw that he glowed too. Very dim and very golden in color, but a glow all the same. I realized I was staring when he met my gaze again. I clambered for something to say.

"Can I ask you some questions?" It was innocent enough. He had asked me a list of questions, now it was my turn.

"Please do."

"Can you tell me more about your first wife, Dezura?" I asked flatly, hiding my feelings about the fact that I was consistently compared to her. He took a slow pause.

"Yes. She was not a mage, of course. She was from a very powerful family from Dunede, the Kul family. We were married very young, far before I took my father's place. It was an arrangement he designed without my knowledge. I did like her as much as I did any familiar person, I suppose. There was no passion between us. She died of complications giving birth to my son. She had been sick for a long time, and it pushed her too far. I did what I could but she insisted on going through with it no matter what she was told. Considered it her purpose, she said. I spent a lot of my years alone grieving that loss. I feel guilty about it still. I may not have loved her as much as I should have, but she was still a person." He was somber, staring at the sky, the glow completely gone. "Maybe it was for the better, anyway... I would not have been a good father then. I was not a good husband. Being king is the only thing I have ever been good at, truthfully."

"That's not true."

"In what way?"

"I have no idea about your capabilities as a father," I faltered, "and you are a wonderful king, but you are also a great friend."

"Thank you, Skye."

I meant it and didn't. He wasn't like Aurelia. She was a friend. He was something else entirely, something so much better. But I couldn't think about that. I didn't get to have a soulmate.

My mind wandered and I found myself thinking maybe we only got along because the star-fire inside us did. His mother had been like me, the same fire. What had happened to her? Her name had been Serana, and that was all I knew. He'd said her lack of freedom killed her, but I still didn't know what he meant by that.

"I have another emotional question."

"Let's get it answered"

"How did your mother die?"

"I was so young they shielded me from it. The memory is faded. I do not know any details except that there was no body."

"I'm sorry."

"It is regrettable. But it has been so long, I have accepted it to a point." He took a deep breath and held it before letting it out as a sigh. I tentatively put my hand on top of his on the railing. He didn't pull away. His glow flickered back into existence.

"I could tell you how the legends say she was born, though. How all the Stardropped and mages happened." He sounded optimistic.

"Is that something Kaniel dug up in his precious books?"

"Yes, actually. He worked very hard at it, and it is a very interesting story." Zandorian smiled and leaned on the balcony rail. "The first Stardropped was said to have fallen to the ground in a great flaming explosion. We know now she probably existed before that and that great explosion was her using her power for the first time, but the first explanation is more poetic. After she entered our society, she was a great protector of the people. She defended against attacks within our own civilizations and from above, whatever that meant. Ordinary young women stood with her, and over time they began to develop powers of their own. They started to call her the Queen of Mages, loosely translated.

Mages began appearing in every generation since. And so did the Stardropped. The first one burned up when she had outlasted the next generation of ordinary people around her…a body was never found. But then a young girl began to use the power. She took up the title, and it was as if the first had never left." He looked at me for a long time, taking in a deep breath. His face took on a much more serious expression.

"Through time each incarnation of the Stardropped was put through everything from slavery to weaponization to being treated as a god." I rubbed at my wrists, checking the chains were not there. "Including my mother, kidnapped from her home country and controlled by my father. Numb to her own emotions by his mage power." His hand became a fist with a dull glow. "The most unusual is one that was kept as a powerful light source that lit a city from the top of a tower."

"So what I'm hearing is we've always been kept in towers," I said it in a flippant tone, but I was becoming angry. My mind was measuring all he told me. It wouldn't let go of the idea that my power was a weapon and everyone, myself included, had known that from the start. I couldn't be anything else. Not truly. The star-fire agreed. It was meant to burn, and they all were lucky it hadn't for this long.

"I suppose that is true… I am sorry about that. That is not your reality anymore, Skye."

"But it was for a long time." I felt the fire rising, spreading to my hands. I fought it down.

"But it will never be again! You are too powerful for anyone to keep you like that again." Ah yes, I was powerful, there it was. I could simply star-fire away any problem I had, from his view. It agreed with him. That's all it had ever wanted to do. I had no problems if I had nothing. "I hope with enough freedom you will be more powerful than anyone in the stories."

There it was again. Comments about my power had started to rub my mind raw, especially after this new information.

"Is that all you're concerned about? How powerful I am?" I asked, trying to keep my tone even.

"Of course not, Skye, I just want you to achieve your full potential."

"Why, though? I've been struggling with that since I got here. The only answer I have is that there's something in it for you and your military. Unless my full potential is a trophy dressed in gold. You've made that clear."

"Skye... that is..." he stumbled for words. He never stumbled on his words.

"So that's it. You want me to be flashy and end the war. Thank you for letting me achieve my potential so I can flatten cities for you when it's convenient." I had to leave, I was too emotional for this. It was taking everything I had to not burn.

After a large amount of trial and error, I made it back to my room. I was too preoccupied to think straight. I grappled with the idea that my power had come here as a hero and devolved into a destructive commodity. I could be a hero again. I hoped to be, but in a deeper, darker corner of myself, something whispered that they didn't deserve it, they had enslaved us. I should let them fight their own wars. Burn them all with star-fire when they got too close.

I couldn't do that. Not to Zandorian, especially. I was angry with him, on some level. It didn't matter how I felt about him. He was the one who kept making my life about what I could do. Showing me off to the world as a warning to other countries. Sure, he tried to help who I was underneath it, but it was an empty gesture if he was doing it only to support my power and not me.

I did feel bad about insulting the gold dress. It had been not only beautiful but also incredibly considerate. I knew it was likely a design he was proud of. I hoped he would forgive me for the insult to his art some day. Or did I? Why did I care what he thought of me at all? I had to let that go.

I found myself thinking this would have been easier if he was the manipulator I had accused him of being. I wished I could believe that he hadn't meant what he'd said and that I wasn't starting to want to hear it. If whatever we had ended any worse than that conversation, I wasn't sure Solde-al would survive. I would slip farther to the star-fire than I ever had, and I would have no reason to fight it.

I didn't want to be in my room any longer. I couldn't go to the library, I'd probably wake up Kaniel and I didn't fully trust myself around books right now. I couldn't go to the study, he lived there. Maybe I could find my way back to the roof? That was unlikely, I'd been thinking about too many other things.

I wandered down to the practice field. I had no idea what I wanted to do there. I pulled a sword off the rack that had been moved against the wall and held it. I didn't mean to heat it up to glowing, but I didn't stop it. I held it a moment before bending it. When I looked back at it, I'd made it into a Z. That made me even angrier, so I crushed it into nothing. I hated it. I hated every feeling I'd ever had.

I laid down on the blanket and pillows and stared up into the sky like we had done before. I wished I was nothing but a star and all I had to do was burn. I was jealous of them. Somewhere, from deep inside my soul, I knew some of them had feelings too. I wasn't the only Stardropped, I couldn't be. They wouldn't think of me as powerful or terrifying. I wouldn't be unusual to them at all. I tried to find comfort in thinking of them as family. But they were still far away, completely indifferent to me. Just like everyone here.

CHAPTER 18

I was embarrassed to wake up on the ground in the early morning. I knew someone had found me because of the blanket that had been laid over me. Thankfully, the sun was barely up and I didn't see another soul. The ground in my immediate space was dry, but as I got up I felt that the rest of the blanket was lightly dew soaked. I threw the blanket away and walked to my closet to start my day.

The anger was nearly stronger than my own mind today, and I was constantly wrestling it down. My hands were just barely not glowing the entire morning. Images and flashes of emotion raged through my consciousness, but I couldn't hold onto them. There was a meeting, so I had to get myself together enough to go.

After breaking the clasp of one of my necklaces, I took the medallion off of it and melted it into putty. I pulled it into two pieces and put them on either side of my front teeth, molding them into points like fangs. If I was an angry monster that couldn't do anything but destroy, at least I could look the part.

I pulled on the closest fitting of my robes, a red one without a back and a slit up the side, gold chains crisscrossing the bodice. I'd put myself in chains for them if I had to.

I made everyone visibly uncomfortable as I walked down to the meeting room. Except Zandorian. Of course. I was starting to think I could have ripped the palace down to nothing bedrock and he would still look at me like I could never do wrong. He was standing with Eran, but he didn't seem invested in that conversation as I walked past them to Aurelia's side. She at least wasn't too put off by my presence either.

"Skye... you're angry today." I felt it lessen slightly, edge gone from its bite. "Is it Zandorian? He looks guilty. You know, I've been meaning to ask you, I don't think he likes me much."

"I'm sure he does."

"No, cause the other day he said he was happy and he wasn't."

"He lies sometimes."

"Is that why you're mad at him?"

"Something like that." It wasn't, but I couldn't explain that too much honesty mixed with avoiding my feelings made a horrible combination. I saw the subtle face she made when she reached out farther with her power. She flinched slightly.

"What is it?" I asked.

"Maybe you should go talk to him. He's... not mad at you."

"You hesitated."

"You need to go talk to him so I can focus on something else. You two are giving me a headache. We can talk later."

"Fine, fine."

I followed her orders. I wasn't sure I wanted to, but if Aurelia said it was best I'd trust her. It wasn't the worst of decisions either way. We had to keep up appearances at the very least. The last thing I needed was the council doubting that my title was justified.

"Skye, how are you?" he asked sweetly. I didn't look at him. I couldn't do that right now. "We are not talking?"

"I'll talk to you, I'm not a child. I just don't particularly want to deal with your pleasantries."

"I can be honest instead," he said with a slow smile.

"Please do." I'd play his game.

"Those fangs are egregious. They are scaring every one of these men, and" he leaned a little closer, speaking in a harsh whisper, "I would absolutely love to know how they taste."

I took three full steps backwards and walked into the meeting room. I sat in my chair and stared at the wall, thinking about anything else. Anything but the mix of feelings that interaction had caused. Unfortunately, he had followed me.

"You said please," he chided. I knew exactly what I said, I didn't need his arrogance.

I took the fangs out and put them on the table in front of him. "Find out for yourself. Now we're not talking."

As other men entered and took their seats, I saw him take them off the table. I said nothing. I would have, but there was nothing to say. I was feeling too many emotions to say something for the sake of it. He made a point of not looking at me, keeping his hands on the table.

CHAPTER 19

I went to Aurelia's house the next day. The high general's house was a stand-alone building separate from the palace but still within walking distance. The houses of the officials all surrounded the palace like planets around the sun, each one with its own arching strip of walled-off land. They were all within another taller gate that ringed the entire palace territory, and I suspected that was why I was allowed to go without bringing anyone else. That, or no one wanted to try to tell me I couldn't. I reveled in the freedom as I walked.

The stone structure of Vitsef's house was towerless and plain, with unremarkable plants and a single fountain between the front door and the road. I hated that I thought it looked cramped- the palace had warped my vision.

A woman opened the door to let me in. She was short, middle aged, and jumpy. I didn't know if it was the effect of my presence or her usual disposition, but

I suspected a mix of both. She flitted away into the house. I took the moment to take in the entryway. It was largely the soft yellow color of a *murdan*. I needed to not think about that. The maid came back a moment later with Aurelia.

"Skye, how wonderful to see you!" She held her arms out for a distance-conscious hug. "What are you doing here?"

"Just visiting. I needed to leave the palace for a bit." I knew it wouldn't sound strange coming from someone who had been in exactly two places in her whole life. I would want to leave. I hoped she couldn't tell that it had nothing to do with the structure.

"Oh, that's great! I'll have to give you a tour. Do you want anything?"

"I'm alright, thank you," I answered. Aurelia looked to the maid.

"Get us drinks," she ordered. I caught myself taking a step back.

"Is that how you usually talk to her?" I had never heard her talk like that.

"Don't worry about it, Skye. She's happy."

I realized what she meant. I even felt her pushing on my own mind, happy energy radiating from her. It made me uncomfortable, but I shoved it from my mind. Aurelia was my friend. She had been for forever.

The maid obediently returned with drinks. I didn't touch mine, setting it on a side table. Aurelia started to lead me into what appeared to be a sitting room and art gallery. It seemed Vitsef had a taste for sculptures of military and combative figures from history and mythology.

The largest was in the center of the room. It was an outstandingly carved realistic depiction of Ashanm fighting with Iliths, the legendary battle between light and dark, creation and destruction. I had always found myself identifying with both sides strongly. I was a destroyer by means of light. The difference between myself and both of them was that I was real, and they were projections of ideals and flaws people found in themselves and the world.

Vitsef came through the front doors while she was talking. He followed by three assistants, sorting through a handful of papers. Aurelia put on a huge smile.

"Hello, dearest!"

He gave her a small nod before walking further down the hall. I saw Aurelia's face change in a way I'd only seen twice. The color faded from her skin and her eyes shifted to brighter red. Vitsef stopped in his tracks. He turned around immediately and scooped her up in an enormous hug.

"Hello, my love! How are you? Do you have everything you need?"

"Yes, thank you so much for asking! Have you said hello to Skye?"

"My queen, how wonderful to see you." He gave me the first smile I'd ever seen him wear.

"You as well," I said. His attitude towards me was completely different compared to only a few days ago. The men with him hadn't noticed, and I pretended I hadn't either.

"I have to work today, but I promise we will go shopping tomorrow, yes?"

"Oh I would love that!" She grinned, and he kissed her in a way I was definitely not supposed to witness. When they pulled away, he started back on his original course.

"My queen," he nodded to me as he walked away. Aurelia turned back to me, her hands folded under her chin and her cheeks flushed.

"Skye, do you want to go visit Cerp? I'm sure she would love to see you."

"I wouldn't be so sure."

"Ah, well if anything it'll entertain her for a few moments. She's like a pet, in that way. Don't get me wrong, I love that you gave her to us, but she is an unusual one."

"She is that." I hated that she used the words "pet" and "gave." Even the word "unusual" bothered me, her tone making it an insult. If Aurelia thought Cerp was "unusual," how did she see me?

Upstairs, Cerprillis's room was completely empty except for a lopsided bed. Her window had heavy iron bars criss-crossing the frame and bolted to the wall. Deep scratches scarred the floor and walls. She uncurled herself from the corner and was in front of us in a second. Too fast, as always.

"Hello, Cerp."

"Skye. You smell like sunlight. And fire."

"Thank you."

"Aurelia smells like flowers." She smiled at Aurelia with her too sharp teeth.

"That's very nice of you to say." She clapped her hands in excitement, "Do you want to show Skye your art?" Aurelia turned to me. "It's been something to keep her busy. She's in here most days."

Cerp flipped her bed up and pulled out about seven pieces of crumpled paper out from under it. She carefully laid them out on the floor, changing their order and turning them every which way. I could hardly see that it mattered, all the pages were covered in deep red splotches and spatters.

"I see you've done another one. They're very nice paintings, aren't they Skye?"

"Yes, I enjoy the red." In truth they were unsettling. Aurelia had to sense my unease because she responded quickly.

"Yes, it is pretty. Cerp, I think we're going to go back downstairs. Say goodbye." Aurelia left the room, waiting to close and lock the heavy door again.

"Goodbye," I said, but Cerp caught my arm. She couldn't hold on long and pulled her hand away quickly with a hiss. She whispered only to me,

"She also smells like leather. It's not a good smell." I nodded and let Aurelia shut the door. I had no idea what that meant, but I knew I had to get out of this house.

CHAPTER 20

The next two days passed slowly. I ate on my own in my room and stayed in the library or garden. I always sat far from where Zandorian might see me in passing. I didn't want to see him again yet. I wasn't sure if it was because I wasn't ready to apologize, or because I wanted an apology.

I was about to take off my necklace and change into a sleeping robe for yet another evening of reading on my balcony when Eda opened my closet door.

"My queen, a note from the king." She held out a folded paper. I recognized the gold edging. I took the note from her, confused. Why was he sending notes in the middle of the night?

Please meet me in my sitting room as soon as you wish, I want to discuss something with you. I will be waiting patiently.

What a way to break our days of silence, a mysterious note with no information except a plea to meet with him. I hoped this was about something like agriculture. I wasn't sure I could handle having my feelings crushed or having to crush my own feelings yet again. It didn't matter. I would go regardless. It was my responsibility.

I didn't have to knock on his door, he was expecting me. The room was dark. The only light came in as starlight from the open windows. My eyes searched the darkness and found his dim gold eyes sitting in his chair by the unlit fire.

Zandorian looked so dejected, alone in this now incredibly cold room. It hurt me to see him like that. Was his mood my fault? Of course it was, I was so incredibly rude to him. Accusing him of not caring about me as a person at all the day after he'd said he loved me.

"Skye," he looked up and I saw the light of my glow across his face. It made him look his age for the first time, catching every line and scar. "Please, sit down." I took my place across from him, keeping my hands firm on the arms of the chair.

"I have had an idea I wanted to ask your opinion on. I value it so deeply... even your indecision is more important than my own feelings," he spoke quietly, as if he were praying to me instead of talking.

"What's the idea?"

He took in a breath. "I was thinking of bringing in another queen." He didn't have to say the words "because you don't love me" I saw them in his face. My breath caught in my throat. My hand went to the Al pendant on my necklace, but I quickly pulled it back. It was still there. Zandorian watched my pause with sincere interest. I found my voice,

"I say no." I was surprised I was saying no, but it was the only thing I could say. He nodded solemnly.

"Of course, then I will not. If you are comfortable, would you mind telling me why?" His face was blank but his eyes begged for an answer.

My brain worked fast in the heavy silence. I had good, sensible, logical reasons that it would be a horrible move for myself and my selfish power.

"I think another queen would undermine my authority. If there are three rulers, it only dilutes our power because it's shared between all of us. If the people hear an answer they don't want, they go asking the other two until they hear one they like. Our concerns could go unconsidered."

"That is an excellent point, Skye. I understand that."

But I knew there was another illogical reason that took me aback as I realized it. I didn't want to share. I didn't want to share my title, sure, but it was so much more wrapped up in my feelings towards him than any other rationale I could cite. It hit me so hard I stood up from my seat, feet beginning to leave the room underneath me.

"Have I upset you?" he asked behind me. Soft and rich voice as clear as ever.

Before I could lie, I was answering, "Yes, but I have upset myself also." And I rushed from the room.

The walk to my room was long and dark, twisting as it did every night I had walked it. Had it always been this long? It had been my first night here, maybe, but it surely had shortened as I'd grown comfortable. Now, the distance seemed to grow three steps for each one I took.

My heart hammered, my hands shaking. Heat pressed on the backs of my eyes but I had not felt this in so long I thought surely it meant they would explode with star-fire, not tears. Tears were wet and hot and the only thing in all the world that could burn my skin as they ran down my cheeks. Why was I crying in the hall? Could I not wait for a closed and locked door? Was I that full of emotion? An emotion I had never felt a drop of now forced itself to be felt with every part of myself, filling me so fully I was crying it out onto the floor. The floor was closer now. I had melted to my knees, palms down on the ground so they would stop their shaking. I begged myself to get up, walk a few more steps down to my room, close my doors. There I could do this. Not here. If I lost myself here, I didn't know what damage that would cause. Surely Zandorian was not far enough away to be unaffected by a firestorm. He'd think I was trying to pull the palace down for what he'd said.

Thinking of him brought on another wave of the feeling that was boiling over. Wretched, ragged sobs was how it escaped me now. My eyes were clear enough to notice that my hands had begun to glow. My arms as well. I pulled them up from the floor and saw hand prints in the stone, burned and blackened and glowing red under my palms. I had to get up. I couldn't burn. Not here.

I reached my room with clumsy urgency. I slammed all three of my heavy doors closed. I looked to the door on the far side of my room, the one that was for emergencies. If this didn't qualify, I didn't know what would. I walked inside and slammed that door too, nearly tumbling down the stairs that took me further underground. It should have been darker than any night down there, but the light from my body did not allow even a shadow. I stood in the middle of the cavernous room, arms held away from my body so they did not clutch and claw at myself.

And I let myself feel everything I had been shoving down. One fact became clear: I was in love with Zandorian Al.

That thought was all it took. Star-fire erupted, consuming me. It burned all it touched, filling the room. The door ripped free from its threshold.

I burned. I burned for a long time, letting go of all my deep seated resentment towards the idea. I didn't need to be afraid of it, because this was the worst that would happen. This reaction was what I was afraid of. I tried to make sense of the one thing I was now sure of, the truth that had caused this firestorm. I was deeply in love. He said he loved me, too. I needed to tell him. I didn't know if I could ever fix what I had done, but I had to try.

My hands were still again. The light faded. On the edge of my noticing I realized my robes had not survived. They hadn't had a hope. That left me in the unfavorable situation of being without them until I went back upstairs which, I had learned, would likely not be empty of Eda. I was a queen, what did it matter if my maid of all people saw me like this? But I couldn't reason away my reservations. I hoped it would become less of a concern with time. After all, I had no qualms about being naked or emotional in front of Aurelia... or, I realized with another flash of heat, Zandorian. With a pang of hurt I remembered that even if I went upstairs and told him everything, I might have already ruined anything we could have had. I screamed into the cavernous empty room. My voice echoed off the walls.

I stepped over the melted heap that was once the door at the bottom of the stairs. It still glowed hot with deep orange light like the rest of the stone in the room. I stumbled up the stairs, hoping the destruction was limited. I ran my hand down the walls in the darkness. Sure enough, at a point well before the door to my room they became cool enough for a normal person to touch. I'd had more restraint than I had thought.

My room was empty, to my surprise. I had started to expect everyone to be here, getting ready to fight the unhinged queen who was going to bring down the palace. That moment had passed. The palace survived my admission of my feelings to myself. Whether I would survive if Zandorian didn't accept them was my next worry.

I slipped on the thin sleeping robe that was draped across my bed like it usually was when Eda had missed me in the evening. It looked less embellished than the others. I was hoping if I burned this one too it would not be an enormous loss. I still felt the fire, but it burned for something else now.

I hadn't sat on my bed long when I heard my outermost door open and close, then the next. At the third, there was a heavy knock. Eda had never knocked like that. I was surely going to be confronted; about the destruction, the explosion, everything. I was in no mood for questions. I had enough questions for myself to fill my evening. As I opened the door, I reminded myself I was queen and didn't have to answer anyone's questions. Except his, I amended as I saw who it was on the other side.

Zandorian still looked dejected, but he had a firm confidence as if he had made up his mind. I did not want to think about how I looked to him.

"I know this breaks our arrangement, Skye, but I wanted to make sure you were alright."

I didn't know if he was referring to the explosion of star-fire or my sudden departure. It didn't matter, I would answer the same way.

"I'm fine." It was not what I wanted to say. I was far from fine. I was thinking of all the hundred ways I could possibly mess this up or had already. My tone betrayed me. He responded to that instead of my words.

"That is understandable. I have made so many mistakes the past few days, Skye. I am being incredibly honest now. I do not value you for only your power. I value you for everything that makes you a person; the most magnificent person I have ever met. I want you to reach your potential because I think all people should, and you especially because," his expression was pained, "I do not want another queen. I want you. I have only ever wanted you. I know you will never want me. That is why I even entertained the idea of..." he faded off as if he was talking about a crime, looking at the floor a moment before regaining his confidence, gathering it in closed fists at his sides. "I am sorry for breaking our agreement again, but I had to tell you. I should not have gone about it this way. I am sorry."

I held the door wide for him to enter. I grabbed him by his sleeve, leading him inside a few steps before letting go. I crossed to my bed and sat down, pulling my knees to my chest. He had nothing to be sorry about. I had to tell him my newest revelation.

"I have to be honest with you, too. I must also apologize. I've been wildly unfair to you. And despite my original intentions upon my arrival here," I took a deep breath, "I am in love with you. In a romantic, desire-filled way I had stopped believing existed. I do want you. I have for a while, but I was afraid. Denying that to myself has led us here and I'm sorry."

"Really?" He crossed to me in two steps. Sparks flew from his hands as he twisted his rings.

"Yes," I said. I couldn't read that response.

He sat down on the bed next to me, a tentative movement he looked to me for approval of. I nodded a little and shifted to sit closer to him. I could feel the heat of star-fire from his body. I let it melt my inhibitions.

"Skye, I feel that same way, I have since I met you." He was smiling. The enthusiastic acceptance of my feelings took me off guard. I hadn't thought of the possibilities of this going well. Not after I had been so cold.

"You can't. You wouldn't have…" I stumbled, more talking to myself than him. He had said he loved me in a language he had thought I couldn't understand. There had been nothing to gain from that. He had said it in other ways everyday.

"I would not have what? Made you queen? Helped you in all your pursuits and supported your feelings? Had a dress made of gold so you could have one garment you would not burn in an instant?" He laughed. "Asked your opinion when I wondered if I should pursue another love in hopes of distracting myself from you because I was so sure you did not feel the same way?" He tentatively put his hand on top of mine in my lap. I grasped it in both of mine, running my thumb across the thin red line tattoos on the back of it. I nodded. What he was saying was right. He had acted selflessly out of love since the beginning. I had made it into a problem. He was willing to forgive me for that without hesitation, a kindness I had never paid him.

We sat there in a heavy silence for a long time, letting the admissions settle. When I met his eyes again he spoke.

"Skye, does this mean I can say I love you?" He leaned closer. My heart beat faster. The way blood rushed to my cheeks and heat rose in my chest made me sure.

"Yes." I let myself smile for the first time in a long time. Before I could say any more, he put a gentle hand on the side of my face and put his lips against mine. It was everything I'd ever dreamed of, no matter how unreal it felt. He pulled away too soon.

"Is that alright?" he asked.

I didn't answer with my words. I wrapped my fingers through the chains around his neck and pulled him back. I curled closer to him, winding my arm around his body. He moved his hand to my waist. I acted without thinking. My legs wrapped around him until I was in his lap. One hand held his jaw while the other braced against his back to pull my chest to his. My hands burned, but he didn't move away. He pulled me closer. He was strong, stronger than I'd imagined. We didn't have to be careful.

We were burning. I didn't know if he had started it or me, but I was glad to know that fire could be sweet. Our robes were gone as if they had never been. Our bodies pressed together with heat and passion, melding into one with smoother motions than I had thought possible.

When the firestorm ended, we were on the bare floor of my room. It was empty, its furnishings reduced to ash. I was in his arms, calmer than I had ever been. I was still the Stardropped Queen of Soldeal, but now I was something better; his.

CHAPTER 21

The next morning I awoke to Zandorian pulling in a new trunk. I watched him, sitting up, still on the floor. He must have gotten up much earlier, he was already dressed and bejeweled.

"I brought clothes, thought you might want more options than the blanket," he said as he threw it open. He wore an enormous smile. I realized he'd draped a blanket over me and put a soft pillow under my head.

"Thank you. Did you bring another gold dress?"

"No, no," he said, smile fading. "Skye, did you like that dress? You talk about it with such distaste." I was surprised he heard it that way, but when I thought back to my comments before, I had never apologized for that insult in particular.

"I'm sorry, I loved it. It was the most considerate, beautiful thing anyone has ever given me. It was just far more grand than I had thought when I put it on, then you told me it was all gold... I was overwhelmed. I'd never had anyone care about me like that, so for a long time I was sure you'd done it for selfish reasons. It was the only thing that made sense," I explained. He waited a long time, folding a robe he'd pulled out of the trunk. It was blue, a color I'd never seen him wear.

"If I had more made, would you believe it is because I love you?" He met my eyes as he said it. Hearing him say it again made my heart jump and the star-fire glow with a warm heat instead of explosive destruction.

"Now I would believe you," I said, letting in another smile.

For the first time I did what I wanted without thinking and grabbed his arm, pulling him back to me. He didn't resist, dropping what he'd been doing and joining me on the ground with a pillow and the blanket that I was now using as a dress.

"I was thinking we should maybe only use the other room." He threw a hand towards the emergency door that led further down. I suspected it had something to do with the fact that replacing all of my furniture would quickly become a pain, if it hadn't already.

"I doubt that will happen every time."

"I would not mind if it did," he said with a wink. I laughed and pulled him closer.

His robe fell off his shoulders under my hands. I saw more of the deep red lines that crossed his skin. I ran my fingers down them while he kissed my neck. I enjoyed the moment before leaning back to ask my question.

"What are they? Your tattoos."

"Oh, I thought you would have put it together. Remember the map of roads and trade routes of Solde hanging in the library?"

"Of course."

"Well, they are that same map but on my skin. It was the best way I could think to keep my country a part of me forever. That, and they hide some of my scars."

"Do you know them all by heart?"

"I should hope so with all the hours I spent looking at the map combined with all the hours it took to transfer it." He smiled wide. "I did not add the labels, though. It felt like cheating to include them."

"Would you ever add to them? What if they change?"

He shrugged as he pulled the robe back over his shoulders. "All things change. If I had gotten a tree you would be asking what I would do should the weather change and trees drop their leaves. It does not bother me. I hope I live to see change. I hope even more to add to them as we grow."

It was true, nothing was exempt from change. We were a great example of that now.

"I may want one. Much smaller, though." I had no idea what I would want, but it felt right. If anything it would be an experience. I was already taking several items off the list of things I'd never done, what was one more?

"If you decide you do, you may have it. Although, we will have to find a creative solution to make that happen. Most needles would not stand a chance." That made me laugh again. He made an excellent point. Cerprillis had actually made a game of trying to stab me with needles when we were younger. All that had come of it was a pile of bent, melted needles and a disappointed Cerp.

I tried to kiss him again but he stopped me. "Can you answer a question for me?"

"Yes," I answered quickly.

"Why did you let me? I had been getting nothing but confusing signals from you, I thought you would never want this."

"I spent my first weeks here expecting you to try without asking. I thought I'd destroy the palace if you tried. I thought of every way I'd make your life impossible if you touched me. But after a while I realized I wouldn't mind if you did."

"I would have never."

"I know. That's why I let you. I wanted to before now, but I was worried about the firestorm if I felt too strongly. I was worried what would happen if we did and it all went bad. I was worried you still had some motivation under it all like a storybook villain."

"I told you I did not."

"You could have been lying. But liars drop their acts and you never faltered." I kissed him once and let my answer sink in while I finally went to the chest and pulled out a red robe that was far too big for me. I pulled a belt off another and tried to make due by tying it around the middle. It was nearly comical, but it would get me to my closet.

"Regrettably, the world does not stop when I am with you. I have to leave. I will see you again at the next possible moment."

"Alright." I wove my hands through his chains again and pulled him back for one more kiss before he left. We both lingered a little too long.

I laid back and stared at the nothingness of my stone ceiling, rubbing at my wrists. My mind was both clouded and never clearer. Being open about my thoughts was good. But had also led to a lack of something I'd never been without before; I couldn't feel a single ache to burn in my whole body.

***

That evening I met him for dinner as usual, but instead of sitting by the fire in the study we took a long walk and ended up back in my wing by the end of it. We sat in the reading nook, curled as close as we could and watching the stars. I held his hand in both of mine and put my cheek to his. He leaned into it, running his other hand down my arm, pulling me closer with each pass.

I'd never been able to do anything like it with another person, and I was starting to realize how absolutely touch starved I'd been my entire life. If this is what other people felt, I understood the appeal of relationships, less than perfect included.

I didn't know if I should ask for what I wanted or how to even begin to do that, but it turned out I didn't need to. He picked me up and carried me to my room. I'd never been picked up before, even as a child. My stomach dropped in anticipation of where I was being taken. The staff had been quick to replace my bed, but that wasn't where we were going. I was being swept off to the room far below us, just as he had suggested. I pulled the chains off his neck along the way, dropping them lightly on the stairs so they wouldn't be melted in what was about to happen.

He laid me down on the stone floor as softly as he would have any bed. His lips met mine, and it was happening again. I was already feeling the same fire as before. The sweet one that only wanted him closer. I let it consume me and guide my actions.

When it faded, I was in a dizzy, calm state of love I never wanted to leave. I could hear his heartbeat slowing and almost drifted to sleep with the sound. It was my new favorite sound alongside the smooth deep timbre of his voice, just like his smoky smell was my new favorite scent and the gold of his eyes was my favorite color. There wasn't anything about him I didn't love, and I was fully and completely willing to admit that to myself now. I was going to allow myself to fully feel everything from now on.

He kissed the top of my head and put a light hand on my chin, moving my face gently so I would look at him. I was sure he was the only one I'd ever let do that. He looked at me a long time before speaking, velvet voice low,

"Forgive me, but this does not feel real. Is this purely a pleasure arrangement or do I dare believe you want to be my wife in every sense?"

"I thought this was the only thing missing from me being that."

"No, no. Love is the missing piece, not sex."

"They're different?"

"Wildly. Like wind and rain. Sometimes together, sometimes separate. Both nice for different reasons."

Moved his eyes to stare at the ceiling without seeing it.

"Zan?" I had never called him that before, but now it only felt right. He looked back at me, the glitter in his eyes swirling quickly.

"Yes?" He asked with a hint of concern. I took a deep breath,

"I love you. *Ai sam nedam.*" I meant it. I'd never meant anything more. He pulled me into a bone crushing hug.

"*Ar sem nedam.*" His voice was rough, but it turned into a hundred sweet whispers between kisses.

CHAPTER 22

The next weeks were the absolute best of my life. I quickly discovered the only thing star-fire wanted more than to rule the ruins of the world was to be near other star-fire. Something between that, physical attraction, and an alignment of our souls pulled us together. I was thankful I could stop fighting it. It wasn't going to end in disaster. That was clearer every day. Expressing the full spectrum of my emotions to another person did not bring about the apocalypse I had been told it would.

He had started calling me *Jer asde ren.* His golden sun. We had been sitting in the library, and according to him the setting sun had aligned just behind my head, meshing with my own glow. That was his story, but I knew it was a nickname he'd been thinking on for a long time, probably since the party. He didn't always say it in Renci, but when he did I was very liable to melt or burn whatever was in my hands. I leaned into my new nickname, wearing as much gold jewelry as I could stand, mostly in the form of Al necklaces. His style had changed to be more simple. We quickly figured out most things he wore ended up burned for one reason or another.

I started to get to know his brother. Eran was the biggest joker I had ever met. He had a story for every subject and situation, most of them ending in a wild night of drinking or a fight. It turned out he had spent his years before the palace taking care of his ailing mother and fighting ex-soldiers for spare change and drinks. He'd gained a reputation of being the best, but that had come crumbling down around him when his mother had lost her own fight. She spent some of her last breaths telling him he was Zindraun's son.

I finally got to hear the story of how Eran and Zan had met. Zan showed me the scar on his arm from the occasion. A young, angry, and grieving Eran had shown up at the gates of a young, angry, and grieving Zan's palace. Eran had fought his way inside and was determined to kill Zan, a feat he hadn't thought would be so impossible. Zan hadn't thought that this arbitrary raving young man would be such a challenge either. Zan won out, but he offered him a job on the spot.

We had our first official portrait together done. In a break from tradition, we both sat on a gilded couch.

Usually only the Al sat while their family stood around them, but Zan had insisted we sit together. We had been dressed in all of our richest finery. Zan had had my gold dress modified, salvaging the usable pieces into a red and gold dress that looked marvelous on the canvas. Once it was finished it would hang in the gallery I had stood in my first day. I was sure I would look much happier in this painting than I had that day.

It had been months since he had first asked for my ideas, but I finally figured out what I wanted to use the grand hall for that wasn't lavish parties: dance practice. As humble as he was about it, Zan was a wonderful dancer. I was, however, beginning to catch up to him. Once I figured out it was easy to move weightlessly if I actually let my feet leave the ground, it became second nature. I didn't need to be pulled around anymore.

We poured more time into teaching me Renci. Between both Kaniel and Zan's persistence I had improved significantly. I had learned basic sentences. Kaniel was also much less frustrating, which was both nice and concerning as it implied Zan had told him too much.

Kaniel was able to answer more of the questions Zan couldn't. He was able to tell me that Aphier, the first queen of Solde-al, had been seen often with a

Stardropped, calling her mother. We knew she was not her biological mother, and that was supported by the lack of golden eyes in every description and depiction of Aphier. But we all knew blood didn't determine who raised you. The reason for her unusual pendant became clear. The reason Solde was called Solde at all, and the reason we all wore stars symbols, was because of my life as Sola. She had made Zenos Al king and Aphier his queen.

I had also started to suspect something about Kaniel that I had never fully put together. After days of listening to him carefully, I deduced that every time the word "remember" left his lips, I did. It was as if the word directly pulled up everything I knew about the subject through a haze. I could never fully grasp the surrounding memory, but I did remember the answer to his questions for a few moments. After I spent time with him, I always had outstandingly vivid dreams that I swore were memories from my lives before, but they always faded quickly. I was convinced Kaniel was a mage, not just the child of one.

When I suggested as much to Zan he dismissed it as him being a wonderful teacher and me being stressed. I knew it was more than that. I theorized that Zan was too used to it to notice; he'd likely experienced it his whole life.

Of all the powers to have, it was one of the more useful I'd encountered. I didn't know the extent to which it worked, but I played with the idea of asking him to help me remember my past lives. After what I had learned about Aphier and the dreams, a part of me wanted to know how that had happened. In the end I decided against it, terrified that if I remembered every wrong that had ever been done to me I wouldn't be able to control the fire that sought revenge. The knowledge from the stories we had were already too much on bad days.

There was also the problem of my last life as Serana. I did not want to remember Zan as my son. I loved him as my husband in this life and that was enough.

CHAPTER 23

Zan had gotten up before me, leaving my room to head to the office. He slept in my room most nights now. The nights that he didn't were nights he had to stay up late and didn't want to disturb me. Sometimes he would wander away in the middle of the night, but he usually came back and made up for it when he did.

I got dressed and made my own way up to the office. I found him hunched over his desk, his eyes dim and his face set in a frown.

"I have regrettable news. I have been requested at a border town. The relationship is shaky, as we have discussed. They are hoping if I am there we can reach an agreement and delay whatever it is that is so inevitable. Or make them rethink their strategy. If all goes well, I will only be gone for five days."

"I'm not coming with you?" I'd hoped maybe I could go with him, not as a weapon but as his wife.

"No, golden sun. Please forgive me for saying this but I think your presence alone would be taken as a threat. I want to keep you away from it as long as

218

possible. They are already too daring, but I do not want to make it worse by bringing you."

"Too much potential destruction?"

"For this situation, yes. When I ask you to join me, know that it will be for a much larger problem."

So that was my answer. I'd never get to go with him because no one else could see me as anything but a weapon. As much as things had changed, they stayed the same.

I tried to keep myself occupied the five days he was gone so I didn't dwell on it. I wasn't worried about him as much as I was about the conflict in general. If it was so bad they had asked for him, things were very bad. I tried to corner Vitsef into telling me more about our situation and his plans, but he pulled out every excuse he could to avoid my questioning. Instead, I went to Nelser who was happy to help. There was a lot to be learned by following the money. We went through our military spending, keeping track of where Vitsef was allocating the most resources and to who the money was paid. Even if he wouldn't tell me what was going on, I could see what he was paying the most attention to.

Aurelia and I spent time in the garden. I didn't want to visit her home again, I wasn't sure if I could handle it. Between her being cruel to her maid, confining Cerp, and her effect on Vitsef, I was too unsettled. Seeing my oldest friend slipping into a darker life bothered me on many levels; the two most pressing being that I was worried about her, and the other that if she was falling into darkness, maybe I was too. I didn't want to let the star-fire have an easier time persuading me to let it run rampant, not after I had found this new level of control. After all, how bad could it be if sweet Aurelia was living that way?

Kaniel bothered me for daily Renci lessons. He kept them short and relevant, always asking Eda to come with me as well, though she didn't pick it up at all. I did manage to dodge my way out of some by telling him in perfect Renci that I had a meeting to go to with Nelser and I didn't have time for him. He took that as enough practice and left me alone for the rest of the week.

I put a lot of time into practicing something I'd never had the control to do consistently- direct my star-fire around or away from something I didn't want burned. Or someone, I hoped.

I used three of the swordsmanship practice targets in the room under my bedroom. Eran was kind enough to help me move them when I asked. I was sure he was far over qualified for the task, but he wasn't upset to leave his losing bet in a dice game with some of our kitchen staff. I would have moved the awkward contraptions myself, they were light enough, but I had been lost on how to take them apart and get them through the doorways.

I had reached the point where I could exclude one target from the fire, no matter how near or far, but the same couldn't be said for a second. I was making no progress. I couldn't vent my frustration either, as that defeated the purpose entirely.

***

It was the first full council meeting in well over a week. It was also the day Zan was supposed to be back. I hadn't heard any news since he left. I awaited updates as eagerly as I awaited everything else from him.

I had to stop a moment when I saw him on the other side of the hall. He handed the last of his armor to an attendant before turning to go into the meeting room, still adjusting the collar on his shirt. He hadn't seen me. I couldn't help but take a moment to adjust my robe and check my reflection briefly, even fixing my posture one more time before entering. I pushed the doors open and heard them shut behind me. Daner was speaking. Apparently they had already started the meeting without us.

I ran the tips of my fingers across Zan's shoulders as I passed him to sit in my seat. It had been a mindless gesture, but I didn't regret it when he looked up at me. After a moment he broke our eye contact and closed his eyes, reclining in his chair. There were two deep cuts on his face. One stretched across his forehead from his hairline to his eyebrow on his left side, and the other on his cheek on his right side down to his jaw. They looked deep enough to leave scars, and I saw the thin threads of stitches. I'd have to ask him what had happened.

I was so distracted that I hadn't been paying attention to the meeting until I heard an outstandingly frustrating question from Daner,

"Do we distribute basic food rations to the affected areas?"

"We should if we have the capability," I answered. Why was this a question?

"We could also put that capability towards something more productive," Vitsef mumbled.

"Forgive me for thinking that if they don't have to worry about whether or not they can afford the limited food they have they can get back to being more productive."

"Affording to eat is motivation," Nelser said. That surprised me, I had started to think we were friends. To his credit, he put up his hands and leaned back in his chair in surrender when I looked at him.

"No, it's a reason to do anything it takes to afford it, including crime and further destruction." They were quiet. I may not have been allowed a vote here still, but I was allowed to argue against their backwards reasoning. "If we help them with the distribution of the basics, they'll have more resources to put forward for improvement and rebuilding. That's what happens when people aren't afraid for their lives. It will be beneficial over time," I said. Zan surprised me by speaking, suddenly much more interested in the discussion.

"I think Skye has the right idea. Let's follow through with that plan." His eyes met mine again, then they drifted to my lips and I couldn't help but remember how his kiss tasted like fire. "That is enough arguing for the day. Meeting over."

"My king, I-" Daner blustered. I knew Zan was not taking anymore time for this discussion. His expression was not the face of a patient man.

"We will get to it later in the week, I assure you. This meeting is done." The men were grumbling and shuffling their feet as they left. I heard one representative joke about the shortest meeting of his career.

One by one they exited the room. I stayed in my seat, waiting to be last in the room with Zan. I waited so long for him to move I doubted I'd read the situation right and started to walk out the door as well. But as I passed he tenderly reached for my wrist to catch me. I stopped and redirected my thoughts to their original course.

"I want to talk to you."

"What about?" The doors closed with a very official latch, and we were alone. In a blink he had stood up and wrapped his arm around me, pressing us together. My cheeks went hot, my heart leaped.

"This isn't talking."

"No, no… a different language."

I balanced on my toes to reach him with a kiss. He met me and lifted me higher. We were kissing with such a passion he let me pull his robe off and throw it to his chair. He lifted me up to sit on the table. I wrapped my legs around his waist to draw him in, not wanting him to ever go away again. His hands pulled my robe down to my shoulders. My bare skin was glowing hot where he touched. I leaned back and braced myself with my hand. Then I remembered I was on a wooden table, and I'd likely just branded its surface with my handprint.

"Should we do this here?"

"Skye, I am king. We can do whatever we like."

"I'm less worried about the social implications and more about the furniture."

"Are you planning on burning?"

"I wasn't, but you know how well I can control myself."

"About as well as I can when I'm with you." He kissed my chest and neck as far as he could go before fabric got in his way. I curled close, very much hoping he would move my robe down further so he could keep going. "Point taken. Unless..." his voice trailed off, but I wasn't one for letting an unless go unexplained.

"What are you thinking?"

"Oh, just that the challenge might make this more exciting." I could see where he was going. The idea of having restrictions on what we could do was something we had never bothered with, but as my hands wandered I remembered what wild felt like. I could feel the desperation in how he breathed and moved at my touch.

"I'm not sure you need more excitement."

"No, no, probably not," he whispered. He kissed from my ear down my shoulder and chest. I felt a deep ache to have him touch and kiss everything about me.

He took my shoulder and my waist in his hands and gently pushed me further into the table, laying me down. His hands finally undid my robe completely. With more desperate kisses and exploration, we were together again. This time there was no firestorm. No rush. We took our time. And what wonderful time it was.

CHAPTER 24

Thankfully, he wouldn't have to leave again for another month. While conflicts were heating up, Solde was able to hold them off. Vitsef hadn't wanted to hear any of my recommendations, but it was working out well enough anyway. We were left with more down time, although Zan spent most of it beating up practice targets as well as Eran and a handful of other soldiers. I had gotten the story behind his newest injuries. A mage that could control eight of her own swords with her mind had given him quite a run that nearly ended badly. I understood his new fixation, but I didn't see how fighting mortals would help him. That was when I decided to pick up my own sword.

I was still a clumsy, unrefined mess, but I was much stronger than he was and he couldn't use bursts of star-fire to push me around. It turned out I could, though. Even if I often subconsciously directed the star-fire itself around him, the force was enough. I'd also discovered I had a gravity that could pull him closer, something I had either never noticed or never needed to use before.

Today we were back on the practice field, this time in less favorable weather conditions. A storm had overtaken the city, refusing to leave for an entire day and night. The rain evaporated before it could land on my skin or wet my pants and shirt, but it had soaked Zan's hair and pants to dripping. The grass was long gone after weeks of fire. Combined with the torrential rain, the field was nothing but mud that gave way under our feet.

I'd quickly figured out I didn't need to spend much of my energy blocking; the best he could do was knock me off balance. I needed to focus on moving and trying to get in opportunity hits. I was getting better at spotting them, but Zan was better at doing it before I did and blocking accordingly.

That was the same challenge I was facing again today as each of my swings against his blade sunk his feet further into the mud. Sparks flew in every direction.

"You can hit harder than that, come on now," he said, adjusting his feet.

I rolled my eyes and hit again with more force. The swords bent around each other becoming more reminiscent of links in a chain. His pulled free from his hands and flew away. I held onto mine. I melted the metal away from the bottom of the new kink in the blade to make it into a red hot dagger. He backed away quickly, heating his hands so his rings glowed hot. That was another thing I had learned recently. His rings were as fashionable as they were weapons in a pinch.

"I'm not grappling with you," I said, shaking my head.

"You are not, you brought a sword hilt." He smiled, nodding to my new creation. I threw it away from myself. I crossed my arms and planted my feet.

It wasn't that I was against hand-to-hand. Not at all. It was more that there was less separation between him and the terribly calculated strength behind my punches. I'd already broken too many slabs of stone this week practicing with them. I would never forgive myself if I broke him too.

"Alright, back to swords, then." He shrugged and put down his fists, walking back to the racks of weapons. I followed.

"I still feel bad every time I break a sword."

"They are practice swords, *asde ren*. It is what they are for."

"I know, but someone still had to take the time to make them."

"I promise they are well compensated for their effort." He pulled another plain sword off the bare looking rack. "One more time?"

"One more," I said with a reluctant smile.

He took a swing before I could pick up a replacement. I blocked the swing with my arm, the metal bending around it.

"Unfair!" I chided in feigned outrage.

"This will never be fair, but I have to try."

My feet left the ground. I sent a star-fire blast that pushed him several yards away. The white light illuminating the entire field brighter than daylight. The windows of the palace rattled with the sound like a lightning strike. He dug his sword into the dirt to hold on to his footing. His skin took on a deep orange glow from within, eyes and hands throwing sparks. He sent back his own wave of crackling star-fire. It bent around my body like a soft breeze. Before he could recover I felt the gravity pull him closer just as quickly as he'd been thrown away from me. He stumbled forward and stopped against my outstretched hand. The waves of fear dropped him to a kneel at my feet.

I hated to see him like this. I pulled it all back, putting a gentle glowing hand against his cheek, his skin drying under my fingers. "I'm sorry."

"No, no. I am still winning. I am sure of it." He pulled me closer, arms around my legs in a hug. I laughed and let my knees fall to the mud so I could be pulled into a proper embrace.

That had truly been the last fight of the night. Usually one more turned into two or three, but Zan seemed to be over standing in the torrential rain. We both changed out of our mud covered clothes and sat down to dinner, back in our usual chairs. It had started to feel almost lonely when Eran and Kaniel weren't there. Six chairs seemed like too many.

"Any news today?" I asked as I spooned vegetables onto my plate. He had a habit of forgetting to tell me when there was. It wasn't intentional, he'd simply gone years without having to share information with someone. He always answered when I asked.

"Not much news, but you should know we are starting to suspect a spy. Thankfully not in our council, but too close all the same. Niode has information they should not about our movements and the only place they could get it is Vitsef. Vitsef insists his home is clear, but we can not be sure." I thought of how squirrely he had been acting in the days Zan had been gone.

"Vitsef has been avoiding me."

"Likely because he does not want to talk too loud. Or, maybe it is because he is an ass," he joked. I would have laughed if I wasn't worried about my best friend.

"Should I be worried about Auri?"

"No, I do not think so. Aurelia is smart. I think I am well founded in saying that I am confident she could manipulate her way out of danger."

"You're right."

It still made me uncomfortable to think about her living with a direct enemy of the country. It was too close. When a spy had been here, that was to be expected. Especially during a party full of strangers. Zan had made quick work of it after what I expected were years of practice finding them. That poor man was rotting in a keep at the edge of the city now after being tried by a lower council. I found some comfort in knowing that if the spy in Vitsef's home met Cerp, they wouldn't be a problem for long.

CHAPTER 25

The next morning I heard the council members before I saw them. They were gathered outside the meeting room as they usually were when Zan was late, but I knew he was already down here since he had missed breakfast. He was never late when he wasn't with me. What were they waiting for? They were arguing but I couldn't pick out details. I heard mentions of ships, storms, and Rolten, but I couldn't find him anywhere among them. Aurelia was waiting with them in puffy robes the color of a warm pink sunset. Even from this distance she was obviously pregnant. The reminder didn't sit right.

I stopped in my tracks when I saw Zifira being led into the room by two armed guards. The men entered the doors and shut them behind them, leaving Aurelia alone in the hall. As I got closer, I saw her face deep with concern. She was biting at her thumbnail, no doubt feeling the emotions of the chaos I'd just witnessed.

232

"What's going on?"

"Oh, Skye." She looked excited, then her face fell back into worry. "It's a shame, Navy Commander Rolten went down with a ship. It was the only ship we lost in the storm. A freak lightning strike or something. He and another man were the only lives lost, thankfully."

"Zifira?" My eyes went to the door where she had just disappeared.

"She was on the ship, of course. She probably was too shook up to fend off the storm, poor thing. I hate that they're probably making her retell the story now."

"I have to go," I said as I rushed away from Aurelia. I pushed open the doors into the meeting room with a bang as they hit the walls. I had to channel my old self. Careful control would be important now.

Zifira sat in a seat at the far end, facing all nine men and Zan. I noticed the lack of Rolten and the sight made my stomach lurch. I didn't need to know anything else about what had happened.

I ran my hand lightly across Zan's shoulder as I walked past them all to stand directly beside her. He didn't react, keeping his hands clasped in tight fists on the table. I was not the only one exercising control.

"What is this about?" I demanded.

"We are here to talk with Zifira about the happenings of yesterday morning," Daner said. He sounded neutral, but I didn't believe he was. They all had their quiet opinions already.

"And why must you interview her? She has just lost her husband. Surely we can talk to another survivor."

"We are talking to Zifira because she is a mage known for angering and calming ocean storms. It seems she would provide us the most insight into why events transpired the way they did," Vitsef said.

"I, as well as others, find the situation suspicious considering her history," Raham added. He was an old man with oiled white hair. He was one of the men who had objected to my ideas most vocally, and the one who had almost always stood at Rolten's side.

"Suspicious? You think she could have done more? Or do you think she caused this so she could endure emotional trauma?" I looked to Zan. He was on the edge of rage as he listened to Vitsef and Raham, his eyes glowing.

"It's not out of the realm of possibility. We are aware she is capable of calming a storm of that size," said Vitsef.

"As well as create one," Raham interjected again. He seemed to be stepping into Rolten's shoes already.

"Are you serious? Asking a grieving widow why she didn't do more to save her husband? As if she's not sitting here wondering that herself! Can you imagine the guilt she's already going through?" I turned to Raham. "And you, saying she created it! How dare you say that about a sister of the queen!" My feet left the ground. "I fully believe that Zifira did everything she could. This is not her fault."

"My king?" Vitsef looked to Zan. They all followed suit.

"I stand by Skye's judgement. She knows Zifira far better than any of us." I knew he heard that I was hiding something. I could see it in how he looked from me to Zifira and back, his jaw tight. "We should let Zifira leave and choose other survivors to interview about the events. That will help us improve ships so that this tragedy will not happen again."

There were exasperated sighs before they agreed to vote. Daner, Nelser, Haullen, his father, and the Southeast representative voted to let her go. I could never guess how much of it was my arguing or their genuine doubt that Zifira was responsible, but I was still thankful to them. Vitsef, the West representative, and Raham wanted to proceed with the trial. It wasn't enough. She could leave.

Zan gave me a nod, and I pulled out Zifira's chair. Her hands were chained together in her lap. I had to pause to calm myself while she stood up. I made a point of pulling her chains off with my hands using strength alone. The cuffs snapped easily. I threw them onto the table with a sound that made the councilmen jump. They fell directly in front of Rolten's former seat. I walked out of the room and Zifira followed only a step behind me.

"Thank you," she said quietly on the other side of the closed doors. Her expression was hard for me to read, as usual.

"Of course, I promised. This won't be easy, though. Once word gets around that some of the council suspects you of- " The doors opened again behind us. "Let's not talk about it here."

I didn't have to wait long for Zan to join us. He looked from me to Zifira with unasked questions. I took his hand and led them both to the royal office in silence. We entered the room and I shut and locked the door behind us.

"Zifira did kill Rolten, but he hurt her," I told Zan.

"More than hurt. He deserved worse than I gave him," she snarled. Her veins turned to lightning under her dark skin, her hair moving in an unfelt breeze.

Zan's eyes went from my face to hers. I saw his expression darken further. In that moment I saw another glimpse of the man that had killed other men for less.

"Zifira, I am sorry you endured what you did, you did not deserve that. I wish I would have taken action myself. I had suspicions he was not kind to you," he said quietly in a much more comforting way than what I expected.

"Could you make Zifira your wife? To protect her in case they pursue this again. They can't prosecute a wife of the king, it's against our laws," I clarified for Zifira.

Zan shook his head. "That is incredibly suspicious Skye, I can not." He shook his head harder, running his hand through his hair. I tried to think of other solutions, but was coming up empty. Then Zan's eyes lit up. "She could work for you." He looked at us as if we were supposed to understand what he meant. "My grandmother Meriah had her own small group of unmarried women to aid her with outreach to the people, and before that Zaphier Al had a council entirely of women to help her make decisions. You could do the same with your sister mages. Make it a front for the committees they denied. The council would not be implicated for actions taken and that was their main concern. The mages' actions would be wholly your responsibility, Skye, but I think it would be well worth it."

It also meant that if Zifira was mine to be responsible for. They would have to call me to trial if they wanted to reopen the issue, a feat that would get them nowhere since I was queen. That kept her safe and gave us both a purpose.

"That's perfect. Zifira?" I looked at her. The lightning had faded.

"After what you did today, it would be an honor."

"Wonderful." He was fidgeting with his rings, wandering to the window.

"We'll need more mages to make it legitimate. Have you talked to anyone recently?" I asked Zifira.

"No, Rolten only let me see Aurelia and you. Even then it wasn't worth his wrath so I never did. I couldn't send letters."

"Well now you can. Let's see if Auri knows where anyone is. The nineteens will be twenty soon enough…" My mind was working out how this would work, adjusting the plans I'd made for my proposal before. This was much different than what I'd intended, but the more I thought about it, the more sense it made to keep my sisters by my side. No one could hurt them. It felt right.

"I have another idea for you. I may have a perfect meeting place. If there are going to be more of you, you will need one," Zan said, finally turning back to us. He put his hand back in mine and took us up two floors to a room behind a heavy wooden door.

It was large and empty, nothing but the unlit fireplace and the windows overlooking the city. I looked up at the domed ceiling and realized we were in the tallest tower. Looking around, I could envision the space filled with mages and their colors, a familiar sight I looked forward to seeing again. But this time all of them would be free.

"You can use this room as a meeting room of your own. It used to be my father's bedroom, but it has been unused for years."

"It's perfect. Thank you." I let my feet leave the ground to reach his cheek for a kiss.

"I am glad it will be used for something much better than what it was." He looked distant for a moment, eyes brightening and brows furrowed. Then he was back, looking at Zifira.

"You will need a place to live."

"I would appreciate that but if it's a problem-" she started. Zan held up his hand.

"No, no. I find this palace has entirely too many empty rooms." He was lying. I knew he was an introvert like me that would have loved to have to see no one but myself, Eran and Kaniel. But so much worry lifted off Zifira's face, I appreciated what he was doing. It would nice to have another one of my sisters live close.

I'd all but forgotten about Aurelia. She must be confused and begging for any information from anyone. She wasn't used to waiting long for her gossip. I left Zifira with Zan to figure out the details of her new life as a free mage. I doubted she'd ever be truly free after what she went through, but it was firmly behind her now.

Aurelia was waiting roughly where I had left her, although Vitsef was long gone. I imagined she had been staying back for this very moment. I quickly became the center of her attention when she saw me, her sewing project abandoned. I sat down on the stone bench next to her, leaning against its low back. She started with her questions immediately.

"What happened with Zifira? Vits told me you wouldn't let them interview her about the accident."

"It wasn't an interview, Auri, it was a murder trial. They had her on trial, and I put a stop to it."

"So… was she innocent?" she asked, leaning a little closer. I shook my head once in the smallest way I could. With recent suspicions, I couldn't know who was listening. She raised her eyebrows then let them fall into a concerned face but said nothing. For once, Auri was speechless. I tried to change the subject before she could ask more questions.

"I'm forming a small group of mages to help the kingdom with community service. Zifira is helping me. Do you want to join?"

"With this one arriving soon, I don't think so. I'm sorry." She patted her belly with a smile. I had all but forgotten about her baby with how fluffy her dress was when she sat down.

"I understand."

"You could probably do some recruiting at the Towers, though. The nineteens will be twenties soon and some of them will probably want to leave."

"I hope so. How are Nerial and Ferona? I haven't heard from them."

"I haven't either, actually. Very rude. I don't even know where to send a letter to find out." She shook her head and picked up her sewing project again.

"Well, wherever they are they're together," I said.

"Obviously. I think I saw them split up once? And it was because they were trying to schmooze men into buying them drinks on a day trip. They'd already spent all their money on candy." She rolled her eyes.

"Did they get the drinks?" I asked. I hadn't heard that story before, but I had heard ones like it.

"Of course they did, you know how Ners is. I did help Fer, though." She laughed and I did too. If there was anything to be said about those two it was that they were the definition of partners in crime.

"Does Zifira need anything?" Aurelia asked.

"I didn't ask her. I think Zan will help her get anything she needs, but I'm sure she wouldn't mind seeing you." She nodded.

"I'll bring her something."

We sat a while longer till she finished what she was sewing. I walked her to the gate and waited as she walked home. I thought about how this new arrangement would work and how quickly it had fallen into place. Most things were starting to feel that way, and it wasn't a bad thing. But it was bringing back the idea of fate, and that was bringing back vague feelings about higher beings I had most certainly met. I was its daughter, and she had taken an interest in me once again. I wasn't sure that was a good thing, but for now it was.

CHAPTER 26

I'd asked Zifira to meet me in the morning today. She'd had five days to settle into her new room and get her bearings, but I wanted to talk her through a more solid plan for what exactly it was we would do. Just the two of us limited our options greatly, but I was eager to get started on something, anything.

I arrived at our bare meeting room to two more familiar faces than I expected. Nerial and Ferona wearing their usual purple and green attire. I was delighted to see them but also deeply annoyed. They had been the most prone to bullying of our sisters and I was not keen to see how that history would translate to our mission.

"I wasn't expecting you." It was all I could say. I still sounded cold with people that weren't Zan on bad days. These two would probably hear that frosty tone more than most.

"Hello to you too, Skye," Ferona said. Nerial elbowed her.

"Nice to see you again!" she said, almost too happy. "You too."

"We left the Towers as soon as news of your ruling reached us. We weren't doing very well on our own, though," Nerial explained, much less enthusiastic, her eyes dropping to the floor.

"The Mother Mages are angry, especially Mother Nai," Ferona had an edge of warning in her voice. Mother Nai was never particularly happy about anything.

"Of course they are, they didn't have the option to leave," Nerial said. These two had always had a way of having conversations between just each other no matter who was there with them.

"They're free to leave now if they want to," I replied curtly.

"You tell them that, my queen," Nerial laughed.

"It's so strange to think of you that way," Ferona sneered.

"Don't you remember what the Mother Mages would tell us? Skye has always been special," Nerial said with a head tilt and an eye-roll.

"If you call being barred from social interaction and punished for feeling my own emotions special, yes, I was. Why are you here?"

"To join this little club. Aurelia told us what you were doing and we would like to help." Nerial gave me a pointed look. I had no idea how Aurelia had found out where to find them, but I was thankful.

"Well I'm glad, but it's not a social club. If you want to help the people of Solde, you're welcome to stay." I wanted them to stay either way, but I needed them to take this seriously. They had a habit of not doing that very well.

"We can do that." Nerial nodded. Ferona seemed nonplussed by her quick acceptance but went along with it.

"I think Aurelia had her mind set on coming by as well," Zifira warned. Sure enough, no sooner than she had said it, Aurelia came into the room, bringing a chained Cerp in with her. She had a large platter of baked goods in her hands and a huge smile on her face.

"Oh good, you two made it!"

We sat on the bare floor. There was no furniture in here yet because I wasn't sure what I wanted the space to be. My sisters seemed alright with that, not hesitating to take the pastries from Aurelia's plate. I sat between Zifira and Aurelia just as I had when I'd stood in line at the Towers.

The whole scene looked very familiar. I had my sisters back. We were all free, but that wasn't good enough. As long as even free mages were seen as nothing but a commodity or liability, my work wasn't done.

CHAPTER 27

Not a full week later, Nerial and Ferona had already folded nicely into the palace routines. Their addition threw the plans I had made into a slight disarray, and that was occupying most of my time. The rest I spent with Nelser following the military spending since Vitsef was still avoiding my questions as if answering them would kill him. Even Zan had started to become annoyed with him but refused to do anything about it. He said he was giving Vitsef the benefit of the doubt since they had yet to catch the suspected rat, a hunt that had taken up much of his time as well. I tried to let it go and focus on what I could control.

Zan hadn't been sleeping much and had let his usually impeccable grooming habits go astray, much like the hairs in his braids. I wished for a way to make it better, but every time I asked he only said I was already helping by existing.

He was unusually tired at breakfast as he looked up from his small pile of papers.

"Skye, apparently I am going to be traveling for the whole day tomorrow and staying on the coast for several days." He waved the letter he had been reading. "For once it is not a battle or a mystery invitation from Wertrick. Would you like to come? It would be an excellent opportunity to bring your sisters and meet with the people. I could arrange some meetings so they could make a positive impact on the community while we are there."

"That sounds wonderful." I caught myself saying wonderful the same way he did. He noticed too with a grin.

"Wonderful."

"Is Eda coming?" I asked. I'd never traveled so I wasn't sure if it was standard for Eda to travel with me. It seemed like it would be.

"If you would like her to, she is welcome."

"I'll ask her." As far as I was concerned, Eda was an unofficial member of my group. Even if I didn't think of her as only my maid, it made sense she would travel with me. I wondered if she had traveled much in her old life. Probably not, from what she had told me about her family. We would be her family if they didn't care enough to write more than one letter a year to her.

***

The carriage ride the next morning reminded me of the day I left the Towers. Now instead of sitting on the opposite side from Zan and struggling to stay sane, I was curled in his lap with my head on his shoulder while he dozed. He hadn't slept at all last night, staying up to send letters ahead so nothing fell apart while we were gone.

The world passed by out the windows as the sun rose and fell. By the time we arrived at our destination, it had been decidedly dark for well over two hours which made for a much less interesting view.

The house we stayed in was spacious but plain. I didn't mind. It was cozy with its sitting areas and little patios and balconies overlooking the hills. It was the kind of place we might live if we weren't ourselves. If I hadn't been made of star-fire, and he had been born an average man.

My sisters and Eda bustled off to pick their rooms. I started to follow before Zan took my hand and led me up the stairs to the top floor. It looked as if the whole level was ours, although it was only a couple of large rooms.

"Do we own this house?"

"No, no, it belongs to the Gi family. They are kind enough to let us use it. You will probably meet Mars Gi tomorrow. We only own the palace and a small house in Renciam." That confused me. I knew about the embassy, but I had never seen anything about a residence.

"I haven't seen that on any of the records."

"That is because it is mine, not Solde's. It belonged to my mother. I will take you there soon as I can, I promise." He kissed the back of my hand. I wanted to ask questions, but I was distracted as I walked farther into what was apparently our room, taking in the colorful decor and wonderful view of the ocean off the balcony. We were followed by two people bringing in trunks of what I assumed were our clothes for the stay. Zan closed the door after them.

"I took the liberty of packing yours, I hope you do not mind."

"Now I'm curious." I opened mine. There were beautiful robes, but under a layer of them I found a few slinky, barely there things straight from the folder I'd nearly been too embarrassed to open. Black and red ribbons. Sheer, thin, and soft fabrics of the same colors. Gold chains I couldn't discern from jewelry. There were too many of them.

"Oh Zan… we're supposed to be here for how long?"

"Six days, not counting travel back."

"And you think I'll wear all of these?"

"You could if we start going through them now."

"You're very confident about that."

"Should I not be?"

"I'm just saying it's bold of you to assume I'll take the time to put it on first."

He laughed and I hugged him, taking a second to kiss his neck.

"Naked is more beautiful anyway."

Somehow we fumbled our way onto the bed. He was over me, still kissing me like it was the only thing he had ever wanted. His hands wandered and I wasn't about to stop them.

Then he pulled away suddenly, completely frozen. I followed his eyes down to his hand. The tips of his fingers were red with blood. I was embarrassed, but my concern quickly shifted to Zan as he backed away from me. First he was the man I'd seen when he'd had that spy on his sword. Then I saw a man who was seeing the dead. His face paled, eyes crackling with fire.

"I know it's disgusting, I'm sorry-" He held up his other hand to stop me.

"It is not your fault." He heated his hand to glowing, sparks flying, but when it cooled my blood was still there. He took a handful of deep breaths, none of them helping. "I can not do this." He left the room in a rush, pushing the door open with such force it hit the wall with a bang, cracking near the handle.

A deep pit of embarrassment formed in my stomach, even if it wasn't something I could control. He didn't seem like the kind of man who would be bothered by blood, but what did I know? He had to have a reason.

I laid back to calm myself down before going to look for him. I pulled a blanket off the bed to take with me. Neither of us were ever anything close to cold, but the feeling was nice. It put a wall of fabric between my thoughts and the world.

He was sitting on the floor of a balcony off of our dark bathroom. He looked calm, the ocean breeze moving his hair. I opened the glass door and joined him, sitting with my back against it. After a long while he looked at me.

"I apologize. I have had blood on my hands too many times and none of those situations were ones I want to remember. Usually I could burn it away, but yours is a unique problem."

"I'm sorry,"

"No, no. Do not be. They are my own ghosts. You are not responsible for them."

"Do you want to talk about any of them?"

He took a few moments to think. "You will hate me if I tell you."

"Never." He searched my face for sincerity and must have found it. He adjusted how he was sitting and moved his hair so he could look at a place just over my shoulder. I leaned on his knees and waited. When he met my eyes and spoke, his voice was the deepest I had ever heard it, completely emotionless.

"The arena my father kept was so I could murder a dozen men every few weeks in front of an audience. His *games* started when I was fourteen. I never did it when I was myself, but when he..." He faded, glitter in his eyes completely stopping until he blinked the thought away. "I rarely used star-fire to do it as that was less entertaining for him. Even swords lost their luster after a few good kills." He flexed his hands on the tops of his knees. The unconscious gesture took on a grim meaning. "You can imagine how much blood was on my hands after I did it his way. Then there were the spies, the soldiers, the diplomats. I was my father's gladiator, spy catcher, soldier, and assassin. I can not tell you how many have died at my hand, and not because I would not want to. I am thankful that even if I have to kill Niode soldiers now, I can give them a way out and burn them to nothing if they refuse. No blood. No struggle."

His words solidified everything I'd ever thought about my husband. I'd seen the numbers, tracing the stars on the records all the way back to the beginning, but he had never talked about it. Strangely, it didn't bother me to hear what I'd only ever guessed be confirmed. If anything, I had to shove the star-fire down as it flared at his admissions. It didn't care about those deaths, it had fueled him to do it. A wave of sadness came with it. He was so kind now, how could that have been the same person? I reminded myself it wasn't. He had been a young prince under his father's thumb, not the independent king I knew now. Most of all I could finally fully understand how he could know what I could do and not think of me as a weapon. He had been one. He knew what being used was like, and he didn't want that for me.

"That's not your fault, your father forced you into doing it."

"It is because I was selfish enough to stay within his reach. I did what the star-fire wanted. Dezura called me a murderer for doing his bidding, and she was right. I did not have the sense to leave and put a stop to it when I should have."

"You were only a teenager, right? You were a kid."

"I knew better, but I held out hope it would stop. That was my mistake. For the first few years I thought if I did well enough he would let me stop. I thought if Dezura and I gave him a grandson he would let me stop. She did too, then she was added to my list of lives taken. Even after that I thought if I fought his war he would let me stop. He never did, it just got worse."

"For a long time I thought if I behaved myself the Towers would treat me normally. Kids think stupid things because they trust the people who are supposed to take care of them."

"He never took care of me, he abused me. Kaniel is my father in every way that matters."

"And the Mother Mages were never mothers to me. They kept me in chains and locked me in rooms to keep me isolated for months at a time. I'm glad you had Kaniel."

"They did what?" he asked quickly. I was surprised he hadn't read that in my file. Granted, they had stopped imprisoning me a couple years ago, but I guessed it was only because my outbursts had become more verbal than explosive with time. The chains, however, had always been constant.

"I wore chains every day of my life after I turned about five." I rubbed where my bracelets had been. "They were largely so they felt like they had some semblance of control over me. And when I got too angry or too anxious or even too happy and burned, they locked me up until I felt nothing. Aurelia would talk to me under the door, but that was all I got for weeks sometimes. They did let me have books, though."

He looked murderous, but when I moved to lean my head against his knees he softened. He put a hand on the side of my face, and I held it there.

"What kept you from leaving? Or destroying them?"

"Honestly? Aurelia. Most of my sisters, even if they bother me. I don't want to think about what I would have done if they had been taken away, and I'd been left alone. I would have been," I paused for a moment to breathe. "I know I said I would have been fine living as a Mother Mage, but the idea of raising those girls to be sold off? I fear I would have gotten a little too comfortable with the idea of ending their lives before the world ruined them or ending the world so they were safe from it." I looked back at him, fully realizing what I'd said. It had been the fire speaking, not me. "I'm sorry, that's a horrible thing to say."

"Do not apologize. I am the one that killed people. You had the self control to make the right decisions."

"You didn't have control at all, that's why it's not your fault."

He held open his arms, and I was glad to crawl into them, my head fitting perfectly against his neck.

He put a hand on the back of my head and ran his thumb gently across my cheek.

"I am going to tear down the Towers for you, I promise."

"Someday, but let's fight one battle at a time. My sisters are free, and so are all the others turning twenty this summer if they want to be. They can come work for me without consequences. That's good enough for now. And believe it or not, my sisters would actually hate to see them gone forever. They had mothers and teachers, I had wardens."

We watched the ocean. I had always loved how it sparkled at night. It was slightly restless tonight, the waves higher. The familiar sound was a constant that didn't care about our pasts, and one we could rely on having in our future no matter what. It was comforting.

"I don't want to dwell on that all night. This is supposed to be a nice trip."

"Right. What should we talk about?" he asked, kissing the top of my head while I thought of an answer. It only took me a moment to remember my thoughts from when we'd arrived.

"This house made me think of something earlier. What job would you want if you had never been royalty?"

"A tailor, a gardener maybe. Something creative but structured. What if I had never made you queen?"

"If I had been born a man, a general. If I was myself I would have been a Mother Mage, obviously. If I didn't have my power, I would have still tried to find a way to be a general, but if that didn't work I'd like to think I could have worked in a library," I answered.

"I would like to think we would have met in a library."

"Me too." I smiled and fixed a stray piece of his hair. "Would you still have liked me?

"I would love you no matter what."

"Even if I was a man?" I asked. He shrugged with a laugh. That was something new. I had never thought he would be open to the thought of men.

"I know I would have loved you if you were a woman."

"Yes, I remember what you told me." He sounded hesitant.

"How does that make you feel?" I asked, hoping it wasn't a bad sort of hesitation. He grinned.

"Like I have been sitting on this floor too long. Let's go to bed." I let him pick me up and carry me back to where we had started. I started to nod off before I even hit the mattress.

I dreamt about a much worse Zan that night. We were on the roof of the palace on a starless night. The ground was littered with faceless dead men and scattered fires. Zan stood over it all, soaked in their blood. I waved to him to get his attention, but regretted it when I finally did. He looked at me with glowing red eyes and an unnatural smile, just like Cerprillis. He put a hand around my throat and asked if he was terrible. I held up my own hands, just as red and dripping. That made him laugh as everything burned to nothing in a firestorm.

***

That was not the dream I needed while away from home. I woke up in the morning in a mostly burned bed, the ceiling covered in soot, and Zan holding me tight to him. I didn't know which of us was responsible for it, but I guessed it was me. I tried to get up, but Zans arms were locked tight. I didn't want to struggle too hard and hurt him.

"Zan?"

"Hm?"

"Can I get up?"

"No." He hugged tighter for a moment before letting go. I went to my trunk. There was a creak and a snap as he sat up in what was left of the bed.

"Today is Ferona's day. Wear something you will not mind getting muddy or walking through a field in," his voice was tired.

"Thank you for the warning. I'm sure one of the gowns will be perfect." I added a sarcastic tone. All I was pulling out were dresses and robes that were far better suited for a hall than a field.

"You do not like them?"

"They're… quite a lot." I sighed and put them down. "I'm thinking about this too much. Should a queen care if her dress and shoes are irreparably muddy, anyway?"

"No, no. As long as she is comfortable."

"Alright. These and this." Both items only had red embroidery on the black fabric instead of gems and gold thread like the others.

"You have never been to a farm before, have you?"

"No, but the Towers did have some nice wineries to look at."

"You are in for an incredibly boring experience. Although, I have never seen Ferona work. Maybe that is entertaining."

"It's entertaining for a while, but it gets old. She thinks so too, I think."

We both got dressed and ate a quick breakfast of incredible local pastries. Downstairs I met the rest of my sisters and a woman giving orders to staff I had never seen before. She had a mess of curly orange hair all piled on top of her head and a stern expression that softened into a smile when she saw us.

"My king, my queen," she said, bending her knee in greeting and smoothing out the front of her dress.

"Skye, this is Mars Gi, lady of the house," Zan said, stepping to the side so I could stand in front of her.

"My queen, very good to meet you."

"You as well, thank you for letting us stay."

"Of course! The Al rulers have been staying with us for generations, you're family. It's good to have you and your sisters too. I've never met so many mages." She did look mesmerized by my sisters, even as they argued with each other like angry birds. I often forgot most people went their entire lives without ever seeing more than one or two mages. That fact didn't help our reputation, and I felt a pang of guilt when I remembered the destruction upstairs. I wasn't helping it either.

"I apologize for," I couldn't find the words. "I'm sorry."

"I am sure Mars knows I am good for a replacement," Zan said with a smile and a wink. Mars returned the grin. She looked lost, but it wouldn't take her long to figure out once her staff reached the second floor.

The front door opened and an old man with rough features and plain clothes entered. I'd never seen him before, but guessed he had a very official reason to be here by the folder in his hand. Zan looked at me,

"Can you summon Ferona? I am not keen to interrupt the current debate." He nodded towards my sisters. With a complete lack of surprise I saw Fer and Ners still arguing.

"Why would I take them? They wouldn't even fit me!" Nerial protested.

"That is a lie, Ners, we've worn the same shoes since we were twelve!"

"No, I don't wear the ugly ones!"

"They're not ugly! That's why you stole them!" Ferona accused. I moved into the fray, stopping between Zifira and Eda. Zifira leaned over to talk to me.

"I took them," she said in the quietest whisper, looking down to show me a toe of the coveted shoes peeking out from under her robe. I quickly hid a smile and looked back to the quarrel. A bit of well-placed drama stirring was not lost on me, but we had more important things to do.

"Nerial, Ferona, stop it," I snapped. They fell silent. "Ferona, come here." I had to blink and reconcile how much I sounded like a Mother Mage as I led Ferona back to Zan and the newcomer.

261

"Ferona, I would like you to meet our head of agriculture for the West. He will help you decide where your power would be most useful today." Zan stepped back, putting an arm around me. The old man blinked and broke into a grin, holding out a hand.

"Pleasure to meet you, Ferona. Can't say I've met a mage with a power I've looked forward to more." Ferona must have found him charming or markedly improved her acting as she took his hand with a smile.

"What are we growing today?" she asked. He took out his folder and started listing crops and soils and whatever else they both seemingly found incredibly interesting.

I looked back to Zan,

"Are you going with us?"

"No, no, I have my own meetings."

"And I'm not going to those?"

"You should stay with your sisters. I will tell you about everything when you return, I promise." He kissed my forehead, holding my hands. "I will be sad to miss Ferona's work, though. I may have to ask her to do the same to the palace gardens. I would love to see them at their full potential." I nodded and went back to my sisters and Eda, herding them into a small group so we could follow Ferona and her new best friend.

We went around to several fields, each one Ferona took from a regular or sad looking harvest into a thriving expanse. After a few, she was done, tired with a headache but still pleased with herself. The spectators looked delighted, the owner of the land and his family in particular. At the very least, they would remember mages fondly.

***

We sat at a large round table in the front room of the house for dinner. Zifira was next to me and Zan on my other side. He kept his hand on my thigh and I played with his rings as the rest of my sisters and Eda settled down.

Zifira linked her thumbs and first fingers on each hand, going through Ashanm's most common prayer under her breath. I'd nearly forgotten how religious she was. I knew this prayer was one about ending and beginning each day, the links of the days in an unending chain. It was one that Mother Rena had taught us when we were eight. I'd never cared for it. There was a line asking Ashamn to raise the sun in the morning. I knew the sun didn't rise because someone asked her to, and I knew for an absolute fact that she would never be pushed to rise by some king-god that got all of the praise for the light she brought. Zan moved his hand to hold mine, and I remembered exactly which king she rose for.

"Are you alright?"

"Yes, just thinking."

Nerial sat on Zan's other side, Ferona beside her. I would have much preferred Eda sitting by his side instead but tried not to let it bother me.

"My king," Nerial started. Zan cut her off by holding up his hand.

"No, no. You are Skye's sisters, none of that. Please call me Zan."

Zan had told me that he hated his full name and hated formal addresses even more. I didn't understand it. I would rather have everyone call me queen instead of Skye for the rest of my life.

This was probably their first time actually being able to talk to him and I saw them studying him as they took their seats. With the exception of Eda, who was looking at me.

"Does that go for me as well?"

"Of course, Eda. Call us our names."

"Oh, I'm still calling Skye my queen, it's too ridiculous not to," Ferona said.

"It's not Fer. I always knew Skye would end up with someone important. It makes sense," Nerial said with a smug look.

"I don't know, Nerial, you looked pretty damn sad when he ignored you," Ferona said with one hand on her head still. Nerial's cheeks went red. Ferona looked at Zan. "She was pissed. What was it she said earlier that day?" Ferona snapped her fingers, trying to remember.

"Something about her hair?" Zifira suggested.

"Oh yeah, 'a little princess with purple hair! So cute!' You were picking out baby names, Ners," Ferona laughed.

"Hair wasn't a priority I guess, huh Zan?" I asked. He gave me a huge smile and shook his head.

"I am sorry, ladies." He did sound sorry, to a point. "You know why I did it that way? Part of my agreement with the Mother Mages was I had to at least talk to the rest of you. I know they were hoping you would distract me from Skye. As nice as you all are, that obviously did not work for a second." He looked at me while he said it, pulling me close to kiss my forehead.

"Well, I for one never expected Skye to leave before me. Just being honest."

"Oh really? Fuck you too, Ferona," I said with a smile.

"Well, after you scared off that Dunede Ambassador that was eyeing you and that other guy with the ships I figured at least I didn't send them running."

"Oh, I remember the Ambassador. He grabbed Cylia and ran to get away from you."

"He was rude," I said curtly. Zan squeezed my hand and kissed my head again, a little harder this time.

"Aurelia was the one that surprised me. Why didn't she go first? She could twist her way into any man she wanted," Zifira mused, looking directly at Zan. She had been quiet all day.

"Aurelia swears she didn't use her power to go home with that general. I don't believe her for a second. She was getting desperate after Zan took Skye, and he was her best bet," Nerial said.

"Aurelia did what she wanted to do. She's happy." I tried to keep my tone neutral. Aurelia had made her choices and as much as they bothered me I couldn't do anything about it.

Zan shifted and stiffened in his seat. One of the soldiers with us had leaned over to talk with him quietly. His fist clenched on the table, palm glowing deep orange under his fingers. Something was wrong. I was just about to ask what when he changed again, talking to everyone at the table,

"Regretfully I have to leave you for the evening. Ask for whatever else you want."

He kissed my cheek, speaking only to me, "I will be back tonight."

Conversation stopped for a moment as he disappeared out the front door with a small group of men holding lanterns, one wearing a courier uniform. The door closed and Nerial leaned over to me.

"Skye, be honest, is he always like that?"

"Like what?"

"Like, all about you. It's almost like he's trying to make us jealous."

"No, you're making yourself jealous," I sneered.

"He's always like that, even when she's not around," Eda offered. I was thankful for the help, but my sisters weren't done with their questions.

"He's two people, have you ever noticed that?" Zifira asked.

"What do you mean by that?"

"He's kind and sweet then someone says the wrong thing and he's…" Zifira started.

"He's scary. Like a sexy scary, but scary," Nerial said between sips of wine, cutting off Zifira.

"I'm two people too. We're both half star-fire, half rational people. Most people think I'm scary. That doesn't bother me."

"Of course it doesn't. He'd never hurt you."

"I'm not sure he could even if he tried." I knew he could. If he left me, I would never recover from that kind of hurt.

"He's a flirt," Nerial said, taking an enormous sip of wine. She was on her fifth glass and only showed signs of speeding up.

"He's not a flirt, he wants to make everyone happy. It's respect," I responded coolly.

"I can think of something that would make me happy…" Ferona said with a stupid smile. Nerial giggled.

"Don't try it," I snapped.

"Ohhh, she's not sharing," Nerial teased.

"It's not that, it's you. You're my sister." I was repulsed by that thought, "It wouldn't work anyway, he doesn't like other women."

"Oh come on, Skye, he's a king. Don't fall for that. They all like any woman they can get their hands on," Ferona jeered.

"Most kings don't have hands that would burn and crush any other woman." That ended that conversation abruptly. We sat in awkward silence. I wouldn't mind if we could avoid that subject in the future.

"Nerial found someone she likes."

"Fer, don't." Nerial looked down at the tabletop.

"Why not? He's nice. And I know for a fact you like each other."

"It's not anything official," she said with a blush in her cheeks as she swirled her wine.

"It will be soon if you keep hanging on him like you did at that party. He's gonna make it official."

"I hope so." There was more to that story that I wanted to know, but it didn't seem like Nerial was willing to give up much else.

We had a few more rounds of nothing but wine-fueled banter before we started wandering back to our rooms. I took the stairs to mine, not expecting Zan to be there. The room was dark as I pushed the door open, but I saw him as my light lit the space. He was pensive, looking out the windows with his hands firmly behind his back. I wrapped him in a hug without thinking, only realizing that he might not want that as he stayed stiff.

"How was dinner?"

"Good. Ferona wants to sleep with you but that's not a surprise," I said. He shook his head and badly hid a grin, wrapping his arms around me to return my hug.

"Have you ever been in the ocean?" he asked, still looking out the windows.

"You know I haven't. As if the Towers had a beach. I did explode over the water, though. That's how they tested what I could do. I wasn't allowed to touch it."

"Would you like to?"

"Alright, but only if I can do it my way."

"Please do."

I untied my robe and threw it on my trunk and moved the few paces to the open doors. I burned, keeping the star-fire within my body instead of radiating. I took a running jump off the balcony. I flew out over the water. The energy that usually ruined everything around me pushed me forward instead.

I had only done this a few times, each time it was exhilarating. When I looked back, I could only just make out the silhouette of the buildings of the town and the few lingering lantern lights.

I hovered above the water, sure I had left Zan far behind. I was wrong. A quickly growing bright shape flew towards me. He crashed into me and pushed us both underwater.

I struggled to swim and quickly realized I couldn't. I let my body sink under the waves, unsure what direction was up. When I stopped fighting, I was surprised to find that water was no different from the air. I didn't need to breathe, and as I looked at Zan, it was clear he didn't either.

I was sure this was as close as I could get to the weightlessness of the sky. The darkness below us stretched on forever. I had no hope of ever seeing the end of the night sky, but the bottom of the sea I could find. I let myself sink further, helping myself along with my own gravity. Zan followed, though he had to swim instead of sink. I added swimming to the long list of things I wanted to learn with my freedom.

My feet found the bottom, disturbing the sand and rocks. My light lit the world around me, a dark world that went on forever. I looked up and saw the distant light of the sky above. The cold water pushed down and flowed around me like a powerful wind. Zan took my hand as he landed beside me. He let me stay for a long time before I felt him tug upward. I used star-fire to push us back to the surface.

Our heads broke the surface and I immediately missed being underwater. Gravity had little hold on me, but something about the rushing cold reminded me of a home I had never been to.

"I did not know we could do that."

"I didn't either. I knew I didn't need to breathe as often, but I didn't know for how long."

"Seems there is no limit, and if there is it is a long one. Though it was uncomfortable after a while, having to remind myself not to breathe." I nodded, but I was quickly distracted.

The water around us was turning to golden steam by my light. Zan pushed his dripping hair away from his face. My eyes caught on every one of his tattoos and muscles and the way the water clung to his skin.

"You're beautiful," I said without thinking. He stopped for a moment, blinking at me in confusion. "What, am I not allowed to say that back to you?"

"No, no. It is just... I am not. Did you try the wine?" He smiled and moved closer.

"No, I mean it," I insisted, a little annoyed but disarmed when I saw how quickly the lights in his eyes were swirling. I found it hard to believe that he truly had no idea how attractive he was. There was no way he was that oblivious.

"I am nothing but evidence of my years of war and the pain I inflicted on myself at my lowest points." He shook his head. It was my turn to ask him questions with my eyes, and he read them perfectly. "There is another reason I have my tattoos beyond my love for Solde. I got them and many piercings at a point in my life when all I wanted was to feel something. Pain was easy to find. Now, they hide my battle scars." He looked down and rubbed at the inside of his arms, drawing my eyes to more faded scars. Those were not from a battlefield. At least, not one that existed outside of his mind. I put my hands on either side of his face, tilting it to look back at me.

"I love them. I love you."

It hurt that he was convinced they made him less than admirable. A man who had wanted nothing but peace for himself and his country had been turned into a god of war. He simply had the scars to prove he had fought for it.

***

The sand shifted under my toes as we walked across the beach. It sizzled and dried where my skin touched it, but I was enjoying the unique feeling. We walked the winding path through the sand and tall grass back up to the house, our way lit by nothing but the stars and my glow. The water had long since evaporated off my skin, but I was happy to take a towel from Zan to wrap myself in as we entered through a backdoor. Back in our room, Zan looked at me with a deep frown and dark eyes. At first I wondered what I had done, but then he started to explain.

"I received bad news at dinner."

"I noticed."

"We will have to cut this trip short."

"Why?"

"Kos has chosen to bring the war to Solde soil."

"What does that mean?"

"It means I will be handling as much as I can. Hopefully, I will never have to ask you to help."

"I will if that's what we need to do."

"I hope it is not, but I have been suspicious of Kos for some time. I do not know why he has chosen now, especially when I have you. He knows what you can do. He saw my mother do it once but still did not surrender. For the first time I am starting to fear for our capabilities because I do not know what he has that is making him so confident he can handle us."

"Whatever it is, we'll survive it. Solde will win, even if I have to take Niode off the map to do it." The fire flared and clawed at my ribs. I could feel it in my eyes.

"Could you do that and not lose yourself?" He asked the question I'd just been asking myself. The star-fire wanted to do nothing but burn forever, and the more freely I let it go in anger, the harder it was to come back to my own mindset. I didn't have an answer for him.

"I don't know. I don't think so. But it would be worth it." Even if I had to help and ended up losing myself to the star-fire, it would be for him. What would happen after that, I had no way of knowing.

CHAPTER 28

The travel back was heavy but uneventful save one bit of news. Aurelia had her baby. A healthy little girl. As happy as I was about that, I felt bad for Vitsef. A war decree, a possible spy, and a newborn all at once didn't sound like a combination anyone should have to deal with.

As soon as we returned, I went to visit Aurelia. She was visibly stressed, but not because of her daughter. Baby Amalie was a blushing, chubby thing with a few strands of blonde hair. Aurelia said she nearly never cried and- judging by the lavishly decorated nursery I met her in- she wanted for nothing. I would have given up so much to have been able to hold her.

It was Vitsef that was the force of chaos in the house, as I had predicted. Aurelia said she was exhausted trying to keep him calm. As much as I was there for her, I wanted to talk with him. I had the maid take me to his office. I tried not to look in her dead eyes when she left me at the doors.

Vitsef was at his desk, writing frantically, wearing a deep scowl and tapping his foot on the ground so rapidly I thought it might fly off.

"Vitsef."

"My queen." He nodded to me, barely looking up. "Visiting Auri, hm?"

"Yes, but now I'm here to see you."

"My queen?"

"What's giving you the most trouble?" I gestured to the tables and papers, the little models balanced on maps, and the empty glasses that made the room smell sharp.

"May I speak frankly?" he asked, punching the paper with his pen as he wrote before throwing it down.

"Yes."

"Fucking all of it. Rolten's replacement is a brain-dead young man that's only ever had five ships. He's energetic, though, I'll give him that." He took a drink and shook his head. "What I wouldn't give for Skrive's help. Ashanm bless that brilliant man in his death." He held up his drink and looked at me properly for the first time. He squinted like he was trying to solve a puzzle. "Why are you here again?"

"I want to help you. I'm sure you remember my passion for such things."

"My queen, forgive me, but you have no idea what this is like. You can't do this. I can barely do this."

"I'd like to decide that for myself. If what I do fails, I promise it will be my direct responsibility, not yours." He didn't look convinced. "Give me something you don't want. I'll take care of it," I continued. He actually looked into my eyes, setting his jaw. Vitsef looked back to his desk and started shuffling. I waited patiently while he gathered three thin folders.

"These three. Our stationed commanders have sent possible choices and the most current information they have. All you have to do is pick a plan or combine them in some other way. They're desperate, though, be warned. They're writing directly to me which means they're going over about two other heads." He barked a single laugh. "The newest letters arrived this morning but I am much more worried about this," he said, holding up a thick stack of papers.

"What is that, exactly?"

"This is a problem we will be fools to not ask your help with. Tell Zandorian I said that, too. This is information about a movement of fully armed and supplied soldiers I have every reason to believe are meant to overwhelm the Northeast capital. They'll be too much, even with our dear king. Especially if I can't get a few thousand men back from East Livade in time." He shook his head. "I've never seen Kos concentrate his forces in mass like this, he's usually partial to a thin and far spread approach. Zandorian thinks they will have something more than men, probably mages. Kos either severely underestimates you, or he's hoping you won't help. I'm begging that you do."

I was slightly annoyed that Zan had already talked with him about this but hadn't told me anything. I hoped he had a good reason. He had promised I would rule as his equal, and that included hearing about news like this.

"How long do we have?" I asked.

"Two weeks at most."

I nodded and took the three folders he had offered and started to walk out. I remembered I should properly end the conversation. It was the polite thing to do, and I was trying to be nicer.

"Vitsef," I said from the doorway. He looked up at me again. "Thank you. I know you would rather be with Auri and Amalie. Let me know if we can help."

"Thank you, my queen."

Even if I didn't care for his other opinions, I saw a man that was giving up his own sanity for the sake of our success. That I could respect.

I walked back to the palace in the setting sunlight. I watched the orange orb sink lower in the sky with all the interest most women looked in the mirror. A pretty color but it had looked better. The first cool breezes of the evening moved around me as I went inside, through the gardens and up to the office.

I cleared my desk and sat down to do the job I had always wanted. Smaller scale than I had hoped, but I didn't blame Vitsef for not trusting me with anything larger yet. He didn't know what I could do, and neither did I. Not fully. I was left with more tactical decisions than actual strategy. I was confident with either, but I hoped if this went well I could persuade him into giving me more responsibility. I reminded myself Zan had already given me all the grand strategy I could want, even if it did have to go to a vote. I moved my focus back to what I was doing. This had to come first.

In two of the places it was almost on the verge of asymmetric warfare. No wonder Zan had to help fill in the gaps so often, I thought. Vitsef had left these men with nearly nothing against a Niode battalion who, even with a lack of resources, had an organized tenacity I nearly admired.

I let one of the commanders keep their plan. It was a good one, straightforward and left them an opportunity to escape and regroup if it went badly. In my mind, flexibility was always key.

The other two gave me sets of incomplete trash. No wonder Vitsef hadn't wanted to take the time to explain what they needed to do instead. I outlined a new plan for both of them. I hoped they listened. I had no way to know how they would react to getting orders directly from the queen instead of Vitsef.

I signed all three responses, nearly forgetting that I could add the Al star after my name and title. I took great satisfaction in it as I scratched it onto the paper.

I heard the office door open. There was a pause, then I heard it creak on its hinges a couple more times.

"Skye, may I ask what the door did to you?" Zan asked with a slight amusement in his voice.

"Hmm?"

"The handle. It is completely crushed."

I turned around. Sure enough, the outside door handle was crushed to the shape of the inside of my fist. "I'm sorry, I didn't mean to. I was thinking about something else."

"It is alright. May I ask what you were thinking about?"

The thoughts came back, a little bit more of a bite to them now that I felt I had nearly taken care of my other responsibility for the night. I took a deep breath.

"Why didn't you tell me about the planned Northeast invasion?" I asked. Zan shut the door carefully, face falling.

"Ah. I was not intentionally hiding it, I was fully planning on telling you. What I did not know was if I would ask you to help when I did. I did not want to ask you to do it, but I am not sure I could risk it without you, either."

"Vitsef begged me to help when I saw him today," I said. He nodded.

"It is still up to you. If you do not want to I would not blame you." He cautiously moved closer to my chair. "I know how hard it is for me to do what I do and not... slip."

I knew what he meant. He knew if I burned enough to eliminate this problem, I might not be able to keep myself from destroying everything else. I could ruin the armies of the world and rule the ashes more easily than I ruled Solde. No votes, no restrictions, no laws. Unbridled star-fire and anger would be my only council members.

I had to fight the thoughts down. Even thinking about it made my resolve softer. He was watching me with concern, and I remembered what I must look like. I rubbed at my wrists, almost wishing for the reminder that I had spent years without destroying my wardens. Surely I could bring myself back from destroying our enemies. I stilled my hands and spoke with as much authority and confidence I could.

"I'll do it, but not because anyone asked. This is my country. The world needs to know what happens when they move against Solde and their Stardropped queen."

CHAPTER 29

I'd wanted to call an official meeting of my sisters, but Zan had held me off for three days, making enough excuses I was suspicious he was planning something. Whatever it was, it must have been over and done as I told him my morning plans while doing my makeup. He said nothing to dissuade me, instead fluffing the pillows on my bed.

I opened the door to let us in. The first thing I saw was an enormous table and chairs had been placed in the middle of the room. The table was made of a deep gray marble. The chair in the end was also stone. It had a higher back than the rest, intricate carvings of stars covered its surface. At the top was the star of Al, inlaid in gold.

"Oh this is amazing." Nerial slipped past me, heading straight for a set of plush chairs and couches arranged around a fireplace. Zifira and Ferona followed her.

My eyes lingered on the bookshelves and paintings. Each painting depicted a mage caught in the act of doing something extraordinary. I loved to see their colors and styles from throughout history.

My favorite was the one of a woman I knew instantly as Zan's mother, Serana. Her hair was a shocking white in long braids, and her skin an exceptional dark warm brown scattered with barely visible freckles. Full lips and long pointed ears adorned with pearl earrings. There wasn't any one feature she obviously shared with her son, but her eyes were familiar. They were mine. Except mine were angry, alive. Hers were dimmer, sad. Her expression was a blank one, the corners of her lips downturned. The artist had made no effort to capture her glow, and it made me wonder if she had had one at all.

"Oh wow, she's gorgeous. She has hair, though. Why don't you have hair, Skye?" Nerial asked at my side.

I shrugged. "We still have biological parents. Maybe mine didn't have hair."

"That is not entirely true." I turned around to look at Zan behind me, a little surprised he was there. He hadn't come with us, but I hadn't heard the door either. "When she burned her hair fell out. Her hair grew longer because she did not burn, is our best guess."

"So it's my fault I'm bald. Good to know." I wrapped him in a hug. He had been in the garden, I could smell the flowers on his robes and breathed a little deeper.

"I am just as much at fault, I think." He kissed the top of my head. "Do you like the room?"

"It's wonderful. More than I ever expected. Thank you."

"Of course. Funny enough, I was having that table made for the meeting room, but I think it suits here much better. The temporary table will have to stay there a little longer."

"Wait, what was wrong with the other table?" Nerial asked.

"I did not care for it," Zan said. I had to hide my smile against his chest.

"I wish I could do that. Just get rid of something cause I didn't like it anymore and get a new one."

"What would you get rid of?" Zan asked her.

"I hope your bed, it's disgusting what you do to Eran," Ferona said between laughs.

"Stop talking, Ferona!" Nerial's face was turning deep red. "He's Zan's brother," she hissed, quickly walking back to Ferona to bat at her hands and get her to stop laughing.

I was left in a silent shock. I had known she'd been with someone but I had not expected Eran. I looked up to see Zan's face. His eyes were wider, but he shrugged. Apparently his brother hadn't told him the news either.

"Ferona just wishes she could get one of them for herself," Zifira said.

"Yeah, like you wish you could get Quidet to come live here," Ferona snapped back.

"Quidet? The shapeshifter from the year under us?" I asked. I had met her, of course, but couldn't picture her. She changed her looks slightly each day.

"That's the one. Zifira is in love with her."

"She is welcome here if that is what she decides," Zan offered. He looked back to me, "I brought you these. Just arrived a few minutes ago."

He held up three thick letters. I recognized the edging from the papers I had taken from Vitsef. They were the results of my orders. I read through each one, laying them out on the table. There were more pleasantries than I had expected from two, and one gave me a curt line about why he was confused to not be hearing from Vitsef. That didn't matter. What mattered was that the execution of each plan had turned out beautifully in our favor.

"Does Vitsef know about this?" I asked.

"If he does not he will soon. Good or bad?"

"See for yourself." I laid them all out for him to read and stepped back. It took him a long moment but eventually he added it all together, his eyes glowing a little brighter.

"You did these?" he asked.

"You sound surprised."

"I knew you could do this, without a doubt, but I am surprised Vitsef gave them to you."

"He was desperate to be rid of a problem, I offered to solve it."

"Solve it you did."

"What did Skye do?" Nerial asked, returning from her scuffle with Fer.

"Nothing," I answered, trying not to draw her attention further.

"It is not nothing, *asde ren*. You won us three conflicts."

"It's not a big deal. I can do better than this," I said, scowling at my papers.

"Okay but like, what did you do?" Nerial sat on the table and picked up my letters, holding two of them upside down. I took them from her hands.

"I directed three small groups through some minor conflicts, that's all" I said.

"Skye has always been a tactician," Zifira said. I was surprised she even knew that word, she'd never expressed the slightest interest in my hobbies. I imagined she'd learned it while she was with Rolten.

"I just find stratagem and military history interesting. Three small victories doesn't make me a tactician."

"Whatever you call yourself you are very good at it. I am sure the men you helped would agree," Zan said with a reassuring smile.

"No, I need more practice. These were easy. I need a challenge."

"We could play more of that game you like so much," Nerial said with a laugh. She didn't know how it worked.

"I will if any of you will actually play against me."

"No one can play strategy games with you and you hate chance games," Ferona said, appearing at her side.

"Because you cheat. You move tiles while they're falling," I said, pointing to Nerial. Both of them would cheat any game, even if all they got was the victory, but Nerial was known for moving pieces with her power to make it happen. At least Ferona had to plan.

"Aurelia cheats at everything and still you play with her," Nerial retorted.

"She can't help it. You can," I said.

"I am willing to bet anything Kaniel would play against you," Zan said with a smile. "I have never been a challenge for him."

"He won't." I shook my head before leaning it against his shoulder. I didn't want to talk about how strange Kaniel was about being alone with me, it might upset him. That, and Kaniel had admitted to reading my file. He probably knew exactly how good I was.

***

The next set of delegations from Vitsef was supposed to be dropped at the office that evening. I was looking forward to them, but I was getting impatient with waiting. I needed something else to do.

I only had one more shelf I hadn't gotten to in my mass reorganization of the office. I was sure I'd never seen Zan use any of the books or files on it, but I thought it would be best to be thorough. The bottom shelf was only dusty books. I didn't know how much I could do with them. Still, I started to pull them down and make a pile. The out of order years on the spines gave me hope for more order still. As I grabbed the last few, there came a small thunk and the sound of paper rustling. I looked behind the books, expecting some rogue notes or maybe a set of doodles as I'd found so many times before. This time I found a file hidden behind them.

I pulled it out carefully, trying not to drop any pages. As I held it in my hands in the light, I saw that it wasn't just any file, it was mine. My name was written across its front with swirling red letters. This was the file that the Towers had given Zan when he had asked to come meet the mages. Why had he never shown it to me? Maybe because I had never asked? But why would he hide it so well…

I flipped it open on my desk. The first page was a formal form. My name, my age, my height, my power. Star-fire. It had a huge star drawn next to it that pulled so many questions to my mind. Now I was certain they had known who I was. But I was distracted by another detail. The large "Do Not Let Out" written over it all in a handwriting I knew belonged to Mother Nai.

How much had Zan had had to fight to get them to let me go? Or hadn't they tried to fight the king? Flipping back I saw they had a collection of letters, all in Zan's handwriting. The oldest one surprised me. It was from seven years ago when he was still a prince. The next one he sent was from two years ago, explaining that he would get me soon. Judging by the next one, they had disagreed strongly. So he had fought them. For years. I counted the rest. Twenty three more, all the way up until the three days before he brought me home.

The next page was the agreement to take responsibility for the actions I took outside of the Towers. Then there was my price, a sum so large I couldn't comprehend that the mages had asked for it and doubly so that Zan had paid. At the bottom I saw his careful signature. Zandorian Al in red ink with the Al star.

I flipped farther back. I knew they kept track of who a mage's parents were, but we were never told. I found the page and found exactly what I had hoped I wouldn't see.

> *Mother- Deceased*
> *Father- Deceased*
> *Family- No living family*
> *Cause of death- Mage's power*

I closed my eyes and shoved down the images of me burning my own parents to death. Had I exploded in their home, leveling it with them inside? Had I killed them separately?

I was thankful when the door opened. I was shaking with the effort of holding in my feelings about these revelations. They felt like a storm, and I couldn't do that here, even with my resolve to let them run free.

"Skye? What is wrong?" He was to me in two steps. I cried as much as I could without fire. He held me close, ignoring the burns I made in his clothes. His hand left my back, and then I heard papers shifting.

"There is a reason I hid that. I am sure you are angry." He had to know I wasn't angry. I was upset, but for once I was not angry. I wiped away tears.

"They weren't ever going to let me out of the Towers no matter what. Even if you wanted me. They knew about you and who I was and they lied. They wanted to keep me there," I whispered. As I said it, it felt less real and more like it was from a past life. It had been a past life, at this point.

"They did. They were set on not letting you out. But not telling you about my plans was not their fault. I asked them not to tell you about me. I did not think they would tell you nothing about who you were and that... I am sorry."

"Why did you ask them to do that?"

"Honestly, I did not want you to feel like you had to be mine. I meant what I said that first day, you could have been anything. You could have left. I wanted to be sure it was an unbiased choice, completely yours."

I thought of how much different I would have been if I had known. I could have swung two ways. Either I would have felt like I had superiority over them all as the next queen, the pride eating me into something even more power hungry than I was, or I would have confronted them for daring to keep a Stardropped queen in chains and left early. Either way I would have come to Zan as a monster. The star-fire would have won. Instead I had kept it quiet so I could settle for a life I didn't want. Now I had one I wanted, and I was able to use it for some good. I was crying hard again, my hands burning against my eyelids.

I fought the worst scenes away and looked back at Zan. He had been right to ask them to not tell me, and he had been right to free me and let me choose him in my own time. He had freed me the way that was best for everyone.

"Thank you for fighting them. I'm glad I left."

"I did what had to be done for a woman like yourself."

"Your father didn't do that."

"No, he did not. I will never forget what he said about the Stardropped." Zan fought a creeping sneer. "He said a Stardropped was either used or became a user. He chose to use my mother, but I chose neither for you. I hope you do not choose to be a user, but I can not stop you." He wiped tears off my cheeks with the back of his hand. I wanted to change the subject.

"You really don't like your father." I knew why. He'd abused Zan for years. Maybe it was the soreness from learning that mine had been dead before I knew how to speak that made me say it. Maybe I wanted a reminder that not all parents were ones worth having. Either way, I felt Zan close his hands into fists against my back.

"I value what my father did to a point. I am skilled at what I do. But he was the worst man I have ever known."

"How did he die? No one ever talks about it." I had never heard one whisper of Zindraun's death from anyone outside of Zan, Eran, and Kaniel. None of them spoke of him without extreme disgust.

When I looked at his face it wasn't the one it had been before. His lips were curled in the start of a snarl. He stiffened, leaning away from me,

"Do not worry about it, Skye." His voice had the undertone of a growl.

"But isn't that something I should know?"

"No, it is not," he said, not looking at me anymore. I saw sparks in his eyes. I watched the smoke rise, but I wasn't going to let it go.

"But-"

"Skye, stop!" He roared with all the fury of thunder. I jumped back, pushing my desk with me, my hands igniting reflexively. He took a few breaths and softened, putting up his quickly cooling hands. "I am sorry, I lost myself. It is not something that is talked about for a reason." He pressed his fists into his eyes, molten gold running down his palms and between his fingers, rings half-melted messes.

"You killed him, didn't you?"

"Not on purpose. We were on a Niode battlefield. I made a mistake. I had no idea how close he was when I used the firestorm." I heard him say those words but I didn't believe him, it sounded too rehearsed. I let that hang in the air between us. The light in his eyes flickered as he wiped the gold drips off of his face. I didn't blame him.

"We both killed our fathers, I guess."

"You did not know what you were doing, you were a baby." He shook his head.

"Doesn't mean they're less dead," I said with a shrug that was far more neutral than I felt.

I saw the beginnings of tears in his eyes. I weaved my fingers through his, curling closer to him. He put his arms around me to hold me there. His heartbeat slowed, and his temperature gradually dropped.

"I understand if you don't want to talk about it- but he was a mage. What exactly could he do? You said he made your mother numb."

"He could make you feel almost empty, like your body was not fully yours. You were just watching life happen. It felt like being in a dream. Worse, because you knew it was happening and were completely indifferent about it, even after it was over."

"That's terrifying."

"It was. He could only do it to one person at a time, thankfully. He did it to me so I would kill for him. I could handle it one way or another. But my mother... I do not think she ever felt a thing when we lived here. I think that is why Kaniel insisted we spend so much time in Renciam. It was so she could feel something." He took in a sharp breath leaning in close to speak in a deep whisper, "Skye, I did kill him, but it was for you. The month before I did it, I heard about you at the Towers. When I brought it up, he said he knew about you already, that he was waiting." His eyes sparked and he hugged me even closer, his hands glowing against my back. I was glad I had worn a backless gown. "I could not let him do to you what he had done to my mother. I had to free you, and that included making sure my father was not a threat. Forgive me."

"Oh..." I hugged him tighter in return. There was nothing to forgive. As always, he'd done what was best. I was crying again, this time with the knowledge that if it hadn't been Zan, it could have been his father. A man that was the very pinnacle of every preconceived notion I'd ever had about what men who bought mages were like. He would have been the man I had feared Zan was when he'd taken me home, but a hundred times worse. I was glad to be crying into the chest of my loving, infallibly loyal Zan. I was glad to feel his kisses on the top of my head and his hands keeping my shoulders from shaking too much.

He let me cry it all out before he got up and went back to the top of my desk. I stayed on the floor, curled up, leaning against the chair. I heard shuffling papers, then a pause.

"How closely did you look at this?"

"What do you mean?" I shifted to look up at him.

"I am sorry to bring up your parents again, but I never noticed this symbol. Though, admittedly I have never given your file much attention."

"Let me see it." He handed over the paper, sitting back down beside me. I ignored the words. In the bottom corner and faded from age was a stamped symbol. It was the outline of crossed swords. It looked incredibly official and startlingly familiar. I knew it, but couldn't place it.

"What does that mean? Is that a family?"

"Ve. One of the most powerful in Solde. At least they were. My grandfather..." I assumed the end of that sentence was somewhere along the lines of him having all but a handful of them killed. That sounded like something paranoid Zian would have done. He continued, "Does not matter. I had known that the last of them had died, but I never asked about it. I was so young when it happened, and my father forbade any mention of the name." His brows stitched together and I saw something happening in his mind. He had more pieces to the puzzle than I did. "Point is, I think you had a title far before I had anything to do with it, Skye Ve."

I remembered reading the name Ve now. They had ruled the Northeast for close to four centuries before officially merging with Solde-al about a hundred years ago. After our newest democratic system of representatives was established about forty years back, they fell into obscurity. Or maybe that was where my books at the Towers had run out.

I wanted to know why that symbol was so familiar. I couldn't remember seeing it in any books. Maybe I could ask Kaniel to help me look for it. He would find more information much faster than I ever could. Maybe he could use the mage power I suspected he had and help me remember. While I was thinking, Zan was looking at me like I was the only thing in the room.

"What?"

"Nothing. I just like the idea that I would have had you either way, Stardropped or not."

"You don't know that."

"Oh, I do." He had a smug smile.

"How?"

"The first part of my life might have played out much the same, but the key being you would have never been taken to the Towers. We would have met at a party since all the old families attend. Maybe I would have actually enjoyed parties."

"That's assuming I would have liked you at all."

"You would have said no to a king?"

"I did. The third thing I ever said to you was no. Did you forget?"

"But a hundred no's later I got a yes."

"Because I decided, not because of you."

"I know. I can never thank you enough for that." I let him kiss me as thanks. Still, my mind was adjusting to this new information, a process I would much rather go through in my room in case it turned into fire.

"I'm going to bed. This is- I need to process this."

"Alright. Do you want me to join you soon or would you rather be alone?"

"Of course I want you there." I kissed the top of his head and left.

I went to my closet to change out of my dress and into something better suited for sleeping. As I pulled on a thin silky thing I looked over to my jewelry and something clicked in my mind.

The small silver ring. It was exactly where I had left it. I picked it up and looked on the inside. Sure enough, small and faint were the Ve swords. I had had a hint all these years and never put it together. Or maybe the Mother Mages had made it so I never could have. It certainly seemed like they had been determined to take Zan's request to the extreme and never tell me a thing.

CHAPTER 30

Zan had to leave suddenly the next evening. I knew it was because we were on the edge of losing one of our most important farming communities. Niode had followed through with the threats of bringing the war to us, pushing too far onto our land. Still, two weeks started to feel like an eternity the moment he left. But this time I had plans. I wanted to make up for the years I'd known nothing. I wanted to know exactly who I was.

My first stop was the library. I was going to research everything about my blood family. I had envied Nelser Hu and others like him for being able to trace their lines back to greatness. Mine couldn't possibly contain anyone greater than what I was, but I wanted to know who I would have been if I hadn't been chosen by the Stardropped power.

I found Kaniel lurking on the third floor, sorting through scrolls for what I guessed was one of our historical collections. He noticed me. I saw it in his pause as he sorted, but he didn't turn around.

"Kaniel, can you help me compile all mentions of the Ve family?"

"The Ve family? That sounds incredibly familiar."

"It did to me as well. I only remember vague facts from my reading."

"May I ask what sparked the interest?" He turned his body slightly but still didn't look at me.

"Zan and I were going back through my file and discovered I am actually Skye Ve."

"Ah, that makes sense. Mages do tend to show up in the old families."

"Really?" I had never heard that theory. I had heard others, like that our loyalty belonged to whoever bedded us or that we were drawn to powerful people like fire to kindling, but I'd dismissed those. This one made sense.

"Yes, it used to serve them well. Then the Towers happened, and you all sank to the lowest level until someone else made you something else. Not to be insensitive," he added. That made me angry. I was and never had been the lowest. I bit back.

"No, I know it applies to you too. You're a mage, too. But you were born in Renciam, a place with free mages. You were a man with such a subtle power you could get away without suspicion here." That got him to look me in the eyes.

"I was born to nothing, and my talent helped pull me to the top. I was lucky and cunning." He had an edge of a sneer in his normally neutral expression. "I aligned myself with powerful people and helped them recall their lines with a simple word. I reinforced their knowledge while they dreamed. It is amazing how much a person can learn when they never have to lose knowledge to the haze of sleep. I tutored royalty far before Zan became my focus. Before that I helped myself graduate early with the highest of honors Renciam's academies had to offer. Most people never figured out exactly what I did to help them. They only cared that it worked. So, I lived as a free mage in Solde-al, but it was not effortless. Especially putting up with Zindraun. Not only was he drunk most of the time, he was a coward. I looked him in the eyes and told him exactly what I thought of him. But he never figured out I was more than a tutor and translator for his prized weapons." He laughed a single joyless laugh.

"Did you help Zan kill him?"

"Hmm, in a way I suppose I did. I raised Zan with morals and a sense of justice. Seri gave him the fire to bring about that justice how he saw fit. Together, with Zan's sense for opportunity, Zindraun met the end he had earned." He tilted his head. "Zan repaid him for everything he put him through. I am sure he has told you about all of that."

"Not all of it."

"He will. Give him time. It is painful, but he will be better to have another soul to talk with about it. He has done his best to be better about how he handles things, but he has only talked to me for so long. I was there for most of it so it helps very little if we only compare notes about the past." We both looked at each other for a long moment before Kaniel cleared his throat and turned to go downstairs. "Let us get to work, then, Skye Ve."

I was grateful I'd asked for help after he brought books from eight separate areas around the library. From everything he helped me bookmark, I was able to pull together a history.

The Ve family had originally taken power from a handful of local lords, united under the idea that combined force would make them all great. Our swords symbol had come from that same extensive military. It was what had made us great, even if it had never benefited the lords they had promised glory.

After ruling what we now called the Northeast region for about thirteen generations, they had chosen to assimilate into the Solde-al states instead of holding their own against them as a small nation.

That was a smart choice from what I could gather about their situation at that point. They were also noted as strongly opposing the establishment of the representative system. That made me angry. If you have four hundred years to improve a nation and it largely stayed static or slipped to be worse, it was time to hand off the power.

I discovered the name of the man that had been my father. He had served on the Solde council in what was now Vitsef's place. It was a name I had heard Vitsef bless only days ago, a coincidence that made me laugh out loud. Vitsef had had no idea he had in fact been helped by Skrive that day.

Skrive Ve had been the only thing standing between Solde and ruin at the hands of Niode for his nearly fifteen years on the council. He also had quite an extensive set of essays written against him for some of the decisions he had made, particularly ones that had led to losses, financial and otherwise. Kaniel pointed out that portraits were done of all council members. I had a good chance of finding Skrive's in the palace somewhere, assuming neither Zindraun or Zan had gotten rid of it.

I wasn't going to call my family good people, but the star-fire loved the idea of ruling with an iron sword. I reminded it I had a steel and gold sword now, and more power than my ancestors could have dreamed of.

"Are you nearly done for the day?" Kaniel asked after several long hours.

"Not just yet."

"That makes sense- Seri stayed up late as well. She said it was the time of stars."

"She's right. I think I'm only diurnal because the Mother Mages kept a strict schedule. Or maybe it's because that's when the sun is out." He nodded. Now was as good a time as any to ask the question that had bothered me since I met him. "Kaniel, how well did you know her?"

"About as well as any person can know another."

"That's not an answer," I pressed. He sighed.

"I know her favorite book was a poetry collection called Flowers and Stars that I would read to her. I know she only ate while we were in Renciam. Her favorite candy was *ren alsha heshan*... sunlight honey made incredibly spicy by a man named Birgan at a corner stand. I know the smell of the oil she used to braid her hair away from her face. I know she loved to sing, but the only time she ever did was to get Zan to sleep." He looked on the edge of tears, voice wavering. "I know who would make her glow as brightly as you do when you are with Zan."

"Was it you?" I asked. He smiled the first smile I'd ever seen from him.

"Most days."

"Who was it the other days?"

"You know that answer." I did. Only one soul could ever do that, and we'd both cared for him more than anything else.

I wanted to know more but I could tell I was losing him to nostalgia. His eyes were unfocused, looking at the reflection of the library in the dark windows.

"Do you miss her?"

"Everyday. I wish I could say the feeling dulled with time, but it still feels like a knife to hear her name."

"I can't imagine how that feels. I don't know how it feels to be stabbed." I tried to joke, but he stayed serious.

"You do, I think. Rem–"

"No, don't. I believe you. I don't want to remember it," I interrupted.

"I understand. I apologize. Sometimes it is more of a reflex than a conscious decision. I have never met anyone with such a delicate sense of memory."

"Serana wasn't?"

"No, no. She asked me to help her get everything back. It was a terrible decision I should have never helped with. It pushed her further into herself and made her situation all the more unbearable. I am glad you are choosing not to."

"Or I do remember in some way on my own, and that's why I don't want to make the same mistake."

"That is possible."

I had always vaguely remembered things I shouldn't. I knew facts I had no way of verifying, and I felt loss for lives I had never met. But my focus was still on Kaniel. It had to be so painful for him to be surrounded by reminders. To sit by me and know that I was one sentence away from being his Serana again.

"Kaniel, I'm sorry I'm not her."

"Do not be. I had my chance with a Stardropped. Zan deserves you far more than I do."

"If it helps, I'll try to remember both of you in my next life."

"Please do. Remember us as we are." For a moment the lights in the room got slightly brighter, the colors melding together. The feeling faded quickly. I shut my book and got up from the table. That was more than enough to call the evening over.

"Goodnight, Kaniel."

"Goodnight, Skye Ve."

I left the library and went to my closet, taking in how beautiful the palace was at night in the warm lantern lights. I took my time changing into my sleeping robe and taking off my necklace, letting all I had learned sink in, but I fell asleep quickly once I was back in my room.

My dream opened in a dark room. I was facing a heavy iron door and ten men in Solde armor, each one illuminated by my light alone. Looking down, I saw the chains. My wrists and ankles pulled against shackles, four sets of heavy chains anchored into the stone walls. The only thing I wore was a skirt made of chains, glowing red hot where the links touched my burning skin. I had another tightly around my neck, an Al star medallion against my chest.

The doors opened with a bang, making me look up again. My eyes fell on a familiar face. It was Kaniel, but he wasn't himself. He was younger, fitter, with long dreadlocks and a worn green robe, a notebook tucked under his arm. He stood in the doorway with another man I hated deeply. I could have snapped my chains like nothing, killed them all for doing this, but my desire to do it melted away as Kaniel introduced himself as my translator. They had brought me him, and that was enough to spare them for today.

I still remembered it perfectly as I woke up. It was the most vivid dream I had ever had and that made me sure it wasn't a dream at all. That was Serana's memory of meeting Kaniel for the first time. The parallels between it and how I had met Zan made me shudder as much as the differences. At least my chains had been taken off.

CHAPTER 31

Vitsef had nearly flipped his opinion of me after my instruction had won us those three conflicts. I hoped the news I brought him today would move him completely to my side. If he couldn't fully respect me, I had a feeling he would respect my name.

I didn't take my usual seat in his office the next day, and it had nothing to do with the fact that it was covered in papers. I stood in front of his desk instead.

"So, I realize we're here to work, but wanted to ask you about Skrive Ve first. You brought him up the other night. How did you know him?" I asked. Vitsef slowly put down his pen and looked up, adjusting his glasses.

"Skrive Ve was my mentor. I knew him for years, working with him on the first Solde council as a much younger man. Ve was ruthless and stubborn, but Ashamn gave him a power over war no one else had. He was the only reason Solde didn't fold. He only lost three times, and each one was a sacrifice for a bigger prize." He held up three fingers for emphasis. A smile had crept onto his face. "Genius of a man. Why do you ask?"

"I recently learned I am not only the Stardropped Queen of Solde-al, I am also Skrive's daughter."

"Ashamn's blessing… I can't tell you how much sense that makes. I knew their daughter had become a mage, but I'd never had the chance to ask about what happened to her or what her power was or even her name. No one else cared, especially not Zindraun. He hated your father and buried his death quickly, told everyone not to talk about it. He buried everything about your parents, really, now that I think about it. Even gave me my job the same day as I watched them take down Skrive's portrait. Fuck." He swallowed hard, looking at me closely. I hoped he wouldn't bring up exactly how they had died. We both knew. And I knew why Zindraun had buried their deaths. He knew that a firestorm meant Stardropped, and he wanted to keep it quiet so no one but him and the Mother Mages knew about me. That was, until Zan found out. I was sad my parent's memories had gotten so wrapped up in Zindraun's scheme that they had been forcibly forgotten.

Vitsef stood up. "I have something to show you." He started walking out of the room quickly. We passed the room with the statue of Ashamn and Iliths and onto another with deep red walls.

"Did Aurelia show you this part of the house?"

"Can't say she did."

"Just as well, it's not as interesting if I'm not there to tell you who's who. She can't remember for the life of her." He stopped in front of a painting crowded with figures dressed in old military uniforms.

"These are your parents here," he said while pointing to the figures in the middle. Sure enough the resemblance was obvious. I had his height and her exact face shape and nose. Both of them had light brown eyes, my mother's slightly darker. Her dark blonde hair was braided over her shoulder, and she was significantly younger than Skrive. My father's curls were black-as-night and reached all the way down to the chain of his necklace. A Ve medallion was in place on his proud chest. They both wore dark, dusty gray-blue outfits.

"This is me, if you can believe it." Vitsef pointed to one of the men off to their side, directly beside my father. He looked maybe twenty-five, at most.

"What was my mother's name? I couldn't find it anywhere."

"Oh, Yarcella. I'm surprised though, she was quite the business woman. And a cousin to the Xi family, but that's not much of a claim to fame," Vitsef scoffed.

"What business?"

"Weapons manufacturing. She ran the largest private forge in Solde. There absolutely was no better match for both of their careers."

A sense of loss bloomed in my chest. I had never met them, never so much as known their names, but I knew we would have been a good family if star-fire hadn't made me into this. But star-fire was what made me a queen, no matter what Zan said. They seemed like the kind of people who would be proud of me for that.

"There might be some other interesting people in here for you. The Ve family was involved with the Solde military from start to, well, you." He gave me the kindest look I'd ever gotten from him. I looked around for a moment, but when I looked up at the enormous painting of him and Aurelia, a piece that completely dwarfed the one of him and his first wife beside it, I couldn't leave the room fast enough.

CHAPTER 32

I woke up later than usual to the sound of Eda opening my doors. Even after the portrait incident, I had been staying up late with Vitsef the past couple days. Sometimes Auri and Amalie sat with us, though Amalie had as much of an idea what her father and I were saying as I understood of her mother's rants about upholstery fabrics. I was glad for the days the rest of my sisters came with me so Aurelia would have someone to talk to.

"Good morning."

"Morning," I said as I got out of bed to wash my face.

"You have new robes in your closet."

"Thank you, Eda." I didn't think much of it. A handful arrived every other week or so now.

"I think you might want to see them." As I looked at her instead of my mirror, I saw the barely controlled excitement on her face.

"You think so?"

"I really do." Eda smiled wide. I smiled back and put down my makeup to see whatever was so giggle inducing for my maid.

I opened my closet doors to a sight Eda had been right to say I should see. Three more gold dresses on mannequins. I'd known Zan had been planning to have more made eventually but I hadn't been expecting three so soon. Again, each one was a work of art. One was tight and simple, nothing but a single layer draped nicely. One was similar to the one I'd worn to the party but in two sections, top and bottom with a drastically shorter train.

The last one was only loosely fit to be called an outfit. It was more accurately a collection of swooping chains and a dress section that would only barely cover my torso. I recognized it from the folder in the study. It was my favorite. I knew he'd had it made because it was his favorite too.

I liked them even better because I now knew they were not only recycled gold from the first one, but that the first one had been made from every bit of golden vanity art, jewelry, or trinket Zan's father had ever commissioned. Zindraun had kept every bit of it away from Serana, so now I wore it with pride and triumph.

It did draw my mind to metal work, though. My conversation with Vitsef had only made me more curious about sword making. If I had a propensity for what my father did, maybe I had one for my mother's occupation as well. While I hadn't spent years reading and practicing swordsmithing like I had strategy and military history, I had someone who had.

"Eda, what are you doing the rest of the day?" I asked as I played with the incredibly small chains on the third dress.

"I was going to help in the forges. We're working overtime to arm our borders as heavily as possible."

"I remember. Could I help?" I asked. She thought for a moment.

"I'm not sure it's currently the place for royalty. It's not safe."

"I'm not worried about my safety," I said with what I hoped was a warm smile.

"Forgive me, of course not. We'd be honored to have your company."

I got dressed quickly into the plainest thing I could find, which of course still left me decidedly overdressed even as I forwent my usual Al necklace.

I accompanied Eda down to what I guessed was her usual route of transportation, one of the plainest carriages we owned with only two lean oxen to pull it. They were not the red coated, fit animals with polished horns I was used to seeing in front of our carriages. Still, these were cute. I wished I could pet them.

We sat inside and I settled near the window. I wanted to see my city. Eda looked slightly uncomfortable with the silence, so I tried to lighten it.

"Eda, can I ask you a question?"

"Of course,"

"How does everyone know where I am all the time?"

"Ah, can I speak frankly?" A small smirk pulled at the corner of her lips.

"Yes," I smiled to encourage her and negate whatever intimidating aura I still had. She looked down at the small bag in her lap as she answered.

"There's a saying at the palace. If you want to find the queen, you listen to your gut. You go whatever direction it begs you not to go until you find her."

"Wow." It didn't surprise me, it made sense, but it was blunt.

"It's not that you're disliked, it's more to do with the sense of panic you radiate when you don't mean to."

"Right, I figured. I've been working on it."

"I've noticed. It's been much less pronounced recently."

We were in the far eastern part of the city, a place I had heard was largely manufacturing and family-owned stores. That seemed to be true from what I could see. I was glad we had taken a plainer carriage until it was clear I would be drawing attention no matter what once I got out.

I got lots of looks, far more than usual. I didn't mind for once, I couldn't blame them for being confused why I was there and interested to see me at all. Most queens didn't venture out among their people often and I was particularly guilty of that. I would make sure to turn that trend around, especially now that I had my sisters.

I followed Eda around much as I had followed Zan around my first day at the palace. She pointed out the different sections and equipment, from furnaces to the individual specialties of some of the smiths that were working. One feature drew my attention more than the others.

"Transfer ladles carry the metal from the primary furnace to the smaller ones where we can work with it." She pointed up. The large bowls moved above us slowly, at least twice as tall as a person. They held my attention most of all. I watched them pouring it into molds for what Eda said were stock to be stretched and shaped into blades. The orange glow was beautiful.

"Eda! I could use some help!" one of the men called.

"I'll be right back." She walked towards him, throwing out her hands in a question. They talked for a moment. She shook her head, rolled up her sleeve, and reached into the forge.

I looked around for something to do while she handled whatever that was. There had to be a way for me to help in a place meant for heating and shaping metal, I'd done it for years. Never with tools, of course, but I imagined my hands could do the same.

I felt very bad about the swords I had ruined as I watched them work. So much effort and care was put into each one, even the plain ones that would go to our lower ranks of soldiers. I was mesmerized watching them to the point I hardly noticed when Eda had returned to my side.

"You wanted to make a sword?"

"Yes. I was hoping you could teach me."

"It's not easy, but I'm sure you'll learn quickly. Being who you are doesn't hurt, either. My biggest trouble when I first started was my arms getting tired. I don't think you'll have that problem."

"Probably not."

"You might have a problem accidentally burning your steel if you work too hot, though. I'll teach you to avoid that. Let's start with a knife and go from there."

I watched her work with my full attention. She narrated her actions and I tried to take in what I could. It was all beautiful in a rough, dirty sort of way. There was something basic about it, ringing true with tradition and art and sheer will power to make a hunk of heated steel into something with so much more potential. Finally, once it fully resembled a blade and a tang for attaching a handle she held it out to me.

"Want to give the edge a final sharpen?"

I ran my fingers down the edge, pinching it into a sharp point. She put it in the quenching water, pulling it back out and putting it on the anvil. She let it cool a moment longer before touching it. She ran her finger across the blade edge carefully.

"Passable?" I asked.

"Absolutely. Twice as sharp and a fraction of the effort. If you weren't queen I'd hire you in a second." That was high praise. But I couldn't enjoy it for long. Suddenly, there was yelling and a horrible bang in a different part of the building. I moved towards it without thinking.

My eyes found the biggest problem first, ignoring the men rushing past me to escape. A cascade of molten metal flowing from a tipped ladle. I burned, keeping the star-fire close to my body so it only made me into a bright white form and not an additional problem.

I ran through the white-hot river to get closer. The side was no longer connected to the rail. I jumped to hold up the tipping side, righting it so it stopped spilling. The hot metal ran down my back, but it was more like a warm shower than a deadly spew of molten steel.

"What do I do with this?" My voice was as loud as a lightning strike. No one answered me, so I took the easy route. I ripped it down completely, bending the rail with it as both sides were freed. I set it on the ground. I could move it later, it wasn't heavy.

Eda was the first to approach me as I stepped out of the disaster zone, holding up her hand so she didn't have to look at me directly. I would have dropped my light but I wasn't keen to be stark naked in front of everyone.

"You're right Eda, this is not safe at all. What caused this?"

"Honestly, we're not sure. Perhaps it wasn't properly attached to the rail?" She looked back to the others. Everyone was squinting against my radiance, keeping a large distance. There was one man standing in front, he spoke first,

"Impossible, these are on a closed loop, they don't come on or off unless maintenance removes them."

That was apparently not impossible as it had just happened, but I wasn't in the mood to argue with him.

"Well while you figure it out, I'm going home to put on some clothes. Eda, you can stay here, it'll be faster. Make sure everyone's alright," I said. I wanted to get out of the way more than anything. They couldn't see anything while I was around. I left through the large open doors.

Once outside I jumped into the air, taking off towards home. I was still slightly uncomfortable with traveling this way, but walking and even running felt impossibly slow in comparison. The view was beautiful as well, what I could see between the streaks of fire. Not many people had ever seen the world this way.

I was back at the palace in a minute. I landed in my hallway, thankful for the openair design. I went to my closet immediately, weaving between the curtains so I didn't burn them as I kept up most of my glow. Inside, I put on the simplest robe that would be easy to take off again. I guessed I would have to be iron-melting hot again to be of any real use to the cleanup.

I went up to the mage room. I knew Zifira would be there. She treated it like her personal living room. She wasn't very adventurous, but I couldn't talk since I wasn't either and didn't have the excuse of working through trauma like she was. The door was open when I got there, the soft sound of her playing her new flute drifting out to greet me.

"Zifira! Help me find Nerial and Ferona. We have to go," I said from the doorway. She obediently put down her flute and followed me.

"They're in the kitchen, I'd bet anything," she said. Nerial had few truer loves than cooking, and Ferona was happy to eat whatever divine creation she made.

We did find them in the kitchen. Ferona was sitting on a chair playing with some potatoes so they bloomed and multiplied in their basket. Nerial seemed to have taken over. Across the whole kitchen objects moved on their own while she focused on a mixing bowl full of flour. I watched the uniformed kitchen staff move around what she was doing and I was surprised to see that she was helping them all rather than being in the way. I felt bad to bother her, but this was only our second official outing, I wanted everyone there.

"Ners, Fer, we have to go," Zifira said.

"Why?" Ferona asked, unconvinced.

"Because there's an accident at the forges we can help with," I answered.

"Why are we going with you?" Nerial asked, the same tone of being deeply inconvenienced. In her case it wasn't misplaced.

"Because the point of you living here is social outreach, remember? The more the public sees mages being helpful, the better."

***

By the time we made it back to the forges, it was crawling with people. The whole section of the accident was closed off. I ignored the barriers and went inside. I asked Nerial to come with me and she agreed with a huff. Her annoyance wouldn't last long, she had always enjoyed an opportunity to show off.

I rejoined the conversation of who I guessed were the highest authorities. They all moved away to give me a wide breadth with the exception of Eda. I couldn't fault them for it after what they had seen. No matter how far I tried to turn down my artificial fear, I was sure they had their own.

It didn't sound like they had reached any conclusions about what had gone wrong. The more I thought about it, the more suspicious the whole thing felt. How could so many experienced people have no idea how something had happened? Why had the only large accident in over a year happened the one day I was visiting?

"Can we help clean it up?" I asked.

"If you can, that would be great," answered the most authoritative man, looking confused.

"She can handle it," Eda said, giving me a smile.

"Where should I put the spilled material?" I asked.

"Put it back in the ladles above if you can? Everything will need to be reheated... repurposed..." I saw him working through the logistics and figured that wasn't my expertise enough to help with.

"Can we find Nerial an apron and face mask?"

"What?" Nerial scrunched her nose.

"I'm sorry, do you want to be burned? It's a forge, Ners. You can give up fashion for a moment."

"Fine." She shook her head and followed one of the men to a rack to find the right equipment for her. I looked back to Eda.

"Do you mind holding my clothes?" She laughed.

"That's what I'm paid to do."

I disappeared behind a wall and pulled off my robe, tossing it back out to Eda and pulling up my burning form again.

They opened the doors to let me into the larger room. The outside of the sea of steel had hardened and cooled, but not by much. This wouldn't take long. I melted it all again with a huge star-fire blast that I tried to focus only on the floor. I started lifting it off the ground with gravity. The molten steel spun itself into different spheres around me as it swung into my orbit.

This is where I needed Nerial. She had a fine control of objects and I didn't. I looked back to her with a nod. She took the signal and pulled each one into one of the empty ladles above us. It looked much better, even if the temperature of the room was still unlivable now that the doors were closed.

I walked back, thankful that they opened the doors for me so I didn't have to touch them. I looked to the group who were still arguing.

"Anything else?" I asked them.

Eda shook her head in answer, everyone else following suit. I walked back behind the wall and held out my hand for my robe. Eda handed it back to me and I pulled it on quickly. Clothed once more, I walked back to Nerial who had discarded her equipment with no small amount of relish.

"That wasn't so terrible, was it?" I said, adjusting my collar. Eda started to do it for me which I appreciated since I had no mirror.

"I guess not. Sweaty, though," Nerial complained, pulling at her skirt.

"I'd imagine." I started to walk back out, wondering what Ferona and Zifira had gotten into while we were cleaning. Just as we were about to step back into the street, I heard someone speak.

"My queen?"

I turned towards the timid voice. For once, I had to look up to the face of someone who was addressing me that wasn't Zan. She was a woman made of muscle. Her deep green hair and pointed ears told me she was a mage, maybe ten years older than me. She was beautiful, but also sweaty.

"Yes?"

"Can I speak with you?" She looked nervous despite her enormous stature, eyes darting to everyone within earshot, settling on a hovering Nerial.

"Ners, can you go get Fer and Zifira?" I asked. She nodded and walked away without complaint. I looked back to the mage, "Lead the way."

She walked me a short distance inside, around a corner and into a room I assumed was used as an office based on the desk and loose papers. I stopped and waited for her to catch her breath. I tried to not be horribly intimidating, consciously softening my face.

"I unhinged the ladle," she said all at once. I fought to keep my composure. She had to have a reason.

"Why? You put everyone in danger."

"Yes and no. I waited till the floor was mostly clear. I wanted-" she swallowed and swung her arms with nervous energy. "I heard about your mages from

328

Eda. I know what you're trying to do, and I thought if they could see you save the day…"

"That's incredibly reckless."

"Not my best idea, I know, but I had to get everyone's attention. Especially yours, my queen, because I don't want to work here anymore." She looked dejected, like a child waiting for a scolding. I wasn't about to put her through that for wanting a way out.

"What's your name?"

"Yelyn."

"What's your power?"

"Take a guess." She flexed and I nodded. I'd heard of a handful of mages with outstanding physical strength.

"Help them fix this mess. But when you're done come to the palace and ask for me. And bring whoever signed for you. I'll take over your contract."

"He'll want paid."

"I'll take care of that," I said. She beamed and tried to hug me, but I dodged to avoid burning her. She didn't know that and turned bright red.

"Oh I'm sorry," she apologized. "Stupid," she mumbled under her breath.

"No, you're alright, I just can't do hugs. I will see you soon." I tried to smile warmly.

I gathered my sisters and took the carriage ride back. Ferona and Zifira had done little but meet people and explain who they were, but any exposure was good. The more exposed to mages the people were, the better.

I told them briefly about Yelyn, swearing them to secrecy about her involvement in the accident. Zifira had her own secret to keep and Nerial and Ferona had told me little about what they had done to survive when they'd left the Towers, but the topic cast their eyes to the floor without fail. Everyone had their secrets. I trusted them to keep Yelyn's.

Back at the palace, I went with them to the mage room to wait for her and decide among themselves who she'd stay with till she was settled. It seemed like it would be Zifira, since Ferona and Nerial already insisted on sharing a room. Zifira wasn't a hugger either. I hoped Yelyn could live with that.

I stayed and wrote a letter to Vitsef. I hadn't had time to think, but when I did I realized I had a solution for one of the challenges he'd asked me about. It would help, but it still did nothing to address the bigger problem of the pending Northeast invasion. I had no solution for that conflict except the one I had settled on. If they crossed our borders, I would be there to meet them. It filled me with anxiety and fire, but it was the only way. My thoughts were interrupted by a gate guard at the door.

"My queen, there's a man and a mage at the gate for you."

"Alright." I put down my pen and made the long journey down.

I opened both front doors. Sure enough, there was Yelyn and a boxy man with a file folder in his hand. I let my aura of fear proceed me. Not by much, but I needed this man not to question me or push his luck. I was trying to be more amicable, but mage buyers still had no place in my good graces.

"Gates open, please," I called to our gatekeepers.

The gates swung open and both of them entered to close the distance as far as they dared. Yelyn made it closer to me, standing between us like a child between mothers.

"My queen, thank you for what you did."

"No, don't thank me. It was an accident, I did what I could," I said. He nodded.

"Here's everything we have on Yen. Not too much." He handed me her folder, finally moving closer. It was significantly smaller than mine, but I guessed mine dwarfed most. I flipped forward to her price. I'd much rather talk to Yelyn about what she could do than read about her. I found her price easily, a sum much lower than mine.

"Is this what you paid?" I asked the man.

"Yes, and I'd like half back, if you please? She's only been with us seven years."

"Is that considering the damages from yesterday?" I looked at Yelyn as I asked. She shifted her feet and hid her hands.

"No, but we'll be getting money for the repairs from the weapons manufacturing budget," he answered.

"Good, I'll make sure of it. Half is fine on the stipulation that you or anyone you work with never gives so much as another day's wage to the Towers. I don't want to hear that you have purchased a replacement. No more mages at the forges unless they choose to be there."

"I'm sure that's agreeable."

"Wait here." I handed Yelyn her file as I wished someone had done for me. It was probably better that Zan hadn't, though. It wouldn't have gone over as well then as it had a few days ago.

I had only ever walked by the vault, but today was the day I'd open it for the first time. I knew it took a key, but I had no patience to find it. As I looked up at the obscenely large metal door, I almost looked forward to finding a way around the lock. My hands heated to glowing, and I wedged my fingers into the seam between the door and the wall, far enough to feel the iron bar that turned to lock it. My hand melted it, and I pulled the door with the other. It gave easily, swinging open. I stopped briefly to scratch the word "Sorry" into the door just above the burned places with my nail.

Looking around the inside of the vault, I felt better about the price Zan had paid for me. I doubted he missed it. Wall to wall, floor to ceiling chests of gold, artifacts, statues, gems. All of it glittered as it reflected back my light.

Thankfully, it had a system of organization to it. Some of the larger chests were labeled with a monetary amount that made my head hurt, but nearly none of the smaller ones were. Great. I pulled one down and opened it, sifting through to guess how much was in it. I would probably end up being too generous by not counting every piece, but I knew it was better in the hands of the people than it was sitting here. I put the chest under my arm and walked back to the front door.

Yelyn and the man were still waiting in the nearly gone sunlight, the lamps from the gates throwing them into a warm glow. Yelyn had sat down on the ground. I felt bad for not inviting them in but changed my mind when I realized I didn't want any more mage buyers in my home then there had to be.

"Here, that should be more than enough." I set the chest down and kicked it towards him. It slid to a stop at his feet. "Yelyn?" I looked at her. She got up and followed me inside, an extra bounce in her steps. She didn't so much as wave back to the man that had come with her and that alone said enough.

My sisters gave her a surprisingly warm welcome. I was filled with a spiteful pride that this was working. Yelyn was our first addition from outside of our year, and I was ready to see who else would find us.

CHAPTER 33

From the letter I'd gotten three days ago, the day after Yelyn had joined my sisters, Zan was due home later this morning. It had said a handful of other things, just enough to reassure me that the situation was under control and that he missed me fiercely. That point had been clearest of all, illustrated to the point that I had burned the letter in my hands.

I picked out the simple gold dress, the single layer one with a low back and slits up either side. It was the best way I could think to show him that I liked them.

I waited at the front gates and tried very hard to remain composed when I finally saw him. He looked rugged and full of concern. His walk was heavy, his beard gone wild, and his hair still in a braided bun it had likely been in for days. The edge of his pants under his armor was frayed, stained darker than when he had left. This was the Zan that battle saw. How I absolutely loved him.

My feet left the ground before I could tell them they couldn't, making my running hug more of an attack. He hugged me tight, ignoring the horrid sound my gold dress made against the metal of his armor. I tried to control myself but my hands betrayed me, warping his armor slightly where they touched. I chose to put my hands on the sides of his face instead.

"You look tired,"

"I am, golden sun, I am. More importantly-"

"My king," a man interrupted at his side. I couldn't place his job. Zan's teeth clenched before he whispered in my ear.

"Go. I will come find you." His voice was a desperate growl.

Under any other circumstances, from anyone else's lips, I wouldn't have considered doing it for a moment. But with the way he looked, the sure power in his tired voice? I was back off to my room as soon as his arms fell to let me go.

I didn't have to wait long. He shut and locked my door behind him. I was a little sad his armor had disappeared but I understood. I didn't blame him for wanting one thing he wore to not end up melted or ash. That thought completely disappeared when he stopped and burned for just a moment so his clothes burned to nothing.

336

"Take off your dress."

I undressed and watched as a layer of his mannerisms softened.

"It is so good to see you again." He leaned down and kissed the back of my neck just below my jaw, taking in a deep breath through his nose. "So good."

I ran my fingers over every line and scar he had, more pronounced by the ash and stress. My toes curled and my hips moved with the idea that he had been in real battle. That he had been facing its horrors and still the first thing he wanted when he came home was me. Me like this, but still me.

The entire interaction was different. He had been rougher with me. His grabbing tighter, his movements more forceful, his sounds closer to growls than moans. He didn't kiss me like he usually did. Now he lay at my side, his face smoother and his breath less ragged. I still held his hand, gently pulling on his fingers.

"I am so sorry. I had to. I would be lying if I said the thought of seeing you when I got back was not the only thing keeping me together the last few days," he said quietly, looking at the ceiling.

"Don't apologize for that." I couldn't think of a single thing he should apologize for.

"You liked this?"

"Yes, I did…" I couldn't think of a way to describe exactly how much I had. When I thought I might be able to fumble my way through an explanation, his expression gave me pause. He looked so guilty. I rolled over to be closer to him.

"Zan, you know you can do anything you want, right?"

"Please do not say that." He shook his head.

"I did and I'm not taking it back. I like when you tell me what to do."

"Skye, I spend the rest of my life telling everyone what to do…" He closed his eyes, that rough whisper back in his voice.

"That's why you're so good at it," I responded. He stayed still as a stone for a long time. Then he opened his eyes and softened as he looked in mine. He sighed. It had worked.

"Are you sure you want that?"

"Very sure." I wanted him to do it because I trusted him more than I'd ever trusted anyone. Whatever it was, it would be perfectly considered.

"Alright, but remember you said that." Then he was getting up and walking away, grabbing a robe from the stash he kept just outside my first door. He looked distracted.

"You're not staying?"

"No, no, but I will be back."

I didn't want to leave my room. I had no doubt he would find me as easily as everyone else always did, but I didn't want to take a chance. Not many hours later I heard a heavy, familiar knock on my last door. He had cleaned up some, new clothes and beard trimmed back.

"I wanted to try 'this telling you what to do' idea. Come with me." I tossed the notebook I'd been writing in on my bed and followed.

He led me down a hall I'd only been in once. He opened a door I'd never given notice and went inside. It was a narrow spiral stairway. I followed, keeping one hand on the wall to keep myself oriented. It reminded me of the ones in the towers and I tried to not let that distract me. When the stairs ended we were on a landing with one wood and iron door.

"I will be just a moment." He disappeared inside.

I waited just long enough for me to start wondering what this could possibly be. I'd never been to his room. Was this it? It seemed too informal for that. I'd always imagined it would be behind one of our most beautiful and complicated doors.

When he opened the door again he was only wearing a small cloth wrapped around his waist. He had his hair tied in a neat knot on the top of his head.

My eyes followed the red lines down and across his body.

"Remember what you said?"

"Yes."

"Then get in here." That voice was back. He shut the door and locked it behind me.

I walked into a small and cozy room with a handful of defining features including an enormous metal bathtub and several decorative boxes in the middle of the floor. The air smelled unimaginably good. Light from the sunset filtered in through the arching windows, the outline of the Al star thrown across the floor. My glow was the only other light in the room.

"Take this off." I took off my dress again and left it on the floor. He lifted my necklace up and off. I stood for a moment before he grabbed my hands and held them behind my back. I was very gently pushed to the edge of the tub. The water was topped with small red flowers and a hundred herbs.

"When was the last time you had a bath?" he asked, kissing my neck.

"A couple days ago…" Truthfully I wasn't sure. I couldn't think straight.

"Get in. Be quiet." He dropped my hands. I obeyed.

"It's really cold." I wasn't complaining. It meant everything that he had considered that I would turn warm water to steam in minutes.

"Are you supposed to be talking?" he said with a grin. I had never been good at staying quiet when I was told to be, but I would try. He folded my dress and put my necklace carefully on top, setting both to the side. Then the mystery boxes were being opened. It was food. A proper picnic as I watched him open them all, each dish in a small metal bowl.

"Fruit?" He held out the bowl of grapes. If he was offering me food this was certainly not going the direction I'd thought. I took them, but I couldn't mask my disappointment.

"This isn't what I was thinking you'd have me do."

"Absolutely nothing was said about it being sexual."

"I thought that was implied." I hated that I was sad, but the whole thing was entirely too romantic.

"Skye, I can not tell you what to do. Not like other people." He gently moved my face to look at him. "It would be incredibly easy for me to have whatever favors I wanted from anyone I wanted within these borders. But not you." He kissed my forehead.

"But I want you to have what you want."

"I want you to be happy and healthy and fulfilled. That is all I have done tonight. And I did not even have to give up seeing you naked." I fought a smile. "If you absolutely hate this you can leave."

I didn't hate it. It was wonderful and thoughtful and the food was delicious. I felt him get in the tub on the other side, refusing to look over. I picked at what was left of my food. The rolling boil of the water filled the room with heavy steam that smelled better than anything I'd ever smelled before.

After a long time I crawled into his arms. If this wasn't what I had thought, I could at least still enjoy it. Sure enough, I was being covered in kisses.

"I love you so much, *jer asde ren.*"

"Zandorian Al, you are impossible. I love you too." I meant impossible in the way that I couldn't comprehend how he was this wonderful.

***

We made our way to the library after a long time, settling into the reading room devoted to stars. It was on the third floor, one of its walls only windows. A telescope was set to watch the stars, a feature I'd neglected in my star navigation research and would never forget about again when I saw how it made the sky I'd always admired all the more dazzling.

Zan sat on one of the deep blue couches to work on a sketch in the dim light of my glow while I looked out the telescope, scratching notes onto papers sandwiched between book pages.

"I heard about your incident at the forges. I am sorry I did not ask about it earlier," Zan said during a lull of my note taking.

"It was less an incident and more of a mage rebelling to get my attention."

"Really?"

"Her name is Yelyn. She's one of my mages now. I took over her contract."

"Should I ask for any more details?"

"There's not much else to say about it."

"I am sure there is, considering I know less now than I did when I brought it up."

I quickly explained the situation the best I could, downplaying the part where I ripped down the enormous ladle while being drenched in liquid steel and arguably caused more damage than before. I hadn't been thinking about it properly at the time.

"That is eventful." Even with my omission of detail, it didn't seem to have been lost on him. He was looking at me with eyes full of fire, but I couldn't read what kind. I continued as if I hadn't noticed.

"So anyway, I paid for her from the vault, I hope that's not a problem."

"I know. Not a problem, that is what I would have expected. I do not think the door saw it coming, though."

"Sorry," I said, repeating the word I had scratched into the door. Property damage had been the theme of that day, it seemed.

"No, no. It made me realize you need a lot more keys. Unless you like to ruin the doors?"

I rolled my eyes while we laughed. As it faded I saw that look again, and I realized exactly what it was. It reminded me of something else that had happened while he was gone.

"Are we going to talk about that letter you sent me?"

"I think today summed up the sentiment I was trying to get across." He winked. "You should probably burn it, though."

"I started to burn it about halfway through reading it."

"Wonderful." I loved the way he said that word almost as much as I loved how he said my name.

CHAPTER 34

The war had been brought home, and Vitsef had every reason to believe the amassing of soldiers we were currently facing was the one we had been fearing. We had been preparing to move out tomorrow in our own small party, myself being the most important member. We had to travel to meet them. Zan lamented that we had to travel instead of flying, but I reminded him we had the time anyway. They wouldn't be within our borders for three more days. I was willing to give them the extra time to sober up and maybe turn back before they made the mistake.

The air at dinner the night before we left was heavy. I was actively trying not to think about fire or destruction, instead working on a set of orders to send at the last minute tomorrow while I ate. I hoped we wouldn't need them, but it made me feel better.

Zan looked up from his food occasionally, watching me carefully and thinking hard. I let it go.

He had so much to think about right now I doubted it had anything to do with me.

Our evening slipped into night quickly. Zan worked his way through a stack of letters that demanded replies while I pushed forward with my plans. Finally, I finished them. Knowing there was nothing else I could do, I forced myself to put down my pen. I went to Zan's side at his desk, sitting on the arm of his chair.

The scratch of his pen was no longer the sound of writing. He had traded in words for lines, working on a sketch. For once it wasn't a dress or robe, instead a beautiful garden scene.

"I didn't know you could draw like that."

"I never used to, but I like the different elements it employs. It is a good break from clothes alone."

"It's very pretty." I smoothed the braids at his temple and kissed them. When I pulled back he was looking at me again with the same intensity he had at dinner.

"What?"

"Do you want to sleep in my room tonight?"

"Yes," I answered quickly. He had never asked me that before. I realized I actually had no idea where his room was since we'd always stayed in mine. He wasted no time taking my hand and leading me to the back corner of the study. He gave one of the shelves a hard push and in it swung, revealing a small set of stairs.

"The study was actually my school room growing up, then it became a sitting room for Dezura and I, then it was my own room to burn in until it became what it is now. This has always been my bedroom. I much prefer it to any other. It is far more secure and secluded, truth be told. Except maybe yours."

"I don't think the location is what makes my room safe," I said. He laughed and we started up the stairs. At the top he opened a heavy iron door similar to the ones in my own room.

It was small but lavish. Slightly cluttered but not dirty, just like the office had been the first day I had been there. The whole west-facing wall was made of windows that looked out over the sea. Plants lived in pots on every piece of floor direct sunlight would reach. It smelled like fresh air in the gardens. The walls were a mosaic of iridescent titles in flower patterns that reflected the falling sunlight. The bed was large, plush, and covered in pillows. The bed frame and headboard were dark stone, built into the wall in sweeping arches. I appreciated that most.

"It's nice," was all I could say.

"It is not somewhere that has always been a nice place." His hand pulled at his sleeve again. "But it is much better with you here." He gave me a sad smile and pulled me close. "Skye, I never let us properly discuss an important topic."

"Which is?"

"Children. Heirs. I have never actually asked you if you would like to have any. Or, rather, never let you talk about it. It is of course very much expected of me, but…"

I had tried to bring it up before since we had made it a possibility, but he'd shut down the conversation, going off the assurance that it wouldn't matter as long as I burned as I had every time. The avoidance, I imagined, had everything to do with his trauma with Dezura and didn't push the subject. I was elated he was bringing it up.

"I want children, I've said that in less words. Before I met you I'd settled that my life would be spent as a Mother Mage raising the daughters of others. The idea of them being my own is an idea I'm open to." I was more than open to it. My heart fluttered when I thought about it. More people who I could love without fear of hurting them. Even better if they were anything like their father.

I remembered the tiny hands of the baby mages when they arrived at the Towers. I had wanted to play with them so badly, be their mother when their own had given them away. But I had never been allowed near them. I'd resigned that if I had become a

Mother Mage I would have been raising late teenagers instead, the ones who didn't need motherly love, but discipline and direction.

"Labor does not scare you?" His question brought me back to the conversation. I could see him holding back horrible memories, fighting to stay in the conversation. He didn't look at me.

"I'm the Stardropped. I'm as close to immortal as our world offers, I'm not afraid."

"I am glad to hear that. You can imagine that I am much more afraid."

"I know, but you shouldn't be afraid for me. I'll be alright." I laced my fingers through his. "Why do you bring this up now?"

"Tomorrow we go to battle with our oldest enemies. I imagine they have a new, horrible thing they perceive as an advantage or they would not be challenging us. I am hard to kill, but not as much as you. I may not come back, and if I do it may not be in the same condition I am in now."

"Don't speak like that." The last thing I needed was to think about losing him. He stopped my emphatic head shaking by putting a hand against my cheek. I looked up into his glittering gold eyes and tried to tell myself it would be alright.

"You asked why, I am telling you. It is the same reason I wanted you here with me. I do not want to lose one single possibility tonight. It might be the last night of any possibility at all." He gave me a tentative kiss. I chose to make it into a hug and a kiss while my mind struggled to adjust timelines and ignore the possibility that he wouldn't be there to see them. I must've been too distracted because he leaned away and watched me with concern.

"You are thinking too much."

"It's hard not to when we have conversations like that. You should be concerned if I wasn't thinking at all after that."

"That is impossible, you are always thinking."

"Apparently too much."

"Too much for tonight, yes. Let's not plan this, hm? Whatever happens will happen."

"Alright, no plans until morning," I tried to joke. He smiled.

"Thank you, *asde ren*."

"You'll have to keep me entertained, though. I plan when I'm bored."

"Hmm, I think I can do that." I was picked up and given another kiss I could actually focus on. This one was far better, ending with falling back on his bed and nearly being swallowed by the pillows.

"Please do your best not to burn these pillows, they are my favorite."

"Even the lizard skin?" I grabbed one and held it up, its strange leathery texture something I would not want anywhere near a bed.

"Yes, especially that one." He laughed and pulled it from my hands, throwing it across the room. I was far from out of pillow ammunition, but I couldn't think about it anymore. I had to concentrate on not giving in to the star-fire that flared where he touched. I didn't burn that night. Not even a spark.

CHAPTER 35

We didn't have as far to travel as any of us would have liked. Vitsef had narrowed it down to a very specific track of land. I was glad to hear it was secluded. We were both still baffled about why Kos wouldn't be guarding that information carefully. If we knew where he was sending them, I could defeat them before they had crossed the border by more than a mile. It didn't make sense, but that didn't mean we could ignore it.

We were headed to the northernmost part of our Northeast region. It brought me a strange comfort to know I would be back on the land my ancestors had possessed. If I had to rip part of Solde to nothing, at least it would be a part I historically would have had the right to do so with anyway.

I said my goodbyes to my sisters and Eda in the early morning, making my way down toward the front doors. Eran and Nerial stood just behind a corner before the gardens. Eran had her hands in his, and she looked at him like he was the best thing she had ever seen. They were so absorbed in their goodbye they didn't notice me pass. Is that how Zan and I looked to others? I realized with a cringe that we were likely much worse. As if to punctuate the thought, I felt a very familiar hug wrap around me from behind.

"Ready to go?"

"Yes," I said, turning in his arms to face him, much less concerned about how other people saw us.

"Good." He held out his hand, something small and gold in his palm. It took me a moment to recognize them as my fangs from the day of my temper tantrum. "Thought you might want these." I was shocked he had kept them, and even more surprised he had thought to bring them. It made me happy. I took them and put them on, melting them back into place.

"Absolutely terrifying," he whispered. They couldn't have been too fear-inducing because he did not hesitate in the slightest to kiss me.

***

We met the rest of our traveling company at the front gate. Our group was not made of the best fighters, but inarguably the hardest working and most devoted men Solde could offer. I appreciated that every one of them had been willing to leave their usual positions and join us. We were all getting into something we didn't fully understand, and I admired their bravery when we had told them just that.

One figure among the fray was in fine armor like Eran and Zan but I couldn't think of who it would be, especially with the dark blue sash. It took me a long moment to recognize it was Kaniel, and I was only certain once I heard his voice. Just like Zan's, I'd know his voice anywhere.

"Why is Kaniel coming with us?"

"Because I asked him to." I didn't push it. He had his reasons, and Kaniel didn't look as out of place as I would have guessed he would.

"Skye?" Vitsef asked. I looked at him but crossed my arms and pursed my lips. He amended his address quickly, "My queen?"

"Yes?"

"Good luck. It really is a shame I won't be able to see it."

"Let's hope you never do."

"Ashamn willing. I look forward to some peace."

"You don't mean that, you'd be bored," I joked. He shook his head, snickering.

"So would you. Believe me when I say you're your father's daughter. You'd make him proud." He nodded politely and walked away. I was glad he was staying. We needed him here to manage the rest of the theater so the situation didn't worsen, even if that meant he wouldn't know immediately what happened on our mission. Aurelia and Amalie needed him too. It made me sad that I couldn't say goodbye to them, but they had been unable to make it to see us off, according to Aurelia's note.

"You have the weirdest friendship with him," Zan said from my side.

"We're not friends. He respects my parents, not me."

"I think he respects you. You do his job better than he does."

"That's not a reason for him to like me. I want that job and he knows it."

"If that's what this is about-" he started. I put a finger on his lips to stop him. Zan had the power to demote and promote anyone on the council that wasn't an elected regional representative. I knew what he was suggesting and it felt like cheating.

"Don't you dare."

"You said you wanted it."

"No, not like that. I'll figure it out myself, don't demote anyone... not while he's still with Aurelia. I'll focus on my mages and ending this war. Then I'll worry about sitting on the council for the next one."

"I doubt there will be another. No one will dare."

"We said that about Kos, and now we're here." We let that hang in the air as we departed.

We traveled through the city in the opposite direction we had gone to go to the beach house. I watched it disperse into farm lands and brief swaths of forest. Once, when I had asked Zan where we were, he pulled down the collar of his robe and pointed to a spot on his tattoos. That kept the trip from being nothing but impossibly heavy. Just as I finished that thought, he was looking at me with a much more serious expression.

"I did want to ask you how you are actually feeling."

"What do you mean?"

"I mean you are probably going to kill a lot of people. That can not be sitting well."

"It's not in my own mind. But the star-fire…"

I knew the ruthlessness of the star-fire that kept him from much more severe problems. If some part of him was alright with what he had done, even a small part he had to shove down, it was one fraction of him that allowed him to live with himself. I hoped it would be the same for me. I didn't know the details of the horrors that haunted him, but I knew enough to know he had come out of them much kinder than anyone else would have, star-fire or not. I hoped that was the same for me as well. I was working at it.

***

We set up camp just before sunset. We had taken the most direct route, and that left us with a stopping point that was in the middle of nowhere. I didn't mind. The countryside had a better view of the stars than anywhere else I had ever been. I asked Zan to sit with me a while after we'd helped the soldiers set up. Neither of us wanted dinner tonight.

We sat in silence as I stared up at them, just as we had most of the journey. Zan took to rubbing his thumb and finger together to make sparks like he did when he was concentrating. I held on to the fact that my favorite star, the midsummer star, was at its brightest shining directly above us. I didn't know why it was soothing, but it did as much to comfort me as Zan's hand in mine. There wasn't much for us to talk about. Or, at least, nothing pleasant.

After a couple more long hours Zan pulled me towards our sleeping arrangements, looking tired and anxious. Our tent was slightly larger than the others, but it didn't make a difference once I saw the cramped inside. The cot wasn't obnoxiously uncomfortable, but it was comical to call it a sleeping place compared to the palace comforts I'd grown used to. It was hard for me to sleep.

The soldiers sang drunkenly outside, Eran's voice rising above the others in a much more pleasant tone than I would have guessed, even if the lyrics were slurred. Alcohol wasn't allowed, but I wasn't going to remind them. They were allowed to have fun tonight.

Zan had fallen asleep quickly beside me, able to ignore the noise much better than I was. I imagined he was used to sleeping through noise like this when he was away. I listened to his breathing and the dull glow of his eyes behind his eyelids. Sometimes he would mutter or growl and turn, sparks flying. He never slept well, but tonight was especially restless. No wonder he always came home from the front so tired.

***

The next morning came quickly, though it could only loosely be called morning. We were up before the sun, and that made me feel uneasy more than the actual realities of the day.

I wore plain black pants and a shirt instead of a robe or a dress. I was here for one purpose and it wasn't to look pretty.

We reached our destination just after midday, though it was hard to tell with the overcast sky. According to Zan, that was the usual Niode weather, and we were right on the border to begin to share their clouds.

This time we didn't help with camp. We had more important things to accomplish. Zan, Kaniel, Eran, myself and a handful of higher ranking soldiers broke off into a smaller group, hoping we could get closer without attracting any attention at all.

We had a small hike before we were officially in position, but it didn't bother me. I was taking in the unfamiliar terrain and tried to imagine my ancestors walking the same land into battles as unbalanced as this one. Well, not quite that severe, that was impossible. The Ve family had never had a Stardropped. If we had, we would have ruled Solde instead of the Al family, just as Zenos had with Sola's help. That wasn't my goal now. I already ruled Solde. I was here to send a message to Niode and anyone else listening. I wanted to end this war for my people and my country and most of all for Zan. He had fought enough, I thought as we reached our apparent destination.

"They're supposed to be coming towards us from over there. They'll have to be in a pass between mountains by now. They'll be easy to find." Zan pointed just over a ridge of low mountains. I nodded. I tried to keep the star-fire quiet, but it was tearing at my ribs to escape. "Are you ready?" I couldn't answer.

He seemed to understand, taking it as an answer. "Go, Skye." Zan dropped my hand, again my only anchor to my mortal title gone.

I was allowed to be controlled by the star-fire now, the raging heat that was angry Niode would dare challenge me. I let it free to light my skin. Never before had I been able to use my power so freely. I ran farther away from everyone, each step I left the ground for longer. When I looked behind me and could only just see them on the top of the steep mountain face, I took that as a safe zone. I heard the approaching forces, the rhythm of their steps. I took off like a shooting star, a small explosion pushing me faster than I'd ever gone.

I finally saw the Niode men below as I came over the last ridge. They halted their advancements as my light hit them, reflected back up by their metal. Just as well, moving was pointless now. I remembered I had to offer them a choice. It was the right thing to do, as trivial as it felt in my fire cursed mind. I landed, keeping up my glow. I wasn't sure I could have stopped it if I tried.

Looking at them now, they weren't as well equipped as we had guessed, but then again neither was the rest of Niode. They'd likely scraped the bottom of their resources to put this together at all.

"Turn back or be destroyed," I said simply. I was surprised at my own voice. It wasn't mine. It was a hundred rolls of thunder twisted into words.

A man in front stepped forward. I assumed it was one of their generals, but I couldn't be sure. I knew nothing of what the light gray cape around his shoulders meant, but I would take his word as my answer.

"No," he said, trying to stay confident. I expanded the feeling of impending doom to include the rest of them as I looked past him to the other men. For once, it wasn't artificial at all.

"Anyone else? You will not survive." I called out, my new voice so loud I had no doubt they could hear. The soldiers shifted and shuffled, but no one moved. That was answer enough.

I shot back into the air. A pang of guilt rang through me, just like Zan had talked about. It still hurt to know I had to end them, even if I had offered them a chance. Any reservations I had disappeared to nothing as I let the star-fire completely free in a life-ending, earth shaking explosion.

I had leveled it. Any sign of life was gone, stripped to bedrock. I had to try to pull the fire back. But it wanted this to be my view forever. Everything should look like this. Fire and melting stone that was swinging into orbit around me, not another soul to be seen, all of them paying for their injustice as the fire enveloped the world. They hadn't deserved a choice at all.

Those thoughts weren't mine and I was terrified as I felt myself agreeing with them. I strained with it, trying to fill my mind with every reason why I couldn't do this forever. They faded as soon as I could find them.

Zan would be heartbroken that I had chosen eternal fire and ruin, but that thought burned away as the star-fire reminded me he would forgive me. Forgiveness I didn't deserve but I would inevitably get. I knew how he looked at me when I was like this. It was love and envy. He would want to burn with me, he would let it consume him, too, and we could rule a new world. We could be this and be together; he would be the king of star-fire.

I reasoned that I couldn't destroy my friends or my sisters. But were they exempt from my wrath? Why should they be? They had been complacent while I was kept in chains. Happy while I was told to never feel or have goals or a life of my own. I'd only recently found I could do all of that and not destroy like I'd been told I would, but here I was, doing just that. The Mother Mages had been right and so wrong. Now my goal could be making them all pay for how they'd treated me. My life could be this, burning and exacting my revenge on anyone and everyone. This was how I was supposed to be. This was my true purpose, I saw that now.

My efforts weren't working. Nothing was working. I didn't have reasons to stop. I wasn't myself anymore, I was star-fire and rage. I had slipped too far. I was nothing but the Stardropped now.

CHAPTER 36

As the reality of what I had done started to sink in and consume me, I felt a familiar, inexplicable calm wash over me. It pushed and pulled the fire back, conquering its anger.

The firestorm cooled and I landed on my feet. I began regaining my own mindset. Something that wasn't rage began to push through. But it became numb. The numb I had experienced at the towers. The numb I had felt my entire first day at the palace. The numb that came with a potential outburst whenever I was with someone I had spent most of my life with.

Aurelia. She was close. But why was she here? How was she here? Had she been somewhere else this entire time, waiting to pull me back if I couldn't do it myself? Had Zan done this? I wanted to feel anger at the idea that they had so little faith in me controlling myself, but I felt nothing. I could only wish I did. I was slipping again, but it wasn't the fire. It was consuming numbness.

But I could still think logically. It was why I liked strategy. It didn't care about emotions. Logic brought me a conclusion I had never considered. One I should have seen since it was so obvious. One that made my whole being recoil. She wasn't interested in helping by keeping me calm. She wasn't helping us.

The problem had been Aurelia the entire time. She was Vitsef's spy, Quailen Kos' source, and my blind spot. Now she had me trapped, alone and so numb I couldn't use star-fire. She was here for me in a much more sinister way than she ever had before.

As I put together the pieces, I heard her voice behind me,

"Good show, Skye! Your best work by far! I was getting a little worried, you were so much angrier than usual. I helped you out, hope you don't mind!" Her smile was huge, her eyes bright, her hands held out towards me. Her fingertips were pure white. This was taking a lot of effort for her, and that kept me hopeful.

A crack and footsteps sounded on my other side. I stole a look as I backed away. The force field mage, Kos's wife Clarina, dressed in white and determination. That was my confirmation they were working together. They both closed in. I wanted to do anything to escape this, but I couldn't move. My limbs went heavy with hopelessness and the air crushed in around me, becoming a cell barely bigger than my own body. I wasn't sure I could overpower it, especially not while I felt like this.

"Does that feel more comfortable? I know how you love keeping yourself contained. I helped you do it for years." Aurelia stood at my chest, looking up at me like I was a new dress in her favorite colors. "Kos thinks I'm going to deliver you to him and kill Zandorian. But that sounds incredibly unpleasant. I've had a better idea. Do you want to work for me? This whole nasty business could be over. We could be best friends conquering the world. Wouldn't you like that?"

"That was not the deal," Clarina hissed. Aurelia held up her completely white hand and she went quiet.

"I was talking to Skye. Don't be rude, Clarina. Skye, do you want to work together? Please?"

The star-fire rose at the idea of conquering the world. But I remembered I already had that, and he had never asked me to work for him.

"No."

"Why not?" she pouted.

"I am the Stardropped Queen of Solde-al. I serve no one."

Her whole demeanor changed. Her warm rust eyes glowed to red. The color drained from her skin, leaving her white and gray. She pushed to change my mood. The attempt was strong but clumsy. I pushed it away. I was still numb, but I would not be moved to anything else. Aurelia sneered and pushed harder.

"Are you sure?"

"I'm a queen, I don't need your help to have it all," I said. My voice was calm but I heard gravity in it again. That set her off into an attack.

"I was supposed to be queen! Me!" It was the kind of outburst I'd only seen a handful of times from her, and every time the emotional roller coaster was unbearable. She could have walked up to another monarch and had them instead. That wasn't the whole story. I let her breathe to calm down, hoping I could get her to keep talking. I wanted to understand why someone who I had called my best friend and sister would do this to me. If there was one thing I knew about Aurelia it was that she loved to talk.

"But it's fine. I have you. For a long time you loved me, and I thought that would be enough for me to use you when I was made queen. But that plan was flawed. Then you were queen and you loved Zandorian. I could work with that. You might be indestructible but not in your own mind." She smiled and her eyes went brighter. She was pulling on my fears of weakness and failure and inadequate self-control. Worse, she pulled on my fear of losing my new life and the person who had given it to me. She was right. I wasn't indestructible as long as there was one thing that could make me as weak as any mortal. "Now I'm thinking if I broke what you love you could be controlled still."

The sadness and truth of it filled my mind but I realized what was happening. She was pulling me deeper into it. I had to change the subject.

"So you made me love him so you could threaten his life and control me as your backup plan?" I knew that was beyond her capabilities, but she would love to correct me.

"I didn't make you love him, you did that yourself. I didn't make him love you either, he'd already had you picked out for years when he arrived, I saw it. There was nothing I could do to get him to pick me instead. He was only thinking about you, the idiot. He was so sure and so were you. I felt exactly how hard you fell and how badly you wanted to appear like you didn't want him. Both of you put on a good show. You even had yourself fooled."

I hated that she was back to the truth. But there was only one way she could know what she was saying.

"You can read what others think."

"Of course I can! Controlling emotions wouldn't be much of a power if I couldn't tell what they were going to be!" She laughed a lifeless laugh "Why do you think I was in charge of you and Cerprillis? I saw what you were going to do a second before you did it so I could calm you down."

She'd confirmed another bit of information I'd guessed at. Aurelia had little sway with someone who was completely sure of their choices. Vitsef hadn't been, so she had been able to slither her way into his mind.

"You're a horrible person," was all I could say about that.

I made the mistake of looking in her raging red-orange eyes as I said it. Waves of resentment and exhaustion rolled off of her, as well as flashing visions of the Mother Mages yelling at her. One memory of a conversation, Vitsef's face and her hysterical anger. "Skye thinks she's so damaged! She thinks she's so much worse off than I am because of what they did! And Ashanm forbid anyone else try to tell her they have problems too! Guess who got in trouble every time she got angry? Me! I spent years keeping her numb. Do you have any idea how exhausting and unfair that is?" Then Aurelia's hand was on the side of his dead-eyed face. "But that's alright, right? I'll make them pay for it, right?"

The vision shifted, this one looking up at Kos and Clarina who stood only feet away in reality. The party whirled in the background.

"I heard you have a war to win. It's an incredible coincidence that I can make that happen for you," Aurelia said with all the confidence of a woman who had already won.

"Who are you?" Kos asked, the initial anger and confusion in his face fading at a rapid pace.

"Oh, you can call me Auri. I'm High General Vitsef of Solde's wife and the new Stardropped Queen Skye thinks I'm her best friend. Nice to meet you. We're going to be great friends."

The visions faded and I was looking at her clearly again. Her hold on my emotions had faded. She was too angry to keep me neutral, continuing to yell.

"You're not better than me, you're a horrible person too! I know exactly how often you think of ending the world. Killing people because you feel like it. You and your husband, both of you do it. He's done it, too. I've seen what he's done, Skye, he deserves the death I'll give him." She was wrong. I had to remind myself of the deep remorse Zan had always expressed for everything he'd ever done. He didn't deserve to die. I wasn't sure he could die, and I needed to remind her of that.

"You can't kill Zan with most means."

"I'm not worried about that, there are other ways to kill a man. His own hand is one of them. He's tried it before and it won't take much to get him back down to that low."

Another wave of hopelessness slammed into my mind. She wanted me to feel that way and I wasn't going to give her that. My hands and arms began to spark. Their reflection in her glimmered in her eyes. The star-fire was sure I could overpower this force field if I pushed it far enough, but when it went down… was I capable of killing Aurelia? The thought made my mouth dry. My mind swirled with memories of our whole childhood.

She'd said she would destroy me if she could. She had threatened Zan and my country. She had shown me how she really felt about me. But I couldn't pull my mind away from the hundreds of good moments we had had. They were slowly twisting as I recalled them. I remembered they had felt good, but now they were so forced. The color was draining from them, just as it did from Aurelia's skin. I hadn't been feeling my own emotions in any of them.

"Now, I have to go get your king. Be good," she said.

She popped out of existence in a flurry of purple light. The teleportation mage. She was helping them too. That made sense. Any other time I would have wondered exactly how this was working, how deeply it was planned. But all I could do was worry about Zan. He wouldn't know how to resist her manipulation, I realized with horror. He would come willingly without giving a thought to it. He thought she was my friend.

I looked at Clarina. Aurelia was too far gone, but maybe she wasn't.

"You're alright with this? You know you're going to die?"

"Anything for Kos." She sounded resolved, but I wanted her to question her motives.

"Anything for a man? A mortal?" I asked. She thought for a moment, scowl deepening.

"Anything for my country, my sisters, and my husband. Same as you," she said, holding her head high. I couldn't blame her much for her loyalty. She was right.

"I respect that," I said.

"Same to you. If circumstances were different I might have been your friend. Though, I hate the one you seem to have."

"We still can be. This isn't irreparable," I offered. She shook her head.

"No. I would rather die here. A hero's death." Her scowl cracked. "Quailen would never forgive me if I came back from a failed mission."

Before I could say anything more, Aurelia popped right back into the space she had left, pulling Zan with her. He was the last person I wanted to see right now. If he was here, she had her claws in his mind.

"Skye has been working with Kos, she just told us. We've properly restrained her, my king." It made no sense, but Aurelia didn't need logic. All she needed was to give him just enough doubt for her to ruin him.

I watched as his face went slack with disappointment. No, something deeper than that. He looked like I had died and taken his life with me to the grave.

"Skye... why?" It was an empty sound from a hollow man.

"I didn't. I never would, you know that. It's Aurelia, please fight her."

"Don't listen to her, look at me." She turned his head to look in her eyes. I couldn't imagine what she was showing him. Every horrible thing I'd ever done, most likely. His knees hit the ground, and silent tears fell on his cheeks while his eyes dimmed to brown. His hands clawed at the long vertical scars on his wrists we never talked about. That was what she was making him relive.

The thought came back. Was I capable of killing Aurelia? I had to. Even leaving her alive wasn't an option. Alive she was impossible to keep under control. She could charm her way out of any jail, persuade anyone that I was the traitor, weasel her way into another country and do this all again. She had to die, and I had to be the one to kill her.

Once I made the choice, I realized with a twist in my stomach, I wanted to. She heard my decision, looking away from Zan.

"You wouldn't."

"There's nothing I want more." She could hear how my thoughts were consumed by the idea of burning again. I hoped it consumed her too.

"I'll kill him first!"

"Aurelia, I hope the mage that gets your power next is a better person." I looked at Clarina maintaining the force field. She gave me the smallest nod. The forcefield dropped. Her mind was made up.

"What a weird thing to say," Aurelia laughed, but it was empty. "My power stays with me until I die." She looked scared. She was trying to get me to doubt myself, a last desperate attempt. She had completely forgotten about Zan. Good.

My feet left the ground and fire filled my eyes. Small rocks left the ground with me, swinging into a soft orbit around my body. I was burning again. My voice sounded like a distant rockslide.

"You get your wish, Auri. You'll never be an old woman with no one who loves you."

I didn't feel anything but star-fire after I said those words. This fire was not anger or revenge, it was me letting go of every emotion I'd ever had about Aurelia.

Every conversation reduced to ash.

Every sweet moment ruined beyond recognition.

Every memory of her burned in the storm.

When all of it was gone and my feet touched the ground, I felt empty. The star-fire faded into nothing. My consciousness was fading with it.

Zan was there, back on his feet and his tears dried, arms and fingers bloody. I leaned against him. He wrapped his arms around me to hold me up. I kissed his cheek, then I was gone.

CHAPTER 37

All I saw was white. Then it was black. Black with billions of pinpoints of light. Trillions of stars. My vision became clearer. They weren't all stars. So many were galaxies, living and moving. I was one of them, spinning in this infinity.

It was quiet, but loud in a way my physical body had never felt. It was like wind from the sea: ceaseless, strong, and cold.

It pushed louder somewhere at my side, if I could call this directionless form a body. Round dots circled around me. Planets. It looked so familiar. I looked closer at one that caught my attention, the action like flying and focusing a telescope. I knew those land masses, I had seen them in another life. A life I had just started to love. I had to go back. I still had a purpose there. I loved this planet, that collection of green land, because that's where he lived. Zandorian Al. That's where I was supposed to be, not here.

There was a lurch that felt like free fall. My vision went white. Someone grabbed my hand and the feeling sped up. I hit solid ground with a familiar force. I had fallen from the stars before.

***

"*Jer asde ren.*" I heard that soft, dark silk voice. He was kissing my face before I had even fully opened my eyes. I sat up slowly, still trying to remember what a body felt like. I was in my room back in the palace, under my blankets

"How long was I down?" I asked, rubbing my eyes.

"It has been about two weeks," he answered. I knew I had to rest after using my power, but I had never been down more than five days. Then again, I had never used it like that before.

"It didn't feel that way."

"I am sure not. You were starting to scare me, your glow was so dim."

"It wasn't though. I was the sun again…" I sounded insane but as I looked at him fully for the first time I didn't see judgment. I did see drastic change, though. The man in the seat beside my bed was still my Zan, but he looked very different. All his hair was gone, his beard reduced to long stubble. He had a new gold ring through the side of his nose.

"Your hair! A nose ring?" I knew I had burned all his hair away. I turned his head every which way to check for more changes. My fingers found a very long and wide scar on the back of his head I had never seen before.

"That one was serious," I mumbled.

"That one is from my father. I keep my hair long for a reason."

"But now we match." I ran my hands over his head and kissed his forehead.

"Yes, we do."

I was able to sit a moment and remember exactly what had happened. It was all a blur, becoming more vivid as I focused on it. Remembering Aurelia's words and images felt like a nightmare. Like so many nightmares I'd had, I was sure there was truth to be found in it, even if I didn't want there to be.

"Please tell me it worked," I said to Zan. He shifted in his seat, taking a deep breath. I braced myself for bad news, but the light in his eyes made me sure it was alright.

"Well, we know either Kos is dead or has completely abandoned his position."

"He's scared because his plan didn't work. He bet everything on Aurelia." Her name made me wince as I said it. It tasted so bitter now.

"That makes the most sense, yes." He looked at me with concern. I swallowed hard and made my hands into fists around my blankets.

"So the war with Niode is over?"

"I would say so. Their forces surrendered and we took power. There is no reason to be at war with ourselves."

"Took power?"

He gave me a smug smile and tapped at his new nose ring, the glitter in his eyes flashing. I'd seen Kos with one as well, but he had had a long and ornate chain that connected to his earrings. I wondered if this was the casual version.

"Their existing succession laws are aligned with military power. I have you, so I have their throne," he paused to look at me a moment, "well, you have their throne, I should say. We have a lot of work ahead of us, of course, especially you. I have restructured one country; this one is yours."

My mind started working through exactly how I wanted Niode restructured. Every flaw Solde had in their system could be fixed for Niode's clean slate. If their ruler was determined by whoever held the most military might then I was about to have a job much better than Vitsef's. All I had had to do was kill his wife. I swallowed that sick thought like a sharp stone, the truth of it scratching my throat as it went down. I looked back at Zan, trying to mirror his smile.

"But at this point I am enjoying being an emperor."

"Emperor Zandorian Al. That feels strange to say."

"I hope you can get used to it, Empress Skye Ve." He kissed my cheek. "Speaking of, I have this for you. A present from the people of Niode-al." He pulled out a box from beside his chair for me to open. Inside was a necklace with large shining clear stones set in silver.

"It is a piece traditionally worn by their queens. I think it suits you," he explained.

"It's beautiful," I said, but my mind was too distracted by the larger implications of everything to truly appreciate jewelry. I set it in my lap to play with how the stones glittered in my light as I asked my questions. "What's going to happen to Livade?"

"Honestly we may be taking that over too. At the party Dortes Weh had asked me to take power when he passed. I have not decided where I stand on that, but I have until he stops kicking to decide. As a country they can start healing now that the war is over and we will help them as if they are our own, of course. I want to make it a complete democracy, though, regardless. I will be helping Dortes with that now that he can do something other than hope to survive Kos' newest onslaught."

"You won't be helping me with Niode?"

"Of course, but I do not think you will need my help as much as you think you will."

I nodded and didn't look at him. What I was really worried about was how often he would be gone. If we were splitting our time between three kingdoms, I'd never see him. I had just figured out how badly I wanted a baby, so the timing was as poor as it could have been. Or maybe it was better this way. I had a country of my own to rule now. Maybe that would have to be my child for now.

I was still grappling with what I had done. I had killed all of those citizens of my new country and even their queen. I had lost control and the only thing that had pulled me back was Aurelia, who was dead. Aurelia was dead. I had killed her. As much as I knew now that had been a choice she had made herself, I was still caught up in the ramifications of her death. She had a family.

"Aurelia's daughter and Vitsef? How are they?"

"Surprisingly well. I had known he had a soft spot for Cerprillis, but I did not expect him to marry her immediately after..." he paused, studying my face. I physically recoiled. I'd never liked Vitsef much, but I still wished I could have wished him the best. I couldn't now. I was absolutely sure it was going to end badly.

"She's going to kill him."

"From what I hear she is incredibly well fed." He made a repulsed face, scrunching his nose. "But their daughter is doing well. She has been moved to live with her aunt who has two other young children."

"Probably for the best." I hoped she would get to grow up happy. It wasn't her fault her parents were twisted people.

"That is what I thought," he said.

Zan let me think before he took the Niode necklace back, setting it on his seat. He slid into bed beside me to wrap me in a hug. I leaned into it, happy to have my anchor back so I didn't fall into my own mind.

"I could never describe how happy I am to have you back." He kissed me sweetly.

I didn't say anything. I wasn't sure I was back, or if I was even myself. I knew I had slipped and Aurelia had pulled me back, but I had slipped in other ways when I had burned that second time. I had slipped enough to not regret killing her or Clarina or anyone else as much as I should have. There was no guilt in it. I had gained so much from it all. The star-fire was quiet because it was placated for now, but when it was strong again it would want more. I wanted more already.

CHAPTER 38

Five days later we decided we could leave Solde and I could officially visit Niode-al, or as Zan called it, Niode-ve. I wasn't sure how long we would be there, but I did know we had a government to restructure and plenty of fires from raging radicals to put out. As daunting as it should have felt, I was nothing but excited. Finally, I had a chance to do something on the scale I had always dreamed of.

Zan was at his desk in the sitting room making preparations for our time away. I was reclining on the new couch, writing as much as I could in my new star covered notebook with black paper, using my gold ink on its pages. It had been my project the past few days, helping me recount the events I'd lived through without losing touch with the present. The only thing better for that was the sound of Zan's voice, a sound that demanded my attention.

"There is yet another presentation that needs to happen. The Niode people have been anxious to meet you. Think you are up for that?"

"Let's do it." I smiled at him as much as I could, and he returned it. I didn't want to get it over with like I had my first one. This one had a sweeter flavor. I had earned this one.

"I had thought about flying but I thought you might have a better time if we could see the countryside, meet locals, see some landmarks. What do you think?"

The star-fire was quiet, so I nodded. I didn't want to wake it up. This would be better. I should meet everyone while I was still less volatile and intimidating.

"I'm going to bring my sisters. Maybe they can help along the way. Solde will still be their home base, but until we can get something started with the mages from Niode and the Keep, I'd like them there."

"Of course."

I knew everyone would come except Nerial. She had disappeared into wine country in the Central region with Eran for the month. I didn't blame them for wanting to take the time away. My biggest concern was the timing of their inevitable wedding and if I would be able to leave Niode to attend.

***

We saw everything along the way to our new home that Zan had promised to show me. My favorite sight was a temple to Ashamn, but I liked it because it was clear that they had made it with respect to Iliths as well. The Niode people treated them as beings of life and death, peace and war, not as good and evil like Solde. Both Iliths and Ashamn had a place in the world, and Niode's militant cultural undertones made Iliths that much more revered. Zan made a comment about how strange it was to see their depictions dividing the temple and myself in the middle, glowing with light but draped in darkest gossamer black. I was more caught on the fact that he had been focused on me instead of the rest of the architectural and sculptural examples. I knew where we both stood, though. I was the only real god in that temple.

The people themselves welcomed us with surprising warmth. Word of Zan's generosity towards Niode soldiers had spread here as well. It became abundantly clear that he had intentionally invited converted Niode men to travel with us when we saw tearful family reunions.

Unlike in Solde, the people gravitated towards me instead of away. They were still afraid, but I had brought an end to the conflict that had been taking members of their families for over a decade. They liked my light and warmth too, I guessed. The usual weather of Niode seemed to be overcast and chilling rain. I was always more popular when it was raining.

Today we were going to be arriving at the official home of the ruling family. I was excited to see it. I remembered not being excited to see the palace of Solde at all, but this arrival had more hope. The landscape alone was a stark contrast. The mountainous region we were traveling through was far colder, and the higher we went up the narrow roads, the more of a strange white layer I saw clinging to the landscape.

"What's the white? Snow?" I felt like an idiot for having to ask Zan to be sure.

"Yes, I forgot you have never seen snow."

"It's beautiful."

"I am glad you think so because we are going to be seeing a lot of it." He smiled, and I had to as well.

"What's the word for snow in Renci?"

"There is not a word for it, they call it snow as well."

"Oh, of course." I felt stupid yet again. A tropical country that shared part of a notorious desert wouldn't have much use for a word for snow.

Niode did not have an ocean-side palace with a sprawling layout and decadent decor. My new home was a mountain top castle built up from the rough living stone. It had square towers with pyramidal roofs, each one topped with a pole pointing towards the sky and flying a red flag with the golden Al star. There were many chimneys, the smoke rising from them mixing with the snowy wind.

The cobblestone roads winding up the mountainside were narrow and only low walls separated their edge from a treacherous fall. The road twisted round in front of the large front stairs. The carriages took turns stopping under a covered through way.

Zan helped me out of the carriage while I tried to take it all in. The cool air felt wonderful. I wished I could feel the wind. We walked in through the front doors, heavy things made of wood and iron. My sisters pushed past us just as they had the first time they had traveled with us, gabbing about what kind of room they wanted. Yelyn carried their trunks and laughed a little too easily at everything Ferona said.

I was happy that they had accepted Yelyn as graciously as they had. She had fallen into a place in our family with such easy stride it was as if she had always been there. We never directly talked about Aurelia after I explained what had happened. I had never known exactly how much suspicion they had all held about her true character until then. I was the only one who had been too blind to see it and I was sure she had orchestrated it that way.

I could see the architectural differences even better now that were inside the castle. The rooms had much lower ceilings than the palace's. This castle was made to trap heat, the palace was made to direct the breeze.

Kos seemed to have had an interest in hunting. The rugs were assorted pelts, and the furniture upholstered with fur. The wall decor was painted directly on the smooth stone. The patterns were much simpler than the Solde mosaics, simply blocks of color, but with more diverse subjects. I saw the silhouettes of trees, the shapes of dancing people, and predominantly the shape of an animal I'd only seen illustrated a handful of times. I could remember everything around it. I knew it was big, predatory, and incredibly furry.

"What animal is this? I can't remember."

"Bear. It is Kos' symbol."

"How would a bear fare against the Al's star?"

"Like anything else, it would not have a hope against you. Kos actually kept bears of his own. They disappeared along with him."

"I hope they eat him."

"That would be quite the twist of irony,"

"Have we caught the teleportation mage yet?" We still had very little idea how deep Aurelia had dug her plan, but I knew for a fact that that mage had been involved and had set them on her trail.

"No. She and her husband have been elusive. We have caught many other Kos radicals, though. I imagine that will be a long game to play."

"Will you help?"

"I will give them time. We have very good people working on it, and I would like the peace." I looked at him again and remembered this would be the first time he didn't have to fight a war since he had been a young teen. He deserved peace.

"Let's go this way." Zan took my hand and led me down another hall, back towards where we'd started.

There was a winding spiral staircase, every curve with a new stained glass window depicting scenes from the countryside. The spiral reminded me of the ones at the Towers, but much less cramped and far more inviting.

"This is our room. Kos used it as a ballroom, but I think it is better this way."

It was the same square shape as the towers from the outside, the same dark stone. The fireplace was enormous. Made of white stone with rough edges. As my glow hit it, the crystals in its composition glittered like the ice that clung to the edges of the large windows. Directly in the center of the room, the bed was covered in furs and thick knit blankets. It looked more like a nest than a bed.

"Do you like it?"

"Not sure how I feel about the furs. They remind me of Cerp. "

"We can get rid of them the easy way or ask them to go somewhere else. What would you prefer?"

"I'd hate for them to go to waste, animals died for them." I wanted to distance myself from death for a while, slow the slipping. I was considering only eating plants and fish like Zan did. Enough beings had died for me to be here already.

"Then away they go."

I moved to look out the window while Zan had people move the furs out of the room. The sun was going down, but the low clouds painted the sky a dull blue for as far as I could see. I realized the clouds weren't low at all. We were in their territory here at the top of the world.

The isolation of it was peaceful. I had spent my life lonely surrounded by so many people. Now that I was no longer lonely, I valued being alone. With one exception. The door closed, and I was scooped up into a hug by him.

"Better?" he asked. Only the knit blankets remained, now among them was a plush red blanket I recognized from home.

"Very much," I said with a kiss.

"Wonderful." We devolved into more kisses that became him grabbing at my robe and starting to pull it off.

"What are you doing?"

"I am still trying for an heir to our new empire, if you still want that?"

"I do."

I let him lay me down on the bed. He kissed from my neck to the inside of my thigh. As wonderful as it felt, my mind wasn't in it. I was counting back. It had been a month and a half– well over three weeks too late.

"Zan?"

"Hmm?"

"I just realized I'm late. Almost a month."

He looked at me with confusion, then it sank in.

"Do you think…?"

"Maybe. I don't know how burning like that affects me but considering what we did…"

He kissed every inch of me he could reach. My stomach got the most. I was still lost in thinking. I was weighing if it was my mistake or a genuine possibility. I'd never been sick in my life, so that symptom was out as an indication. That left me with exactly nothing to go on. But if it was true, I was getting a country and a baby, both challenges I wanted to take on.

"Well, if you are pregnant I am done here." He feigned getting up, over acting every motion

"No no no." I pulled him back, laughing. Even if I was already carrying the newest Al, I still wanted this one.

***

Zan got up much earlier than I did the next morning. My only task of the day had been to get dressed before noon, so I took my time rolling out of bed and drifting down to my new closet. Eda was already waiting outside the door.

"Eda, how are you? Are you settling in?" I asked. I hadn't seen her at all yesterday.

"Yes, everything is very nice. A little chilly, but I have my ways of avoiding that." She held up a briefly flaming hand. I laughed as I put my palm to hers and opened the door.

My newest dress was waiting for us. It was white and full, even longer than my gold dress had been. It had a structured top with sweeping shoulders of gathered gossamer fabric. The skirt and sheer cape were adorned with thousands of tiny clear glass beads in wispy crystalline swirls. It looked like snow. I loved it.

It took a concentrated effort from both Eda and I to get it off the mannequin and onto me, the heavy fabric and layers making it difficult. But when it finally fell into place and I was able to see it on myself while she laced up the back, it was every bit as mesmerizing as my gold dress had been.

Zan opened the door while Eda was doing her best to make sure every fold was laying correctly. I recognized the black star-bedazzled robe he wore as the one I had loved when I had looked through his designs. It looked even better on, its strong lines exemplified by his own. He wore a chain studded in diamonds with the Al star on the end, and a silver chain from his nose ring to his earrings.

"I love this." I took some of the fabric in my hands to pull him close, incredibly careful not to burn a single thread.

"I do too. I have been saving it for the perfect occasion. Do you like yours?"

"Absolutely."

"Their queens wear white. I hope you do not mind too much." I remembered Clarina had worn white. I'd wear it for her. She had been as devoted to Niode as I hoped to be.

"I'm not a queen," I corrected with a small smile.

"No, no. You are so much more than that." He kissed my forehead.

"It's beautiful, thank you."

"Of course."

"Necklace?" Eda asked. I felt bad for almost forgetting she was still in the room.

"Thank you, Eda." He took the similar but smaller necklace of diamonds and star medallions from her and put it around my neck. I centered it and let my fingers linger to see how their glow lit the stones. "Ready to rule Niode?"

"Yes."

I put my hand in his and let him lead me from my closet up several ornate curving flights of stairs. I noticed far fewer furs than there had been yesterday and squeezed Zan's hand a little harder. Finally, we stopped at a set of dark wooden doors manned by two Niode men in full armor. They started to push the doors open. On the other side I heard a muffled announcement. "Empress Skye Ve and Emperor Zandorian Al of the Al Empire." I had never liked the sound of my name more.

The throne room took my breath away for the moment it took me to adjust to the cold mountain air rushing in. It had arching windows with no glass, the vaulted ceiling supported by roughly carved columns that held it higher than even the grand hall in the palace.

We were walking across the long room to a raised stage with two thrones, one glittering white stone, the other an obsidian black and polished to a mirror finish. Zan went to the white, dropping my hand so I could manage my dress. I sat on the black stone throne, looking out over the mountains and the hall. My throne, my hall, my mountains.

My sisters and other familiar faces were in the crowd, along with so many new ones I couldn't wait to meet. I watched my people as the Niode priest of Ashamn and Iliths draped a set of thin gold chains across the bridge of my nose and behind my ears, the unpierceable equivalent of Zan's nose ring and chains. With them, I officially ruled Niode.

For the first time, I was completely content with the star-fire in my heart. I wanted to rule it all. Maybe my slip into the star-fire was the second-best thing that had ever happened to me. I looked to my side to see the first. I was back in a tower, but this one was mine and my chains made me an empress.

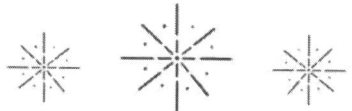

What to read next in the
Stardropped Series

KING OF STAR-FIRE

The story of Golden Sun told from the
perspective of Zandorian Al.

LYDIA MAXAMELIA
ART & WRITING

instagram.com/lydiamaxamelia_art/

https://www.facebook.com/lydiamaxameliaart/

https://www.patreon.com/lydiamaxameila_art

Made in the USA
Middletown, DE
04 December 2025